A New Mantra

A Sood Family Romance

Sapna Srinivasan

A New Mantra
Copyright© 2022 Sapna Srinivasan
Tule Publishing First Printing, April 2022

The Tule Publishing, Inc.

ALL RIGHTS RESERVED

First Publication by Tule Publishing 2022

Cover design by Lee Hyat Designs

No part of this book may be used or reproduced in any manner whatsoever without written permission except in the case of brief quotations embodied in critical articles and reviews.

This is a work of fiction. Names, characters, places, and incidents are products of the author's imagination or are used fictitiously. Any resemblance to actual events, locales, organizations, or persons, living or dead, is entirely coincidental.

ISBN: 978-1-956387-69-8

Dedication

For Shyam and Noyonika Srinivasan.

Acknowledgements

I am truly grateful to the Tule Publishing team for giving this book a chance. Meghan Farrell, thank you for hearing my story and envisioning it through my eyes. Thank you to my awesome editor, Sinclair Jayne, whose can-do spirit makes me want to write more and write better.

A special thank you to Jane Porter, our fearless leader who is an inspiration to all those who surround her. Lee Hyat and Nikki Babri, I appreciate all your hard work that went into shaping this book to make it what it is today. I also want to thank the people who worked on this book behind the scenes, including members of the Tule team, copyeditors, and proofreaders.

I owe this book, and who I am today, to my family. Shyam and Noyonika Srinivasan, thank you for your love, support, and for always cheering me on, no matter the goal, no matter the outcome. I would not be the woman I am today, without you.

Chapter One

SUMMER – August

IT WAS A proud moment in the life of Mira Sood, as she admired the set dinner table before her. A true work of art completed over the course of eight hours. Mira smiled down at it—the seven-course, traditional Indian dinner she'd made... from scratch. From the half dozen samosas to the paneer tikka masala, to the saag, the biryani, and not to forget, the gulab jamuns—deep-fried dough balls dipped in sweet syrup which alone had taken two hours to make. It was a meal fit for a Maharaja. Or in her case, her husband of three years, Jay Mehta. The latter had been acting strange for many months now, and Mira had no idea why. She'd tried everything from asking him about it, to making fresh parathas for him every morning (her mother's advice), to offering to finally take the plunge and bequeath her maiden name for his last name (an aunt's advice), to trying to start a family (everyone's advice).

Mira considered this last piece of advice as she attempted to straighten out a plate. She'd spent the years of her married life shelving away her own dream of working so she could cook, clean, and support her husband's career. Be the "good Indian wife" that tradition demanded. But with her turning thirty, the pressure had been mounting from her family for her to have a child. And so, Mira had (yet again) succumbed to her wifely duties. Did she want to be a mother? Did she think she had the chops to be a good one? Maybe. At least she was willing to try to bring her best to the table. Clearly, having a career wasn't in the cards, so maybe motherhood was her calling. What was troubling, of course, was that Jay had been acting distant. They had vaguely tried to get pregnant, but only so much could be achieved in the absence of intimacy. Nothing had helped shake Jay out of his funk. Hence, Mira had decided to go all out. Tonight, she was determined to get to the bottom of her stale marriage.

When the doorbell rang at seven, Mira bounded up like an attention-starved puppy to open it. Jay stood there with his laptop bag slung across one shoulder, and yup, there was that ridiculous mood. She could see it as plainly as the nose on his face. "Hi, Jay." She smiled, letting him in, determined to pivot toward cheer. "Look what I made. Diwali's coming up in a few days, so I thought we could celebrate early," she said, allowing him to take in the beautifully set table with the dishes all steamy, hot, and smelling irresistible, even to her.

But Jay turned and faced her instead. "Mira, we need to talk."

She was glad to hear those words, because that's exactly what she wanted to say to him. "We do, Jay. Listen, I know you're stressed at work, and I'm sorry if I haven't been supportive enough, but—"

"I'm having an affair."

"Wh-*huh*?" A tsunami-like shock wave engulfed Mira from the inside out. "You're—"

"I'm having an affair," he repeated.

She was hearing him, but she couldn't comprehend his words. "With a p-person?"

"Uff. No, a squirrel. Of course, with a person," replied Jay, shaking his head.

"Oh, m-my . . . GOD!" Mira cried out, her hand muffling her mouth. "You're having an a-affair?" She felt the earth ripple as the ground slowly began to sway under her feet. The women in her family had been prone to anxiety. Her great-grandmother's panic attacks were notorious to the point where, by the end of her life, the old woman had taken to running down the street butt naked every time her nurse tried to get her in the shower. The gene's baton pass down the generations had diluted the severity of this condition, but not enough to stop Mira from having a full-blown panic attack.

Jay rambled on. "Look, I met her on an airplane about a year ago while I was on my way back to Seattle from a business trip, and we hit it off right away. I wasn't even sure what I was feeling at the time, but as the months went by, we got close and—"

Mira felt an explosion inside her head—a potpourri of shock, anger, and realization. "Oh my God, is that why you've been acting so aloof with me? Not wanting to—" She stopped short. She was a conservative Indian housewife, after all. Talking openly about their sex life (or lack thereof) wasn't second nature to Mira. She preferred to imply. "Is this why you and I haven't been *close* in months?"

Jay frowned, appearing almost confused at the insinuation. He offered up a shrug and off-loaded his laptop bag.

"Mira, I'm tired of pretending. Reema just got a new job in California which made me realize, I have a choice to make . . . and I choose her."

The words cut through her heart like a knife "*Reema?*" repeated Mira, incredulously. All this time, she'd been picturing Jay with an uncharted blonde with blue eyes and peach-pink breasts. But the fact that he'd cheated on her with another *Indian* woman was humiliating. Like losing a home game. Clearly, he wasn't looking for someone different. He just didn't want *her*.

By the time Mira surfaced from her deliberations, Jay had stomped away and was in the bedroom packing his suitcases. Instinctively, Mira tried to stop him.

"What are you doing?" he scolded her.

"Jay, this is crazy! You can't just *leave* me?"

"I told you, I don't want to be in this marriage anymore, Mira. I want to live my life with the woman I love, and that woman isn't you. Don't you understand?"

"But I gave up everything for you. My career, my family back home, my friends. I dedicated my life to you."

Jay paused midway through laying a stack of his shirts into an open suitcase. "OK, so I am now giving you your life back."

His words sent a shiver down Mira's spine. She wasn't getting through to him, and time was running out. But giving up wasn't a choice; her marriage wasn't the only thing on the line. Her father had, only recently, suffered a massive stroke which had left him completely immobilized, strapped to a wheelchair, and no longer able to speak. She couldn't risk giving him another (and likely fatal) stroke with the news of Jay's affair. "I'll do anything, Jay, *please*. Don't leave me..."

"Stop embarrassing yourself," he replied waspishly as he continued to empty his side of their closet, packing his things into two large suitcases.

For the next two hours, Mira seesawed between pleas and reprimands. "Please don't leave me, Jay" to "Shame on you, Jay" The lowest point in Mira Sood's life was, hands down, her attempt to body-block her husband, to stop him from leaving her for another woman. But he left anyway, towing her heart through the mud behind him.

"Here," he said, ceremoniously holding up his set of keys to the apartment along with a check for three thousand dollars. "The rent's paid through the end of this month, and I've closed out my bank account. This is your share. It's whatever we had in there, split evenly. It's generous, considering it was all my earnings."

Mira stood frozen, unable to move or comprehend the words hurtling at her like a meteor shower. Jay considered her with frightfully calm eyes, then dropped his keys and the check on a nearby coffee table.

When Jay finally left, Mira sat down on the carpet with her back against the apartment door. The moment felt surreal. Her brain felt numbed by the shock. It was as if she were in a movie, suddenly playing out the life of someone else—someone she did not recognize. Because this neither looked nor felt like the life of Mira Sood anymore. This was nothing like the life she'd dreamed of for herself—the life she'd hoped to have when she agreed to marry Jay and move to America. Three years ago, Mira had been an emotionally secure, twenty-seven-year-old woman who was content with life and *herself*. She'd completed a B.A. in English, worked a few years as an academic counselor at a local school, and then at a call center. Yes, she was still living in a small town in Punjab, but she was happy. She'd never been overly ambitious and always assumed she would eventually marry and have children. As her clock began ticking, her mother and the family elders had begun needling her to get married. "Either you find someone you want to marry, or I will find someone *for* you," was her mother's ultimatum. Mira didn't exactly go out of her way to find someone she could love enough to marry—there were only so many options out of the handful of men in her small town. She'd had a couple of boyfriends over the years, but none of those relationships had been serious enough to stand the test of time. So, in the end, her mother won the "find-Mira-a-groom" race. Jay Mehta was a highly eligible bachelor, living in America. "And he just became an American *citizen*," Mira's mother had beamed. Did Mira love Jay? No, not really. But her mother did, along with the family astrologer who had lauded the match and guaranteed its success. And considering Mira had zero excuses (and zero men) queued up, she was left with the "no choice" choice. This was the norm. Besides which, she'd absolutely no reason to mistrust Jay—he was polite to her friends, he came from a well-respected Punjabi family, he was well-settled, well-educated, and Mira knew America was the land of possibilities. She'd married Jay on account of trust, hoping love would find a way into her heart with time. She'd bungee-jumped into an arranged marriage, hoping to fake it till she made it.

A NEW MANTRA

Lesson learned, Mira Sood. For here she was now, a thirty-year-old, "married-but-separated," Indian woman. Such a phrase didn't exist in her conservative community—a place micromanaged by age-old stigmas and family orthodoxies. As Mira sat sobbing, she tried hard to search for a point of reference. She couldn't seem to remember anyone in her family who'd crossed the forbidden line. Not one broken marriage among the hundreds. Unhappy ones, yes. But they'd all stayed put in their nuptial prisons, preferring to slam doors and sleep in separate bedrooms, speak in sardonic tones and whispered threats, but never daring to break the sacred matrimonial pact.

Mira suddenly felt overcome by shame. She felt like the failure who had dropped the baton and cost the team the race. If word ever got out about her, she'd be shunned by one and all in her family. Her parents would no longer be invited to weddings. Her mother would lose her coveted spot in the inner family circle—the place where stories of gossip not only first reached but were freshly churned for the benefit of the masses.

Mira closed her eyes, trying to shut out her panic-inducing thoughts as she slowly succumbed to a second anxiety attack—she was nauseous, dizzy, her heart raced like a spooked horse, and the walls closed in on her. In the hours that followed, she sat on the couch and oscillated between a jaded, half-awakened state, and moments of involuntary sleep. Amidst her transitions, her dreams felt like flesh and blood reality, while everything she'd known to be real appeared to turn to smokey imaginings.

IT WAS THE pain in her neck that woke her the next morning. With her head throbbing, and her hair smelling like a koi pond from all the tears it had absorbed the night before, Mira zombie-walked from the couch over to the window to look at the dewy world outside. The rain fell incessantly. It had been for three days straight. Typically, on a day like today, with the raindrops softly playing percussion on the leaves amidst a cool breeze, Mira would have taken her cue and banged out a dozen handmade *kachoris*—perfectly crisp pastry shells, with a sweet and spicy lentil filling. But that Punjabi-Indian housewife in her had just been fired. Who was she now, without a husband to cook for? Just a woman with a ladle. Mira's head felt like it weighed a ton, so she let it slump forward to rest against the cool glass window. She had no appetite, but she knew she needed to eat something. She turned around in the hopes of finding some leftovers in the fridge. But then her eyes fell on the fully laid dinner table—it looked perfect from the outside, but on the inside, it had all turned cold. Walking over to it, Mira reached out to grab a cold samosa, which she then stuffed into her mouth with anguish. With her mouth overfull, she went back to the couch and picked up her cellphone.

She felt no shame in desperately calling Jay (many, many times). She knew it was a mistake each time she called. But, at the moment, she felt hopelessly devoid of any self-respect, so she called him. It hurt each time it went to voicemail. It hurt as she left him another message, begging him to call back. And each time she hung up, she felt even more worthless than before. At the end of it, she'd exhausted the hours in her day, finding herself on the couch again, physically beaten, and so desperately heartbroken. She wanted Jay back—even though she knew he didn't deserve her—just so this massive sinkhole he'd left behind in her life would be filled. By the end of the week, it became clear to Mira that Jay wasn't coming back. Her brain had understood, but her heart refused to comply. She continued to dash to the phone every time it rang, hoping it was Jay calling. But it never was.

Mira was now a separated, *unemployed*, thirty-year-old NRI housewife with absolutely no financial prospects, and in dire need of a plan. And along with it, the answer to the universal question that follows a predicament like hers: *What the hell am I going to do now?*

Chapter Two

WHEN THE RING woke Mira up, she could not tell whether it was the doorbell or her cell phone. She'd succumbed to a feverish, dreamless sleep at two in the afternoon on a weekday—she couldn't remember which one. She was groggy, sick to her stomach, and hadn't showered or eaten anything beyond dill pickles since Jay's departure from her life ten days ago. Or was it eleven?

The thing rang again, and this time Mira knew it was the door. She couldn't bring herself to answer it in her present state. She knew if she saw another human being, she would instinctively collapse into their arms and bawl her eyes out, which was precisely why she'd avoided human interaction. The visitor, however, remained depressingly persistent and rang a third and a fourth time.

Pulling her sheets back over her head, Mira defiantly curled back into the fetal position and closed her eyes. But right at that moment, it hit her. *Wait, what if Jay had come back?*

Diving out of bed, Mira dashed to open the door. When she did, her heart instantly sank to the pit of her stomach. Standing outside was her older, wiser, overachieving, all-American cousin, Sahana Sood. Sahana was five feet seven (eighty percent of which was pure legs) and she looked radiant in her high-end corporate work clothes: dark jeans and a blue tweed jacket.

"H-hi," Mira tried to say, realizing the hoarseness of her own voice. Sahana was studying her closely, almost suspiciously, so Mira tried to distract her with a compliment. "You look really nice."

"And you look like a meth addict. What happened to you?" Sahana frowned, inviting herself into the apartment.

"I—er, I'm just . . . I wasn't feeling very well, but I'm all better now." She'd barely come to terms with Jay's affair and his exit from their marriage, so there was no way Mira was planning to reveal her circumstances to a cousin who, incidentally, had a tent flap for a mouth.

"Well, Mom said she called you a hundred times and you didn't answer your phone, so she called me at work and asked me to come check on you in case something bad had happened."

"I'm sorry. Tell Mummyji I'm fine," Mira replied, referring to her auntie. While her parents lived in India, Mira's paternal uncle, her father's eldest brother, Vinod Sood, and his wife, Sharmila, lived in Seattle, Washington. Auntie Sharmila had humbly (and with quiet eagerness) assumed the role of matriarch within the Sood family with the demise of her mother-in-law, Vinod Sood's mother. All the cousins referred to her as "Mummyji." Her husband was the official head of the Sood family and was referred to as "Papaji."

"Okay . . ." Sahana squinted, still looking unsure. "So, we'll see you at the Diwali party tonight, then?"

Wait, what? Mira felt her brain cramp at the reminder.

She and Jay had attended Auntie Sharmila's annual Diwali party since Mira's marriage and her move to the States. "I-I can't go tonight . . . I told you, I haven't been feeling well."

"You just said you were feeling better."

Shit. She was, officially, the world's worst liar. "I-I know, but I might still be . . . c-contagious, and I don't want to spread my germs," Mira said, feeling a sliver of pride at her quick comeback.

"Er, you and I both know my mother doesn't give a rat's ass about germs. She'll drive over here to come and get you if you and Jay don't show up tonight."

Mira breathed out. There was more truth to Sahana's words than she cared to admit at the moment—and just when she thought her life couldn't get worse.

DIWALI WAS AN epic festival in India, regardless of which part of the country one was from. Back home in Northern Punjab, where Mira was from, the Diwali celebrations at her grandparents' colonial-era farmhouse lasted days. The women in the family would pool their culinary talents to create the most amazing feast, while the men would decorate the entire house with *diya* lamps and burst firecrackers all through the night. It was precisely why Mira eagerly anticipated Auntie Sharmila's Diwali party each year—it reminded her of a past she loved and missed.

The clock said it was time to get out of the car—the Honda Jay had been given as part of Mira's dowry when she married him, and which he'd thankfully left behind when he left her for another woman. Mira had been sitting there with the engine running for the better part of an hour, unable to bring herself to step out. Every fiber of her soul ached, and then some. All she wanted to do was remain curled up under sheets—the very *last* thing she wanted to do was nose-dive into her auntie's Diwali party with a bunch of overexcited, hollering, tirelessly nosy relatives.

"God, give me strength," sighed Mira to herself as she unbuckled her seatbelt and ascended the walkway to her auntie and uncle's lavish waterfront house right on Lake Sammamish. God, she could hear the Bollywood beats through the three-inch thick Craftsman front door.

Auntie Sharmila answered. "Mira," she cried, and engulfed her before the latter could respond.

"*Namaste*, Mummyji." Mira smiled and bent over to touch her auntie's feet, as was the custom. She then handed her the large box of barfi she'd brought along with her, as it was traditional to bring a sweet or savory dish to a house party.

"Bless you loads, my dear," replied the older woman. She was dazzling in her magenta-colored chiffon sari. Enormous earrings dangled from her earlobes, and she wore a double-string diamond necklace that Mira was convinced cost more than her Honda.

"Is Jay parking the car?" Auntie Sharmila inquired, her eyes immediately darting past Mira.

"No, h-he couldn't come, Mummyji. He had to work late." Mira felt sick. It was like a horse kick to her stomach, trying to pretend as if everything was hunky-dory when her life was on fire.

"Who works on a Friday night? And *so* late?" Auntie Sharmila pulled Mira into the house and continued to chat her up as she led her to the living room. The place looked beautiful, decorated with marigold flowers and *diya* lamps; the smell of incense and fried food filled the air. It took every ounce of Mira's willpower to keep the tears at bay. Everything around her reminded her of home in India.

The house was bursting with Soods and non-Sood relatives, and they cried out in cacophony when they saw Mira—first cousins, second cousins, cousins she was sure she didn't know who they were; and a bunch of aunties and uncles who were, in some way, shape, or form, connected to either Uncle Vinod or Auntie Sharmila.

"Mira, You're here."

"Happy Diwali!"

"*Oye*, Mira!"

A few aunties came up to her, and she greeted them cordially. "Oh, you look lovely in that sari, Mira," they said, complimenting the meager effort she'd made that night to look as presentable as her bleeding heart would allow. The last thing she wanted was to succumb to her instincts, show up in pajamas, and raise suspicion.

"Thank you." She tried to smile back. She was gritting her teeth so hard, her eyeballs were cramping.

"Come, come, Mira." Uncle Vinod smiled. His accent was evenly split between his decades spent in America and his grounded Indian roots. Rather contrary to Auntie Sharmila, who somehow managed to sound more American than Dolly Parton.

"*Namaste,* Papaji." Mira bowed to touch his feet, to

which he first blessed her, then pulled her up into his arms.

"Good to see you, Mira." Vinod Sood was a tall, broad-shouldered man in his late seventies. He was the oldest of three brothers: Vinod, Mukesh, and Sanjay Sood. In the mid-1960s, Vinod, along with his wife, Sharmila, left the Sood family home in Punjab, India, and flew on the newly inaugurated international Air India flight to the United States of America, in search of the American Dream. He found a job as a shorthand typist, while taking night classes in computer coding. He then found a job at a start-up tech company as a junior coder and worked his way up, eventually retiring as its CEO. Within the first decade of living in the U.S., Uncle Vinod had also managed to facilitate getting green cards for his entire family. And by the time immigration audits discovered the system's loophole, every single living member of the Sood family, including Vinod's younger brothers, Mukesh (Mira's father) and Sanjay, their wives, and kids, all had a shiny green card each. Although Mukesh and Sanjay continued to live in India, they kept their green cards alive with periodic and extended visits to the States.

"Where's our son-in-law?" Uncle Vinod frowned, looking about Mira. At that very moment, Sahana Sood got up from her seat on the couch and began walking in their direction.

Mira was giddy with anxiety. This wasn't going to be easy. She knew that well enough. She'd somehow managed to keep her separation from Jay, and his affair, a secret from her family thus far. But it wasn't a question of whether they would find out. It was a question of *when*. The Soods, especially her auntie Sharmila, not to mention her mother,

Nina Sood, and almost all the cousins in their family were hot and heavy on social media. All it would take was a spark, and that would be the end of poor Mira Sood.

"Is Jay not here?" Sahana asked, joining the conversation.

"Er, Jay's got a migraine so he couldn't make it," Mira replied, praying the subject would get dropped.

"But you said he was working late?" frowned Auntie Sharmila, who had just entered the room with a plate of samosas.

Mira winced inwardly. *Cyanide, anyone?* "Er, yes, he's . . . w-working late with a migraine," she quickly amended. She couldn't think. She hadn't eaten a proper meal in days, yet the sight of the samosas revolted her. "I'm going to get some water," she said softly, and walked away toward the kitchen.

Standing with a glass under the water dispenser in the fridge, Mira stubbornly held back the tears. She could hear the others a few feet away as they laughed, cheered, and danced to music. She needed a shoulder, an empathetic ear, a pillow. None of which this place could offer.

"Mira?" The sound of Auntie Sharmila's voice startled her and she turned.

"Mummyji?"

The older woman moved closer and spoke in a low voice, to stay out of earshot. "How's Jay doing? You had said he was acting funny, or was in a bad mood or something? How's he now?"

It was like facing a criminal investigator and Mira was about to be administered a lie detector test. "He's fine, Mummyji." The less she spoke, the better, realized Mira. And she could not bear to say Jay's name.

Her auntie was studying her with a squint, as if waiting to spot a breach. "You know I spoke to your Ma just yesterday? She was almost in tears, she's so worried for you."

"W-why's she worried?" asked Mira, her heart pounding.

"You and Jay have been married for three years now, Mira, and you are not getting any younger. Isn't it time you and Jay started a family?"

Mira considered her auntie with tired eyes, wondering where to begin answering the older woman's questions. It was as if she needed to climb Everest, but couldn't even find her shoes to get started. Of course, part of her wanted to unburden the load and blurt everything out: *"Sure, Mummyji, I was all for starting a family with Jay, but guess what? He chose Reema."*

However, Mira's auntie appeared content with a monologue. "You are *thirty* years old, Mira," she continued to say. "I had two kids in elementary school by the time I was your age. And why do you think Jay has been acting funny, huh? Men are like big kids, my dear, and having kids makes them more responsible. Take your older brother, Manoj? Happily married, with *two* kids and getting ready to celebrate his tenth anniversary. I hope you are not offended that I'm giving you all this advice? But with your own parents living in India, your Ma is relying on me to keep tabs on you."

Was she offended? No, not really. She was decidedly nauseous. *Livid.* Baffled at the lack of consideration for her private life. But no, not offended. Well, at least her auntie appeared to be asking and answering her own questions for the moment. This allowed Mira to find comfort in staying silent.

She managed a quiet nod, hoping that would satisfy her auntie and end the discussion.

The older woman smiled. "Good," she said, and then reached for the barfi sweet on the counter that Mira had brought over in a box. "Here," said Auntie Sharmila, splitting a piece into two, and giving one to Mira. "Happy Diwali to you and Jay."

Mira pretended to eat some of it, but she shoved the majority of the sweet into the folds of her *sari pallu,* which draped loosely across her left shoulder.

"Mmm," moaned Auntie Sharmila. "You have become quite a great cook, Mira. These are the best barfis you've made, and much better than the ones you brought over last Diwali."

"Oh, good," Mira replied, emotionally dehydrated, and wondering if she should bother telling her auntie they were store-bought.

Chapter Three

IN THE DAYS that followed Jay's departure, Mira suddenly became introduced to a real-world problem—cash flow. Or, in her case, the pure absence of it. Her heartache now needed to scooch over to make room for reality. Jay had been the most diligent of jackasses, wiring the lion's share of his earnings each month to his parents in India the entire time they had been married. Mira was aware of this, of course, and had questioned him when she first discovered it. "They're old, and I'm their only son," he'd protested.

"And I'm your only wife," she'd shot back. The whole thing had ended in an argument. There wasn't a lot Mira could have done, given Jay had his name on their bank account. Other than his check to her for the three thousand dollars, Mira had no more than a few hundred dollars saved up in cash, which she'd stashed away in her closet somewhere to use "in case of emergency." With no job, and no income, "emergency" was, officially, banging on the door.

Mira coped the best she could by prioritizing her main task—she wrote the word "BREATHE" in bold letters on the palms of both hands. She needed reminding, because the act was no longer an involuntary one.

Jay Mehta came from an orthodox Punjabi family—a

fact Mira believed wouldn't impact her once she and Jay had married and moved to the States. Wrong again. Over the months, despite the oceans that lay in between, her in-laws, with Jay's quiet support, began pulling out the bricks from Mira's wall of dreams, one by one—she wasn't allowed to work, she wasn't allowed to study, the purse strings were pulled tight with the reins firmly held by Jay and his mother. Mira's instincts had kicked in at first. She'd fought for her basic rights, which had turned her marriage into a constant battleground. Her fighting spirit, however, died with her father having his stroke. Handcuffed by tradition and her father's condition, Mira decided to stop battling for herself, no longer listening to her heart but, instead, living for Jay. Now that he'd left her for another woman, Mira found herself stranded, emotionally and financially. She needed to find a job, pronto. But there was one other problem. She couldn't afford to pay the rent on her apartment, and she needed to be out of there by the end of the following week.

Sitting on the couch, Mira considered her predicament as she ate her lunch with a rusty appetite—six dill pickles with a side of Coke. Looking around the apartment, she considered the pictures on the wall from her and Jay's wedding. She felt sick to her stomach every time her eyes glanced across one of those frames. She needed to make new memories to replace the old ones. And the first step toward that goal was finding a new home. She knew her options were limited. She still hadn't revealed her circumstances to either her parents or her extended family. So right away she knew Mummyji and Papaji's home wasn't an option. Nor was living with Sahana. Going back to India was out, because that would be like jumping out of a frying pan right into the fire. So, where then? She couldn't move in with a friend, because, well, she didn't have any that she was close to. Anyone she knew outside of her family was more of an acquaintance.

Mira's brain slowly contemplated the third and final option—Laila Sood—the only cousin who'd not bothered to show up to Auntie Sharmila's Diwali party. Laila was the one and only child of Sanjay Sood, the youngest Sood brother. She was the dark horse of their family. A renegade Sood who, at twenty-one, had announced to her parents that she did not believe in the institution of marriage and instead wanted to pursue her passion—becoming a musician. Her parents, and the family elders, tried everything to reboot her brain, using every tactic from emotional blackmail to hiring a Hindu shaman to brainwash her. By the time the dust settled, Laila had moved to Seattle (thanks to her green card) and managed to put herself through college, studying art and literature. She eventually became an American citizen and started her own rock band named Kali and the Juggernauts, sending home postcards and pictures from stage performances. The Soods always appeared supportive, although no one could deny the palpable tension between Laila and the other Sood cousins, and most of all, her Auntie Sharmila, who'd militantly disapproved of Laila's life choices.

Mira, however, had always got along well with Laila, from the time they were little girls digging up dirt in their paddy fields to when Mira moved to Seattle after her marriage to Jay. And above everything, Mira could trust Laila to keep her situation a secret.

Getting up off the couch, Mira walked over to grab her phone. The decision had been made, and it was now or never, she thought. She hit the call button on Laila's number.

"Hello?" answered Laila.

Oh God, this was happening. The most conservative Indian girl in the world was going to ask her radical, pot-smoking, rock star cousin if she could please move in with her. "Hi, Laila. It's Mira. Can we talk, or are you busy?" *Please be busy, please be busy, please be busy . . .*

"Nah, not busy. What's up?"

"I need to talk to . . . *ask* you something, actually. Can we meet somewhere for coffee, maybe?"

"Sure, why don't you just come over to my place? We can hang out and chat? I have a bottle of Pinot I've been meaning to crack open."

"Er . . . it's actually something really important I need to talk to you about."

Laila paused to consider. "Mmm. Whiskey, then."

THEY WERE SEATED, legs crossed, on the floor of Laila's apartment in downtown Fremont with a tiny coffee table and half-filled glasses of whiskey, neat between them. Mira hadn't touched hers, but Laila was well on the way to her second drink.

"Damn, what a scumbag that Jay." Laila shook her head as she absorbed all of Mira's news about her split. "Who else knows?"

"Absolutely no one. And I'd like to keep it that way."

Laila raised a skeptical brow at her cousin. "I won't tell a soul, but you know our family. They live for gossip and they're obsessed with this whole, utopian concept of 'marrying for life.' God, what a bunch of—"

"Forget the family, Laila," interjected Mira. "That's not why I came down here. There's something I want to ask you . . . a favor."

Laila quietly sipped her whiskey, keeping her eyes fixed on Mira the entire time.

"I was wondering if I could move in with you. I need a place to stay. The lease on my apartment is up, and I can't afford the rent on my own. I need to find a job."

"You want to move in *here*?"

"I couldn't think of anyone else to ask."

"What about the family? Won't they find out something is wrong if you move in with me? How would you explain it to them without giving yourself away?"

Mira pursed her lips. There was no way of sugarcoating the bitter truth. "They will find out eventually, I'm sure. But for now, I'm not ready to tell them."

Laila said nothing, watching Mira with quiet, furrowed brows. The latter's heart was galloping away with her imagination. Was Laila about to say no? If she did, what would Mira do then? An image of living in a freeway-side tent was coming more and more into focus. "I don't have much saved, but I'll chip in with the rent. I was going to start looking for work right away, so once I get a job, I'll split it evenly with you—"

As Mira watched Laila shake her head, her heart sank.

"I'm sorry, Mira, but that's not going to work for me," said Laila as she poured out a second, smaller peg into her glass. "There's no way in hell I'm letting you pay rent. Not until you're back on your feet."

Leaping forward, Mira reached out and embraced her cousin, not caring that she toppled the latter's drink over in the process. "Thank you . . ." she whispered. "Thank you so much."

Chapter Four

THE FEELING WAS hard to describe. But the start of the new chapter in the life of Mira Sood felt bittersweet. The past was done. She'd hit rock bottom. Her heart was done breaking (at least for the moment), and it was time for the healing and the rebuilding to begin.

Mira was fully moved into Laila's apartment after she'd packed whatever remained of her life and some valuables into the same two suitcases she'd brought over on her maiden trip from India to America as Jay's new bride. Everything that didn't fit into her suitcases, she'd sold on eBay. She even took the painful plunge and sold her *mangal-sutra*—the sacred, black-beaded necklace with a large, diamond-encrusted pendant which her parents had taken out a loan to custom-make for her wedding, and which Jay had tied around her neck to make them husband and wife, with a mutual promise to love and support each other for a lifetime. It was the only piece of wedding jewelry which her mother-in-law hadn't usurped. It was rather shocking—and a little sad—how it only took Mira three days to deconstruct a life it had taken her three years to build.

When her mother called, Mira was seated on the bed in a room that she now called her own. She answered the phone.

"Hi, Ma." It was the first time the two women had spoken since Jay had left Mira. The logical thing to do would have been to let the call slide to voicemail. But Mira had done that twice already in the last couple of weeks, which had only prompted her mother to reach out to the next best thing—which was, incidentally, the worst thing for Mira—Auntie Sharmila. Mira thought it best to bite the bullet and pick up the phone this time.

"Mira?" cried the older woman. It was eight a.m. on a Monday morning, which meant it was past nine p.m. in Punjab, India. This was prime chat-time for all the Indian mothers whose children lived in the States. "*Hai, Ram!* Where on earth have you been? Why haven't you been answering your phone? Everything okay between you and Jay?"

Face a firing squad on her birthday; make snow angels, butt naked, in an Arctic blizzard; shampoo her hair with Super Glue . . . all the things Mira felt she'd rather do than talk to her mother about her marriage.

"Yes, it's good." Fewer words, fewer mistakes. She'd learned that from her visit to Auntie Sharmila's Diwali party.

"It's good? So, Jay's mood is better? He's happy now?"

"Yes." This was true enough.

"Okay," sighed her mother, appearing satisfied. "And how was your Diwali party? I spoke to Sharmila and she said you looked beautiful in your pink sari."

Mira sat up straight. "What else did Mummyji say?"

"Why didn't you take Jay with you?" Even the phrasing of her mother's questions appeared to sound so unfortunately sexist.

"It's not like he's a toddler in a car seat that I need to carry around and take places, Ma. He's a grown man and he could have come if he wanted, you know. He chose not to." Mira bit her lip to stymie the flash flood of words.

Her mother chose silence, if only for a moment. "There should be no ego in a marriage, *especially* for a woman."

"What about dignity? Self-respect?"

"Mira, just because you live in America now, don't think you can forget your roots and use all these fancy-sounding words. These have no place in our Indian marriages."

It was like trying to lasso a cloud, and the effort left Mira feeling tired. She'd yet to have her morning coffee, so this was hardly the time to discuss feminism with her mother when, clearly, they were both living on different planets.

"Okay, Ma," Mira conceded. "Is Papa there? I thought I'd say hi to him?" she then asked.

"He's taking a nap. The doctor has increased his painkiller dosage, so he sleeps through the day. You would have known that if you visited us more often."

A spiky knot lodged itself in Mira's throat. She'd only visited her parents once after she moved to the States. And she couldn't foresee another visit anytime soon, given she was no longer with Jay. Mira and her mother talked some more. Well, her mother talked, and Mira listened—which is to say, she put the call on speakerphone and began scouting for jobs on the web on her ancient laptop.

By nine-thirty, the call was all done, and Mira had applied to fifty-odd jobs in the greater Seattle area. She'd had to refurbish her old resume, which dated back to when she was in her mid-twenties. A knock on her door distracted her, and she looked up to see Laila's head pop in.

"Good morning, sleepyhead." She smiled.

Mira smiled back. "Hey, Laila."

"Listen, I know you're still settling in, but I really think you need to get out of the house," said Laila, fully stepping into the room.

"I don't think so, Laila . . ."

"We're playing in downtown Seattle tonight . . . the band is, and I want you to come. You've been cooped up in this room ever since you moved in and it's a Saturday night."

"I really don't feel like going anywhere."

"OK, then do it unwillingly, 'cause I'm not taking no for an answer."

Mira sighed inwardly. No one said rebuilding one's life would be easy.

SEIZING THE LAST spot in a long line of parallel-parked cars in downtown Seattle, Mira inexpertly squished her Honda between a VW Bug and a white Wrangler Jeep. Turning off her ignition, Mira briefly eyed the Jeep before her through her front windshield. She'd always loved that particular car and had (in her better days) dreamed of owning one someday. She now absently wondered who the owner of the Jeep might be. *A feisty female executive with a string of nameless lovers and a German shepherd*, she decided with a smile as she exited her vehicle.

As Mira crossed the street toward Seattle Center and the Fisher Green Stage, she tried to ignore how badly she did not want to be here. But she owed Laila—for graciously opening her doors to Mira in a time of need. And that loyalty meant something.

Laila was up on the stage at Fisher Green, having a heated conversation with one of the event coordinators. Making her way closer to her cousin, Mira waited for Laila to spot her. When she did, she waved for Mira to come up.

"You look cute," Laila said as she briefly turned away from her conversation to face her cousin.

"Oh..." Mira considered, sheepishly tugging at her oversize turtleneck sweater, which she'd paired with grey leggings that nestled her curves. Yes, she'd acquired a few extra pounds after her separation and no, she felt no shame in admitting it. She took pride in her nature-bestowed curves—and now they were *curvier*. The fact was, her body responded better to sugar than it did to Advil. And who was she to rebuke science?

"Thanks, although I feel a bit underdressed," Mira replied, looking at her cousin's sequined minidress.

"Just something to please the crowd," Laila replied with a playful twirl. "Anyway, you won't *believe* the gimmicks we're having to deal with here," she complained to Mira. "We're completely missing a PA system for our sitarist—can you beat that?"

"Ma'am," reasoned the woman with an ID hanging from her neck whose face had now turned red. "There was nothing mentioned about a mic in your technical rider."

"Rider, my *ass*—"

"Er, listen, why don't I find out if there's another way to amplify the sitar, okay?" offered Mira, gently grabbing Laila by the forearm and leading her away.

"Ugh! Don't bother doing that useless event coordinator's job. I'll ask Sawyer, our bass guy. He's usually a wiz with sound equipment," replied Laila, with a brief wave of her hand.

"Great. Then maybe I'll walk around and get some soda . . . find a cozy spot," said Mira, pointing to ground level. Being up on stage with a large crowd beginning to gather was making her want to shy away.

"Sounds good." Laila smiled and quickly turned to chat with Sawyer.

The show wasn't until five-thirty, so Mira still had a good forty-five minutes to look around Fisher Green and all the different booths. It looked lively, with both vendor- and sponsor tents scattered across the open grounds.

Mira stopped by the soda stand to first buy herself a cup of lemonade and a giant white chocolate chip cookie with macadamia nuts. As she walked around, sipping her drink, she heard her phone ring. With her hands full, Mira stepped into a random booth and put her cup down, along with her purse, on the nearest table. There were sign-up sheets and some flyers on display, with a treadmill nestled in a corner with someone running on it, and some activewear shoes on racks. By the time Mira fished her phone out of her purse, it had stopped ringing. She gingerly noticed the call was from Auntie Sharmila—the very last person she wanted to speak to at the moment (and also, ever).

Mira took a cathartic bite out of her cookie, inwardly heaving a sigh of relief for missing the call. That's when she noticed the woman in the booth staring at her from the other end of the table. "Are you interested in checking out our running gear?" she asked Mira. The woman appeared athletic, with the kind of taut neck muscles that pulsed under irritation. Mira also noticed that the booth was called BigFoot Athletics, with a picture of BigFoot running with a pair of shoes on. Of all the booths to choose from, this was the one Mira related to the *least*.

"Oh, no, I was just . . . looking," Mira mumbled, trying to hide a mouthful of cookie behind a closed fist. "I don't run," she added.

The woman nodded. "You're still welcome to take a flyer," she said, pointing to the transparent holder that was on display.

"Oh, great." Mira smiled. Not wanting to appear rude, she reached over and pulled out a flyer. She knew she was in the wrong place and needed to get out before she got suckered into buying something she'd never need in her life—like a pair of *running* shoes. "Okay, thank you!" she waved and dashed away, her lemonade tossing in her cup.

Chapter Five

THE SUN HAD almost set, and the crowds were beginning to gather around the stage. The Pacific Northwest breeze felt chilly yet comforting. Laila, with a lead guitar strapped to her body, was checking the microphone as the audience started to roar softly in response. Mira smiled as she watched her cousin in action, wondering if the tingle she felt inside was envy or pride. While she'd been learning to make perfect *rotis* and co-depending on her perfect ass of a husband, here was Laila, who'd started a band, released singles, and built an independent life for herself. Yup, it was envy, alright.

As the rest of the band walked up on stage, the crowd cheered and hooted. Laila thanked the audience and the sponsors as the band got rolling with one final sound check. A lanky guy with gingerbread hair was on bass guitar. Mira assumed this was Sawyer. A blond woman with mighty dreadlocks and scarlet lipstick cradled a sitar like it was a colicky infant. A bespectacled guy with a blond beard was on the flute, and a robust goth chick with a half-shaven head and cheekbone piercings was on percussion.

Mira's vantage point on the grass afforded her a clear view of Kali and The Juggernauts. This was the first time she'd seen Laila's band, let alone watched them perform live. Laila spoke into the microphone again. "We'd like to open with our new single, 'Rama, Light My Cigarette.'" Her raspy voice echoed across the lawns, and the song began to play. And that was when the sound of a deep, male voice caught Mira by surprise.

"Excuse me, ma'am?"

Turning around to face its owner, she instantly felt the air in her lungs crystallize. Handsome was one word for him. *Hot* was another. The man who stood before her had dark-brown hair that contrasted with his Caucasian skin. Thin, metal-framed spectacles softly accented his hazel-brown eyes. And all those features sat atop his six-foot-something, perfectly toned body that presently cooed at her from underneath a black crewneck sweater and denim jeans. To Mira, it was as if her cookie had suddenly transformed into a man. The thought of this caused her to reflexively clutch the half-eaten treat closer to her chest. Not to mention, her thoughts were a souffle of mixed emotions. At one end, she felt desire, realizing how much she missed having a man in her life, but on the other hand, she felt the tug of a man's betrayal. Men were scum, no? Hadn't Jay proved that theory?

"You okay?" the stranger asked Mira. "I'm really sorry, I didn't mean to startle you."

"Oh, yeah, no . . . no, thanks—I-I mean, thank *you*, I'm fine." Wow. Mira could hear her own gibberish, but she felt powerless against the outpour.

"Er, okay . . ." the man smiled, looking amused. "This is yours, I believe," he then said, handing Mira her purse. "You left it at the BigFoot Athletics booth."

Reaching out, she quickly took possession of the purse, pretending there was more than five bucks in it.

"Thank you so much—I didn't realize I'd left it behind," she replied, allowing herself to soak in the aura of this purse-saving hottie.

"Sure, no problem," he said, tipping his head sideways as if he were about to walk away. But then he didn't. "It's funny, though," he then added. "You forgot the purse but remembered to take the cookie."

Mira stared back at him, wondering why this gorgeous man felt the need to state the obvious. Yes, it was true. She forgot her purse, but not the cookie. Big deal, so what?

"I *like* cookies," Mira admitted with pride. She did, and this one in particular, because it had brought her this man, who looked like a paleontologist who modelled for *Vogue* on the weekends and smelled just as good as he looked.

Upon hearing Mira's reply, his brows furrowed with concern, while his lips curled with amusement. "I'm Andrew Fitzgerald, by the way . . . Andy," he then said, reaching his hand out to her.

"Mira Sood," she replied, letting her palm softly sink into his. His hand felt warm and oddly comforting. Looking back at him with whole-hearted admiration, Mira cursed herself for not taking a bit more effort in getting dressed for the event—she looked cute in her black turtleneck sweater and grey leggings, but not good enough to match her purse-saver. She pretended to look down at her shoes when she, once again, heard his chocolate-fondue voice.

"So, you don't like running, huh?"

This caused her to look up at him with a jolt of realization—he had been there at the BigFoot Athletics booth the *whole* time. He'd heard her ridiculous and slightly awkward conversation with the gal who was working there.

Mira shook her head. "I don't *not* like running. I just don't run."

"Got it." He nodded. But there was that smile around the edges of his lips again. *Man*, did he smile good. And looking him in the eye was causing random words to spill out of Mira's mouth. "It's just . . . I can't relate to runners." She shrugged. "I was never much into sports."

Andy pursed his lips thoughtfully but said nothing.

"I mean . . ." Mira continued, "I've watched those races on TV, you know, where these men and women sweat and grunt, and run some crazy marathon distance . . . I don't know, like ten miles—"

"A little over twenty-six, actually," Andy interrupted softly.

"Yeah, okay, *twenty-six*," Mira conceded. "I could *never* do that. I mean, I respect it—sort of, although not really—but I could never do something like that." Mira said, shaking her head, glad her throat was now too parched to let any more words out. What the hell was wrong with her? She'd normally never say so much to a stranger, so what was different about this guy that was making her act like she was on a talk show. . . or a psychiatrist's couch?

Andy was watching Mira intently and looking all too quiet. A few moments passed in silence, following which he said, "Well, it was really nice meeting you, Mira. I should get going."

Oh? *Oh shit!* thought Mira to herself with dismay. Clearly Andy had found her over-enthusiastic views off-putting. The fact that he so suddenly wanted to get away from her was proof. Her heart sank as she smiled back at him. "Yes, likewise . . . and thanks for retrieving my purse."

Andy smiled back, his eyes briefly locking onto hers. "You bet," he replied, and pocketed his hands before walking away.

As she watched him disappear into the crowd, Mira felt a sense of exhaustion. Maybe she'd moved too quickly in deciding to come out tonight. And clearly, she'd forgotten how to interact with the opposite sex. When Laila came down to meet her during a break in the performance, Mira quietly asked to be excused. It was time she returned to reality and to solitude—a place that felt more comforting, less awkward. She needed to return to the place most familiar to her—the kitchen, her pots and pans.

As Mira ascended the flight of stairs to her apartment door, she noticed a large USPS envelope on the doormat, which she picked up before turning the key in the lock to let herself in. As she kicked her boots off, she thought she would take a nice hot bath, then cook up a nice dinner for herself and Laila. Flinging herself on the couch, Mira took a closer look at the envelope. It was addressed to her, forwarded from her old address. It was from the Law Offices of Ruby Wadia. Mira could feel her airways tightening as she slowly ripped the tab off to retrieve the contents. When she did, her heart sank to the pit of her stomach. Jay had served her divorce papers . . . via First Class Mail.

Picking herself up off the couch, Mira dashed into her

room and shut the door behind her as she tried to hold back the tears. Jay had knocked her down a second time, and just as she was beginning to get back on her feet again. She had to know this was coming; her marriage to Jay was dead. But nothing had been made official yet. And that had given her the perfect excuse to hold on a bit longer to hope—protecting her family (and herself) from reality. And now her cover had been blown. There was nowhere left to hide for Mira Sood.

Hyperventilating, Mira doubled over to catch her breath. She needed something to quell the rising whirlpool of resentment and anger inside her. She needed to calm her throbbing head. *Oh Lord*, she needed to tell her family she was getting a divorce. How would she ever face them? And would this be a good time for her to point out that she'd been right in shunning their advice and keeping her maiden name? By now, Mira's head was spinning. She desperately needed *something* to help her calm d—

Rushing back out to her handbag on the living room couch, Mira feverishly searched for and found the wrapped-up, half-eaten cookie from the concert. It was stale, but it was a cookie. And then, her eye caught the paper that had housed it—it was the flyer she'd picked up at the BigFoot Athletics booth. She read it for the very first time. It was a sign-up call for the Lake Union Half-Marathon.

Cookie in hand, Mira's eyes remained fixed on the flyer's contents for the next few minutes. The tears continued to fall, but she hardly noticed them anymore. Marching back into her room, Mira grabbed her laptop. She sat down on her bed, pulled up the race website, and without the slightest flicker of a second thought, Mira registered herself for the Lake Union Half-Marathon. Leaning up against her pillow, she finished her cookie in peace, following which she made her way to the kitchen, determined to remain unaffected by the black hole she carried inside her. Cooking had always been an integral part of her life—the only real skill she felt she possessed, and the only thing that could comfort her in her present state.

Laila, in anticipation of Mira's arrival, had stocked up the kitchen and pantry. Pulling out a large saucepan, Mira threw in some sesame oil, followed by a mix of whole spices (cumin, coriander, fennel, black cardamom), then added some fresh whole okra and garam masala to finish. She cooked some white rice on the side, and then she began whipping up a perfectly aromatic batch of *dal*, which was her great-grandmother's never-fail recipe, known to spiritually heal anything from a broken heart to a broken nose. The dal required patience to make, as it took its time to slow-cook in the sauce made of onions, ginger-garlic, and tomatoes, along with some *ghee*. "If you are patient with the dal, it will turn out exactly the way you want." That's what her great-grandmother, *Badi-Dadi*, would say.

It was only now, on the cusp of a divorce and her thirty-first birthday, that Mira realized that maybe her *Badi-Dadi* wasn't talking about dal, but life.

Chapter Six

THE NEXT MORNING, Mira woke up wrapped like a toffee inside her sheets, her head throbbing, and her face stained with dried tears. Peeling her sheets off, she recollected her bold move from the night before. When she looked in her inbox, she saw the email confirmation she'd received from the Lake Union race organizers, congratulating her on signing up for the event. "Oh *God*," Mira cried, cradling her face in her palms. Why on earth had she let her emotions get so completely out of hand, she wondered with dismay, as her gaze drifted over to the USPS envelope on the side table. Oh. Right. Mira remembered. *That's* why.

With a heartfelt groan, she closed her eyes with defeat. This was hardly the time for her to try a new sport. She needed to find a job, start paying rent. Instead, she'd decided to prematurely hit the self-destruct button on her life with this whole half-marathon business. Mira drew in a breath and thought about the situation before her. She'd signed up (in a pretty non-refundable way) for a half-marathon, which, in all likelihood, she'd never be able to complete. Which basically meant, she had one of two choices—either train for it, give the race her best shot, and fail gracefully, or give up without trying at all, like a Type-A wimp.

Her head throbbed with anxiety, and Mira knew she needed help—a serious intervention to calm her nerves like... a double-chocolate mocha rum cake with a rum-hazelnut cream filling? *YES!* she decided, feeling slightly relieved. Slipping on a pair of yoga pants, Mira drove out to the nearest Whole Foods. In what felt like minutes, she was in the kitchen, going cuckoo-bye-bye with her blender and ingredients. She tried not to notice that she'd splurged and gone for the real Madagascar vanilla beans, instead of just doing the sensible thing and buying the synthetic version. What difference would it make when the cake reached its final resting place—her hips? But it went against her principles and what not, so she'd bought the real thing for ten times the price.

When the cake was baked, Mira cut out a de-stress-worthy slice for herself. The stress-baking had helped calm her nerves, and with the sugar from it now coursing through her veins, she was ready to face some hard facts. She typed "Half-marathon means what?" into the search engine box before her. The results were painfully clear. Mira would need to run 13.1 miles in no more than four hours to complete the race. *13.1 miles in four hours?* Mira shook her head at the idea. She couldn't even run that distance over the course of four *days* if her life depended on it. Heck, she'd never *run* in her life. Not even to catch a bus or a runaway shopping cart. She'd grown up in a conservative, upper-middle-class family in Punjab, where the greatest physical exertion was incurred in taking a shower or feeding oneself at the dinner table.

But then again, how hard could running possibly be? Race day for the Lake Union Half-Marathon was March

15th—still months away, with plenty of time to figure out logistics.

Finishing her cake, Mira washed it down with a cup of coffee. She then spent the rest of the morning online, learning about running half-marathons. By that afternoon, she was convinced she was in way over her head. The pictures of runners on the internet were especially discouraging. Their toned, muscled bodies in no intergalactic world resembled Mira's rice-fed muffin top. And yet, she'd signed up to do what they could.

"Most people start with a 5K," Laila observed later that day, as Mira threw some finely ground spices into a pan of hot oil. She'd decided to make tikka masala for lunch, because that's how Soods trained for a half-marathon. They *cooked* their way to race day.

Mira sighed and stirred in some freshly ground tomatoes to create her sauce base. "It's too late to think about a 5K now, Laila."

"Were you drunk?" asked Laila, with a compassionate tilt of her head. "Receiving a divorce summons is no easy pill to swallow, so if you did get drunk and sign up for a half-marathon, it's nothing to be ashamed of."

"I was sober the whole time," Mira replied grimly.

"Wow. Then you *should* be ashamed."

Mira looked up from sauteing onions. "If nothing else, this will take my mind off Jay and the divorce drama. Besides, I shouldn't give up on running without ever trying it, right?" she said, feeling the rejuvenating effects of her own words as she spoke them.

Laila leaned over the pan to sniff the mixture and

moaned. "Hmm . . . delicious," she said, and then turned to Mira. "I just hope you realize you're majorly screwed, that's all."

Mira shot a reprimanding look at her cousin, who had the bad habit of always being right at the wrong time.

SHEEPISHLY STANDING BEFORE the dirt path of the Discovery Loop trailhead, ready for the first run of her life, Mira Sood felt the adrenaline rush of a shoplifter at a mall. It was cold and raining softly, and the trail appeared mostly deserted, which was comforting to Mira, since she preferred to make a fool of herself in isolation anyway. Wearing a pair of joggers, an oversize sweatshirt, a pair of leopard-print shoes, and a fanny pack, Mira likely resembled a New-Age rapper more than a runner, but the important thing was, she *felt* like a runner.

Armed with a free mile-tracker app which she'd downloaded on her phone (which her research on half-marathons had highly recommended), Mira began walking down the trail, deciding to warm up first. She walked a couple miles, then turned on her run-tracker app and began to run down the trail. Her adrenaline kicked in, along with some anxiety, as she brought an unhelpful image of Jay to mind. And then, almost immediately, she started to lose her breath. Her muscles tightened and her airways began to contract; her heart began pounding wildly. Her pace slowed as the muscles in her legs ached for her to stop. Mira tried to push through it, hoping she could at least manage a decent distance before giving up. But she was gasping for air as her lungs threatened to explode. After a few more seconds of struggle, she sheepishly pulled her body over to the side of the trail. Mira bent over; her hands cupped her knees as she hyperventilated, afraid she was going to pass out. When she finally regained herself, she looked down hopefully at her phone to check her mile-tracker app: 0.2 miles.

"What? That can't be right," Mira cried out. She clearly was out of her mind with this mission to run a half-marathon. She couldn't even run half a mile without falling to pieces. How on earth was she ever going to run 13.1 miles? *Shit.*

She pictured Jay in her head again. He was laughing at her, looking smug. An unusual anger stirred up inside Mira, which caused her to shake her head at herself. She allowed herself to catch her breath, and when her lungs were plump with air, she restarted her mile tracker and began running again.

A new wave of confidence flooded her, carrying her across the next few meters, and then she spotted something that made her gasp. Mira tried to squint against the falling rain. *No way!* she thought with horror. It was him—it was Andy Fitzgerald, her purse-rescuer from the concert, in the flesh, running right toward her. *Holy Mother India!* He was a runner and—oh look, he was *topless*. Mira couldn't help but be drowned in a cocktail of awe and dismay as she watched Andy. The sun now theatrically broke through the vapor-logged clouds and glinted off his delicious runner's six-pack. Mira recollected how she'd shot her mouth off to him at the expo, about how much she couldn't run or relate to runners.

Very, very nicely done, Mira Sood.

He was closer now, which gave Mira a better look at his toned muscles—he *had* to be more than just a recreational runner. Clearly, he had the body of a serious athlete. And just then, amidst her deliberations, Mira felt the oxygen drain out of her lungs. She was beginning to get breathless again, and this time, she was about to fold in front of Andy. Mira cringed inwardly at the idea. She knew she somehow had to push through it and make it past him before doubling over. He was closer still, and Mira knew he'd have caught sight of her by now. For a moment, she thought they locked eyes and expected him to wave back. But then he wasn't looking at her at all. By now, the rain was falling again and hard.

As they approached each other, Mira instinctively shot Andy a soft smile, but he ran right past her without the slightest acknowledgment. *Huh.* The tug of embarrassment was well felt. *Maybe he doesn't recognize me from the other night.*

Running past Andy, Mira couldn't hold on any longer. Her lungs were on fire, and her legs hurt so much, she was sure they would spontaneously detach from her torso at any moment. But as she slowed down to a stop, Mira suddenly felt her right foot slip. The next thing she felt was a sharp pain shooting up her leg as her ankle twisted and her knee buckled under her. Tripping, she spun to the ground like a dervish, landing flat on her bottom in a rain puddle.

Sitting herself up, Mira tried to wrap her head around what had just happened. She couldn't believe how her first run had turned out. This attempt at a half-marathon was supposed to provide her *closure*, a sense of reassurance. And instead, here she was, simmering in a puddle, feeling totally defeated by her circumstances with her mile tracker now reading . . . 0.3 miles.

Mira tried to wipe the schmear of mud and dirt off her knees. She held the latter to her chin like a fetus as the hot, salty tears started to well up in her eyes. It was a mix of shame, anger, and submission that finally made her cry into the crevasse of her folded legs and torso. And then, somewhere in the midst of her emotional deluge, she heard his voice . . .

"Mira?? Mira Sood? From the other night?"

She looked up and was startled at the sight of Andy Fitzgerald. What the hell was he doing here? And why had he chosen the worst possible moment to have a heart? This wasn't happening, and she wanted to die.

"Andy, y-yes. Hi," Mira stuttered.

"I wasn't sure it was you. You okay?"

"I-I'm . . . doing fine, thanks," she quickly replied, suddenly aware of her tear-stained face.

But the man wasn't moving. He simply stood there (still topless), wearing running shorts that exposed the kind of thigh muscles you'd see on a *Game of Thrones* character. He continued to watch Mira, unwavering, with a frown on his face and a fist lodged on one hip, as if he were inspecting a bathroom leak.

"You sure?" he asked again.

She nodded firmly. "Doing great, I promise," she replied, simultaneously feeling the puddle water rising in her panties.

"Uh-huh," Andy replied, looking unconvinced. "Because

you look uncomfortable."

"I'm just . . . catching my breath."

"Sitting in a puddle?"

"You should try it."

"Hah," Andy coughed up a laugh. "I'll take your word for it." He then pulled out a twisted shirt which he had tucked away in the back of his shorts, and Mira watched as he turned it into a ball to wipe the sweat off his brow, then put the shirt on. If there was any doubt in her mind as to how Andy might look taking a shirt off, it came to rest just watching him put one *on*. *Fascinating,* she thought to herself, trying not to appear so obvious. But by now, her heart was racing, and she was sure the expression on her face was giving it all away.

Andy folded himself down on one knee next to Mira as she absently ran her fingers over her ankle. "You really shouldn't be running in those," he said, pointing to her most favorite pair of shoes in the world. "It's probably what caused you to fall in the first place."

"What's wrong with my shoes?" Mira asked, looking puzzled.

Andy appeared to stare back into her dewy eyes. "These aren't running shoes."

Mira clicked her tongue. "If I run in them, then they're running shoes," she explained. *Isn't that how it worked—if you sleep in them, they're your pajamas, if you run in them, they're your running shoes?* "Plus, I really like this pair," she added.

"They're *leopard*-print," Andy cried out with mild outrage. But Mira preferred to take the rebuke as a compliment.

"I *know*." She smiled.

Andy licked his lips, looking both bewildered and amused. He tried again. "Running is a high-impact sport, you know. You can exert about three times your bodyweight with each foot strike. And regardless of your level as a runner, you need to respect the sport, starting with your feet—"

Mira flagged him to stop by waving the flats of her palms at him. "Look, unlike you elitist, super-star runners, I am a newbie and a fairly poor one, so I don't have that kind of money to throw around on *running* shoes, okay?"

Andy frowned. "*Elitist*? You mean, elite?"

"Sure, let's go with *elite*." Mira shrugged.

Andy held back a smile. "Just let me take a quick look at your ankle, alright? I want to be sure it's not broken, and then I will leave you to the comfort of your puddle, I promise."

Mira shook her head definitively. "It's not broken."

"How d'you know?"

"I just know," said Mira, even as she watched her ankle disagree, doubling in size and turning a lovely ombre-violet.

"Look, I'll feel better about walking away if I know it isn't broken."

Mira studied his expression without saying a word. She then nodded. "Fine."

Reaching out, Andy gently put the tips of his index, middle, and ring fingers on either side of her ankle. Using mild pressure, Andy slowly massaged the bone. "Does it hurt when I do that?" he asked, consciously keeping his eyes off her and on the ankle.

"Not much," she replied.

"Okay, can you do a circle in the air for me, with the foot?"

Mira managed a trapezoid and winced the entire time. "It hurts when I move it," she admitted.

Andy nodded. "I'm not a doctor, but this looks like a badly twisted ankle. But I don't believe it's a broken bone."

Mira considered his diagnosis with a frown. "I could've told you that."

Andy let out an involuntary laugh. He cleared his throat to reestablish a more serious attitude. "Okay, I'll get going then," he said, rising to his feet. "I won't bother you anymore if you're sure you want to handle it from here on."

For some reason—maybe the puddle she'd been slow cooking in was finally getting to her—Mira spoke up in a meek voice. "Actually, do you mind giving me a hand getting up, please?"

This made Andy smile graciously. "You bet," he said and extended an arm for her to hold and hoist herself up. She just about managed, placing her weight on her good foot. Now what?

She struck a one-legged flamingo pose for the better part of ten seconds before she needed Andy's help again, just to stay upright. And the cheeky weather had changed its tune, from clouds with sunshine, to rain and hail the size of green peas.

"Actually," Mira confessed with a groan, "I wouldn't mind some help getting to my car."

"Sure," replied Andy, as hail speckled his glasses and his thick brown hair. "Here, you can put your arm around my waist if you prefer."

"Oh, perfect. Thanks." She smiled, hoping she hadn't sounded like a kid who'd just agreed to lick cake batter off a beater. She tried not to focus on how good this man smelled. She'd forgotten the feeling—the touch of a man, his scent. Her wounds were still fresh from her husband's betrayal but, oddly, that didn't discount the fact that she was human.

She obeyed him, although a bit reluctantly at first. Andy's hand instinctively reached for the curve of Mira's waist. "Is that okay for you if I do that?" he asked her, which she appreciated very much, despite the immediate goosebumps it created on her skin.

"Yes, thanks."

"It's only a couple of miles to the trailhead," Andy said reassuringly. But the hail was unrelenting.

"We're each going to end up with a concussion," Mira chuckled dryly. She was starkly aware of the fact that if it weren't for her, Andy wouldn't have to brave this horrible weather in the first place. He appeared to consider her point, looking upward at the falling hail.

"Mira," he said. "I'm just wondering, would you be okay if I carried you the rest of the way?"

For a moment, she looked up at him with disbelief. Would she *what*? Be okay with a white American runner dude carrying her on his back two days after her husband had served her divorce papers? She could die laughing or just *die*. "I don't want you to break your back," she said, deciding to use logic instead.

"I'll be fine, I promise," he replied with a smile of assurance.

Dear God, is this funny to you? Mira questioned the hail-shooting heavens above. She then nodded, only to watch Andy pull his arm away from her waist and bend down on one knee before her with his back facing her.

"OK, missy, hop on before I change my mind," he said with a laugh.

Mira curled her arms around his neck and her legs shyly coiled around his waist; her body shuddered against his, as she felt their skin collide. "Are you sure about this?" she asked herself out loud, to which Andy replied, "I'm absolutely sure."

The hail had ceased by the time Andy carried Mira to the parking lot. Naturally. "Which one's yours?" he asked her, turning his head tentatively to one side.

"The Honda," she replied, pointing to the car.

"Great," replied Andy, but instead, he walked them over to the white Jeep that was parked right next to it. "First, let's take care of that ankle for you," he said, and with a swift motion he had Mira off his back and hoisted up onto the hood of the Jeep.

"Wait, is this *your* car?" Mira asked. Her eyes were following him as he walked to the passenger side and pulled out a first aid kit from the glove compartment before walking back to her.

"Yeah, why?"

"Er, nothing," said Mira, as she realized something. "I think I might have parked my car behind yours at the concert."

Andy nodded briefly as he busied himself with the contents of his first aid kit.

"I had wondered who the owner of this car might be," continued Mira, as she watched him pull out some disinfecting wipes and a long piece of self-adhesive gauze bandage from his kit.

"And? Did you imagine it was a charming, *elitist* runner-guy?" Andy asked, eyes twinkling. He then proceeded to wipe the scrapes on her knee with the wipes, her skin twitching under his touch.

"Actually, I imagined it was a gorgeous *woman* with a German shepherd."

Andy paused to look up. "That does sound way better."

To this, they both burst out laughing.

"Here," Andy said, handing Mira an unopened bottle of water from his car.

She smiled back at him graciously. "Thanks, that was thoughtful," she replied, and opened the bottle to drink. While she did, Andy began wrapping the gauze bandage around Mira's bruised ankle. "This should help stabilize the slacker," he explained, as his hands worked dexterously in securing the perfect wrap around her ankle—neither too tight, nor too loose.

Mira felt his eyes on her as he worked on the ankle. When he was done, he looked up at her.

"So, was this your first run today?" he asked.

Was it really that obvious? Mira wondered with horror. "Yes," she replied. "What about you? Were you out on your one-millionth run?"

A laugh blossomed on his face, extending all the way up to those gorgeous hazel-brown eyes. "I was out training for a marathon."

"Ah, right," Mira acknowledged with a nod. *Of course he was. The handsome bastard.*

"It's one of the best feelings, you know, the high after a run?" Andy then said, with his lips pursed.

"Mmm," considered Mira, watching him pack away his first aid kit. She wouldn't know, would she?

"Do you mind if I gave you some advice—runner to runner?" he asked, cautiously.

Mira coughed up a laugh. "I'm not a runner." She'd tried it, and it was sufficiently chastising. She was done. She had enough on her plate as it was, and the last thing she needed was to challenge herself on a trail and get beaten.

"Well, regardless, you might want to hear me out."

"Go ahead." Mira shrugged. There was nothing this man could say to her that would change her mind.

"Give running a fair shot, and if you still hate it, then don't ever run again."

"Today was a pretty fair shot, in my books." Mira frowned.

"For starters, you're wearing the wrong shoes."

"Not that again."

"If you wear the right kind of shoes, you'll enjoy your run *way* more. Not to mention there are apps that can help you run better. They track your pace and your performance, and you can download them on your phone for free. I think you should at least try those things before you give up, that's all I'm saying."

Mira blessed the notion with an upright palm. "Look, I already tried the app thing, and it only killed my confidence. Plus, I don't know anything about running shoes or what makes a good shoe run well, or however you say it—"

"Maybe I can help. I could take you shoe shopping. Help you find a good pair?"

Mira's heart was in her chest, her head was in a fog, and her ankle was throbbing viciously. The usual symptoms of what happens when a girl like her—an average-minded, mildly self-deprecating, recently separated, thirty-year-old—was offered help and an indirect ask-out by an incredibly hot, elit*ish* runner, right after he'd given her a piggyback ride down a trail. But it was time she came clean with him—and with herself. A man she'd trusted for three years of her life had betrayed her. How on earth was she supposed to trust Andy—a man she'd known five minutes?

"Andy, look, I really appreciate you helping me out today, but I don't think so, no."

"May I ask why?" he asked with soft eyes.

"Look, I don't know you and you don't know me."

"Okay." He frowned contemplatively.

"I'm going through . . ." Mira paused as her brain carefully decanted each word as it came out. "I'm in a bad season of life, right now a-and I was experiencing a moment of weakness when I signed up for a half-marathon." Mira shrugged. "Today, I thought I'd give the idea a try, but running just isn't for me. So, I'm not going to run the race, and I'm not going to need running shoes, either."

Andy produced a single affirming nod. "I totally get it, and I won't be pushy."

"Thanks." Mira smiled back.

"But, if you do change your mind, and want help . . ." he said, pulling a piece of paper from the driver's side of his car to scribble something on it before handing it to her. "Just call me.

Mira glanced down at it as Andy helped her back down. "It's unlikely I'll change my mind, but I appreciate the offer."

Chapter Seven

"WELL, AT LEAST you've regained your sanity," said Laila as Mira sat on the couch, soothing her swollen ankle with a bag of frozen peas. "We Soods aren't engineered to run. No one in our family has ever been a runner—not one out of the hundred clan members."

Her ankle was killing her, but not nearly as much as Laila's truth report. Luckily, the sound of the doorbell caused the latter to turn away to answer it, and when she eventually let the visitor in, Mira almost jumped out of her skin. "SAHANA!" she cried out as her cousin walked into the apartment. "How did you know I was here?"

"I made a few trips to your apartment, and you weren't there, and today, some strange dude answered the door, saying he now lived there? So, I checked with your leasing office, and they gave me your forwarding address." Sahana studied Mira with expressionless eyes as Laila walked back over to join the conversation. "And I know you and Jay aren't together anymore," she said, her words landing on Mira like meteors.

"How?" cried Mira. "Who told you?"

"Well, for one, you've moved in here. Plus, he just updated his social media status from 'Married' to 'In a relationship.'"

The words cut through Mira like a knife through butter. "He . . . w-what?"

"Well done, Sherlock," Laila said, tipping her head at Sahana. "You figured it out. So, what do you want from Mira? A medal for your meddling?"

Sahana threw Laila an admonishing look. "I didn't come here to meddle. I want to help." She then turned to Mira. "Why didn't you ever tell us you and Jay were having problems?"

Mira shrugged. "Because I didn't know we were having problems until he told me he . . . h-he was having an affair."

"WHAT?!" Sahana cried out.

Mira nodded and proceeded to tell her cousin the sordid details.

"You'd better lawyer up," warned Sahana.

Yeah, like I can afford one, thought Mira. "Who else knows?" she then asked.

"Mom suspects something is up between you two, I'm afraid," Sahana said with a shrug. "She's more active on social media than I am. She called me today while I was driving to work and asked me if I knew anything about Jay's status change—it was so out of the blue. But that's when I checked it out for myself."

If Auntie Sharmila ever uncovered the truth for herself, she'd likely never forgive Mira for withholding a secret of this magnitude. Mira cradled her head in her palms. She knew what she needed to do, but it was that very thought that was causing her head to spin. "I have to go see Mummyji tonight."

"Do you want me to come with you?" offered Laila.

"No," Mira said with an inward shudder. "I need to do this alone."

SHE COULDN'T BRING herself to ring the doorbell, so Mira simply stood outside Auntie Sharmila's door, brain numb and ankle throbbing, until the older woman's territorial instincts kicked in and she proactively emerged to open it.

"Mira?" she said, eyes widening. She was wearing her bathrobe and her makeup was off, so she was probably getting ready for bed.

"Sorry, Mummyji. Maybe it's later than I thought—"

"Nonsense. Come in, come in," she insisted. "I was just watching the latest Bollywood hits on that new cable channel your Papaji installed." She herded Mira past the television room, however, and straight into the interrogation room, a.k.a. her breakfast nook in the kitchen. She then paused to consider Mira's limp. "What happened to your leg?"

"I-er . . . twisted it. It's nothing."

"Sit down, Mira," she instructed softly. "I'll make us some *chai*."

Chai. *Great*. A.k.a. the Indian truth serum—a sweet, milky, cardamom-flavored puppet master.

Mira watched in contemplative silence as Auntie Sharmila shuffled in the kitchen before pouring the tea into two cups. She lined the saucer with homemade savory cumin crackers.

"Here," she said, placing the tray of items between them.

"Now, tell me what's going on, Mira. All is not right with you, my dear—I feel it."

"Jay—" she began to say, but the words were firmly lodged in her throat. Mira tried sipping her tea and then continued. "Mummyji, Jay had an affair. He's left me—our marriage."

Auntie Sharmila's jaw dropped, just shy of mouthing a cracker. "An *affair*?"

It was like getting a root canal in the seventeenth century. But through the pain, Mira managed to (coherently and without tears) relate the unfortunate facts to Auntie Sharmila. The latter listened, occasionally chanting "*Hai, Ram!*" every few minutes.

"But why didn't you tell us, Mira? Instead, you move in with that hippie cousin?"

"Laila has been extremely supportive, Mummyji."

"She's a disrespectful rebel who has embarrassed the family time and time again. And she didn't even bother to show up for my Diwali party," Auntie Sharmila said, fuming. "Do you know, she smokes *ganja*?"

A sigh slipped out of Mira. "She's been there for me, and I didn't tell anyone because . . . I was humiliated and angry."

Auntie Sharmila reached out to hold Mira's hand. "This is terrible news, Mira. But there is no point crying over spilt milk, my dear. What's done is done. Now let us think about the next step. That's my advice," she said, steadily.

Her aunt's curiously progressive approach left Mira confused yet touched. "Thank you, Mummyji."

"Absolutely. We are family, and we Soods always stick together."

Mira's heart unclenched, and she reached for a cracker to dunk in her chai. "I can't tell you what a relief this is to hear."

Her auntie watched her. "Yes, but now we should work to minimize the damage to our family."

"Mmm..." agreed Mira. Emotionally unburdened, she could finally savor the sweet taste of the tea. "And I'll call Ma tonight and—"

"Don't mention *anything* to your parents," Auntie Sharmila cut in. "They don't need to know a thing. And we can fix it all before any of this news gets out."

Mira let her teacup come to rest on the table. "I don't understand. How can I keep the news from my parents that I'm getting a divorce?"

"This is what I suggest..." Auntie Sharmila said, gently rocking back and forth in her chair with anticipation. "Your Papaji and I will call Jay's parents in India—ideally it should have been *your* Papa, but he is not in a position to do it, poor man, and your mother can't do it alone."

"But what does it matter now if Jay's parents know or not?"

"Well, it matters, because they can *talk* to Jay. He is their son, so they will know how to bring that rascal back on track. I know a friend's daughter who married a French guy, and they got divorced, then they got remarried under the Eiffel Tower a year later, and now they have *three* kids."

Mira's brain drew a blank. She wished she'd brought Laila along, for she would have known to mete out a perfectly fair response to the garbage spewing out of Auntie Sharmila's mouth.

"Are you listening?" her auntie checked in. "Do you

agree with this plan?"

"But you just called Jay a rascal?"

"He's a *scoundrel*," added Auntie Sharmila, with an emphatic nod.

"You want me to get back with a rascally scoundrel who cheated on me with another woman?" Best to confirm the premise before losing her mind, thought Mira.

Auntie Sharmila squinted back, defensively tucking the edges of her bathrobe around herself. "You and your entire generation think you are so smart... so *modern*. But you have a duty to this family and your parents... especially to your father who is in a wheelchair, unable to move or speak. And now you want to tell them you are getting *divorced*?" cried the older woman. "Men will be men, Mira. Women are smarter and *stronger* than men, so we have to take charge in these situations—"

"By acting stupid?" The words slipped out with ease, and Mira was happy not to hold back anymore. Plus, her head felt like it weighed a ton, and she was convinced if she wasn't careful, it would roll right off her shoulders.

Auntie Sharmila licked her lips combatively. "So, what are you saying then? You want to be selfish and only think of yourself? You want to be a divorcée at *thirty*? What will our people back home say?"

"I don't *want* to be divorced," said Mira, fighting back tears. "But this is what Jay wants. What I want doesn't matter."

"Divorce is unheard of in our family, my dear," her auntie replied firmly. "You're lucky we're having this discussion here in Seattle and not Punjab. If it were the latter, we would have had to move to another town."

"Mummyji, I don't think anyone in this family knows what I'm going through. I don't want to think about Jay anymore, and"—Mira inhaled deeply, for the next part would cause some pain—"I'd rather face the humiliation than get back with him."

Auntie Sharmila's mouth was left open. "So, you're determined to ruin us, then?"

Mira matched her auntie's fiery gaze with a deadpan look. "You have Jay to thank for that, Mummyji, not me."

"YOU'RE HOME EARLY?" asked Laila with a curious frown, when Mira entered the apartment late that night. "How'd it go? Did the piranha eat you up, or did she just torture you with emotional drama?"

"I have good news and bad news," replied Mira, settling into the sofa. "I've decided to run the half-marathon."

Laila appeared confused. "Did you hit your head somewhere? What changed your mind?"

Mira stared blankly at the floor. "I can feel myself sinking, Laila. I feel . . . like a *failure*," she said, breathing in. "I need to run this race to prove myself wrong."

"Okay," said Laila. "And what's the *good* news?"

Mira smiled back at her cousin. "Given how disappointed Mummyji was in me tonight, you and I will likely never have to attend another one of her Diwali parties, ever again."

That night, Mira texted Andy: *Changed my mind. I'm running the race. Does your shoe-shopping offer still stand? Oh, this is Mira Sood, by the way. The woman who hitchhiked on your back.*

Chapter Eight

THAT NIGHT MIRA made the most gut-wrenching phone call of all—she called her parents to relay the news of her broken marriage. The conversation with Auntie Sharmila had afforded her a reasonable preview into what to expect from her own mother. It went down badly. Tears were shed, emotions erupted, just as one would expect. The showdown between Mira and her mother was almost as dramatic as the one with Auntie Sharmila, with dishearteningly similar themes—how men will be men, but the wife had to be their older, wiser babysitter. The older woman had cried, howled, and scolded Mira as if she were eight, not thirty. Ironically, as she scolded her like a child, she reminded Mira of how she was now thirty and too old for a scolding.

Surprisingly, though, the news did not kill her father. In fact, a few minutes after her call with them had ended, Mira received a text from him. He couldn't type complete sentences, owing to his disability, but what Mira received from him made her break down and cry: a single heart emoji. She knew how hard it must have been for him to even do so much, with barely being able to move his fingers anymore. But he'd sent it, probably without her mother knowing. The latter had been less gracious and more furious, both with Jay and Mira. Such was the Sood family custom—where you always split the blame fifty-fifty between the spouses when it was the husband's fault, with the woman incurring one hundred percent of the blame in all remaining scenarios.

The final call was to her brother, Manoj, who lived in Australia. They weren't close, mainly because they had nothing in common but for their biological parents. He was ten years older and had enjoyed all the misogynistic privileges that came with being the first-born son of the family—the freedom to drink, smoke, date, work, study, and ultimately marry the woman of his choosing.

"Hi, Manoj *Bhaiya*," said Mira when he answered the call.

"Mira?" he replied. "What's all this nonsense I'm hearing about you and Jay? You're getting a divorce?"

"Yes," sighed Mira, and painfully hit the play button on her saga for the millionth time. Manoj listened, offering some perfunctory support before hanging up the phone. As Mira lay curled up in her bed that night, she felt isolated and alone. She was surrounded by family, and yet, her failure felt like it was her own, and no one could lighten her load.

SITTING UP IN bed the next morning, Mira checked her emails. She'd sent out a hundred and fifty job applications and absolutely *no* one wanted to hire her. This meant she had to resort to Plan B—the Indian grocery store was hiring. They needed a new cashier and the job would pay minimum wage. She was a leading candidate for the role, since she was on a first-name basis with the store's owner, Jaggu Sethi. It was a last resort, but if nothing else turned up by the end of the week, she decided she would take the job so she could at least start chipping in with the rent.

The swelling in Mira's leg was almost gone, and she could put weight on her foot again. She and Andy had a shoe-shopping appointment that evening, and he'd offered to pick her up. Standing before her mirror, wearing a pink sweater and black leggings, she checked the clock. Andy was due any minute. Laila was sprawled on the bed, watching intently. "Now, remember," Laila said. "It's not slutty to put out on the first date."

Mira cringed. "Laila, I told you, it's not a date."

"Then it's odd why this dude wants to help, without expecting anything in return. What is he, a modern-day monk?"

"Well, you're wrong," said Mira. "And considering how my last relationship ended, I'm off men."

"Why should you deprive yourself of men just because your husband turned out to be a shitless weasel? I remember you were the same way in college. You dated that one loser. What was his name? Yash, or Yaj?"

"Suraj," replied Mira, as a memory of him wafted into her brain.

"Yeah, him," cried Laila. "The self-obsessed, wannabe model who couldn't keep a job longer than three weeks. So, you broke up with him and didn't date anyone for a year. Why do you do that? You get one bad grape, and you toss the entire box of Welches in the trash."

Mira rolled her eyes at her cousin. "Oh, stop exaggerating."

"Anyway," said Laila. "I still think it's weird this Andy guy, who you barely know, wants to help—take you freakin' *shoe* shopping. He's going to ask you out, I know it."

"Well, either you're right, or I am. And tonight will tell, okay?" said Mira, her heart pounding.

ANDY STOOD OUTSIDE the door, looking phenomenal in a black crewneck sweater and jeans. His metal-rimmed spectacles added that soft dimension to his otherwise lean, but muscular frame. "Hi," he said with that smile that invaded his eyes.

"Hello," Mira smiled back. "Do you want to come in?"

Andy nodded and stepped in. "How's your ankle?"

"Oh, much, *much* better, thanks," Mira replied. "And how's your back after carrying me on it?"

Andy laughed. "Better than ever, thanks."

Hearing the bustle, Laila walked out of the bedroom. "Ah, yes—you must be Andy," she said dramatically.

"Yeah, hi," Andy replied.

"Would you like something to drink? Some chai tea?" Mira asked, trying to diffuse any further interrogation by Laila.

Andy's eyes widened with enthusiasm. "I actually love chai tea. But we should probably get going."

As they headed out the door, Mira shuddered as she heard Laila call out: "I'm right, you'll see."

"Do I want to know?" Andy turned to ask.

Mira gargled a sigh. "Nope."

SPORTING GOODS INC. was located in Downtown Seattle, and it was as if Andy Fitzgerald owned the place. Within seconds of them walking in, a guy from the store had walked up to them with a smile of recognition. "Andrew! How's it going, man?"

"Hey, Seth. Good to see you," replied Andy. The two men greeted each other, slapping their palms together or whatever it was that was the equivalent of a "man" shake. "This is Mira," Andy added.

"It's nice to meet any friend of the marathon star." Seth smiled as he and Mira shook hands. With his dreadlocks and glacier-blue eyes, Seth looked like a yogi who'd cracked life's secret code to a happily-ever-after.

"How's Savannah?" Seth asked, turning from Mira back to Andy.

The question caused Andy to check his blind spot with a turn of his head, which is where Mira was standing. "Er, she and I broke up."

"No kidding?" Seth said, raising an eyebrow.

"Yeah, it's old news. Anyway . . . listen, Seth?" Andy said, slapping his friend on the shoulder as if to physically reset the conversation. "Mira, here, is looking for a knockout pair of running shoes—"

"Oh, so, you're a runner, too?" Seth turned, tipping his head at Mira.

This caught her off guard for a moment. *Was* she a runner? The word sounded so "audacious" and "free." And she was unfamiliar with either sensation. Nonetheless, she was tempted to touch the tip of the idea. "Yes, a beginner."

"Swell." Seth nodded. "Follow me, and I can hook you up."

As they followed Seth, Mira leaned in to whisper to Andy. "You never told me you were a marathon *star*."

This made him laugh out. "That's because I'm not."

Seth led them to a wall stacked with all kinds of shoes. He started pulling random ones out for Mira to try on; every single one she slid on felt a million times more comfortable than her leopard-print pair. Mira even ran around the store wearing them, as per Andy's suggestion, and was blown away by the way her body responded to running in a good pair of shoes—it made the running *fun*.

After trying on several different pairs, Mira settled on one, which Andy admitted was his favorite also—a pair of neon-blue-and-pink Brooks Running shoes. They fit perfectly, and Mira knew this was the pair she ought to wear to run her first half-marathon.

"One hundred fifty dollars," Seth said coolly when she asked how much they cost.

"Wait, *what?*" Mira cried with disbelief.

"Good running shoes can be a bit pricey sometimes," Andy tried to explain.

"A *bit* pricey?" gasped Mira. "Andy, I can't afford these."

"But do you like 'em?"

She shrugged. "Yes, but they're way over budget for me."

Andy appeared to nod with understanding, if not agreement.

"Can't I just buy them secondhand from somewhere? Craigslist?" Mira brainstormed.

"Secondhand?" Andy repeated, looking rather intrigued. "Er, no, I wouldn't recommend that."

He then suggested the clearance section. "How about these?" he asked Mira, after much browsing.

She tried them and liked them. They were reasonably priced—still more than she would've liked to pay for a pair of running shoes, but she knew she needed to invest in them. She knew all too well that there was no way her feet were going to carry her across the half-marathon finish line in their present state. "I'll take them."

Andy waited with the weight of his body leaning against the checkout counter while Mira paid for her shoes. When she was done, she turned to him. "Thanks, this was perfect," She smiled, inwardly wondering how she should ask him to please drive her back home.

"Yeah, I think the shoes worked out," he said with a nod. "So, should we grab a quick bite before I drive you back?" he then asked. "I'm *starving*."

"Oh?" Mira shuddered. Would that be okay for her to do? She didn't know. She was still getting used to being Mira-the-ex-wife. But a casual dinner with a new "male friend" felt innocent enough, so she nodded.

"Great! I'm going to take a wild guess and say you like Mexican food?" Andy smiled.

"I love Mexican food. How did you know?"

He winked and pushed open the door for Mira as they walked out of the store. "All my Indian friends seem to love Mexican food. Something about the rice with the beans? Plus, I know this great place."

"Not fancy, I hope?" She couldn't afford that, especially

since she'd just shelled out a week's groceries' worth of moolah on those damned shoes. "Because I'd prefer as unfancy as possible."

"It's a food truck." Andy grinned.

Score. Mira smiled back. But her heart tripped over a sudden realization. Wait, was this turning into a date? *Oh God, was Laila right this whole time?*

Chapter Nine

THE FOOD TRUCK was called Señor Toad, and it stood, expelling aromatic steam, a few blocks down from the Fremont Canal. It was faintly raining, but Mira was too hungry to notice as she savored the idea of the items on the chalkboard menu.

"They have one of the best burritos you'll ever taste," said Andy, as they got in line. "That's what I always get."

"I think I'm brave enough to try their spicy chimichanga with a side of their salsa," replied Mira. "And maybe the raspberry margarita?" she wondered out loud. If she was taking the freeway to "broke," she preferred to do it with a pretty pink drink in her hand. Reaching into her purse, Mira pulled the cash out to hand to Andy.

"Nah, don't worry about it," he said gallantly.

But Mira shook her head. She had to complete the litmus test to establish to herself that this was *not* a date. "I insist," she replied, to which Andy quickly conceded.

Twenty minutes later, Mira and Andy found themselves sitting across from each other at a picnic table along the canal's waters, savoring the taste of fresh-made chips, guacamole, and salsa. The chimichanga Mira had ordered was as delicious as Andy had promised, and her drink felt warm on her throat against the nightly chill.

"So, what changed your mind?" asked Andy. "About running the half-marathon?"

Mira placed a fist over her full mouth as she considered the question. "For one, I couldn't get a refund."

"Ah."

"But more than that, I just felt convinced I needed to run this race to help me get over whatever I'm trying to get over in my life right now," she said, her words wobbly and unsure. She thought it best to turn the spotlight away from herself. "How long have you been a runner?" she asked, reaching to pull out a large chip from the mound.

Andy sipped his drink and smiled as he watched Mira fearlessly heap guacamole on her chip. "I think I started when I was about fifteen, and I'm thirty-one . . . so about sixteen years?"

"*Wow*," cried Mira as she put the chip in her mouth.

"What's wowing you? The extent of my running journey, or the goodness of the guacamole?"

Mira shrugged, looking meek. "Mmm, would it offend you if it were the guacamole?"

Andy laughed.

"So, you've been a runner more than *half* your life, then," Mira said, reaching for more chips and guac.

Andy followed in her footsteps. "Once you taste a runner's high, it's hard to shake off the addiction."

Mira sipped her flamingo-pink margarita. "I wouldn't know," she said, dryly. "Unlike you, I've been a runner for an exact total of fifteen minutes. Which is, what, one *millionth* of my life?" Mira asked, swatting the air. "So, are you like a professional racer or something? If you are, just tell me and I'll leave *right* now," she warned. *No, seriously.*

Andy shook his head. "Nah, I do race major marathons on a regular basis, but I don't do it for money, just street cred within the running community."

"I see." *Street cred within the running community*, soaked up Mira, inwardly. Not a single damn word in that sentence felt relatable to her. "What do you do for a living then, if not racing?"

"I own a tech start-up called 'Cloud-9,'" Andy replied, pushing his spectacles back onto the bridge of his nose. "We offer cloud-computing solutions."

"Sounds very . . . er, *technical*," said Mira. "How big is your company?"

"How small, you mean?" Andy amended with a smile. "We're at about twelve or so employees, and I co-own the business with two other guys. We started the company right out of grad school."

Mira listened intently, hoping the employment question wouldn't go round-robin and land on her head.

"What about you? What do you do?"

Damn it! She just had to go and light a fire under the topic by asking Andy the question first. "I'm, er"—another word for unemployed would be—"in the midst of a career change." *Nice.* Much better sounding than: "I'm unemployed as I have no transferable skills."

To Mira's relief, Andy nodded and decided to change the subject—to a worse one.

"I take it this is your first half-marathon then?"

Gulp. The sound of the truth caused Mira to reach for

her drink again. "Yup."

"That's impressive," Andy said with a shrug.

"*Impressive?*" asked Mira with a pout. "Which is elite-runner code for what, 'extremely stupid'?"

"It's neither stupid nor extreme," replied Andy, shaking his head.

"That's easy for you to say. You're a marathon star."

Andy appeared to wince at the imagery. "Uh, I should remember to punch Seth the next time I see him."

"Why? Is he wrong?"

"He's not wrong. I just don't agree with him." Andy picked a chip up and scooped some guacamole. "I don't consider myself a star. I love to race, and there's pleasure in winning, I'm not denying that. But I don't think winning a race makes anyone a star."

"Then, what does?" Mira laughed.

"*Finishing* the race," said Andy with a glorious smile. "In my opinion, anyone who sticks it out to run across that finish line, regardless of the distance they've run, or their pace, or their runtime, is a star."

Yes, she was listening. And yes, the blood was pumping through her veins as she heard him out. "Interesting perspective, I'll give you that," she said.

"And if you put your mind to it, you can run across that finish line too."

"You think?" she asked with a raise of a brow. Fat, fat chance, but it was nice of him to say.

"Yeah, I really do. And if you ever need a running partner . . . or a trainer, for that matter, I'm happy to play the part."

Mira watched him intently. "You're offering to help me train for my half-marathon?"

"Sure, and I can teach you a few tricks of the trade." He winked playfully.

Okay, that's it. It was time to address the big, fat elephant in the room. "Look, Andy, I really appreciate the offer and everything you've done so far, but there's something I want to get clear with you."

"Okay," Andy said, looking tentative.

"I'm just not ready to da—*hang* out with men at the moment."

A quizzical frown appeared on Andy's face. "*Hang out* with men?"

Inhaling deeply, Mira put down her fork. "About a month ago, my husband told me he was having an affair. He left the marriage and me, and I moved into my cousin Laila's house—"

Andy's eyes widened. "*What?*"

"We were married three years. I placed my trust in him, and he smashed it, just like that," said Mira with a snap of her fingers. Surprising. It had taken her several weeks and a whole lot of pain to admit the fact to her family, but absolutely no time or effort to open her heart to this perfect stranger who sat before her.

"*God*, Mira." Andy's frown deepened as his hands released their grip on his burrito. "What a fucking jerk!"

"I don't know why you offered to help me with the shoe shopping and now with the training. And if you think about it, you'll understand why I'm finding it hard to trust any man right now, and I'm absolutely not ready to . . ." Mira was lost in pursuit of another synonym for "date."

"Okay, just back it up for me here," Andy said, wiping the sides of his mouth with a paper napkin. "I'm sure you picked this up already, but I just survived a pretty nasty breakup myself. I'm not nearly close to reentering the dating scene, either."

Mira frowned. "So, you want to help me purely out of the kindness of your heart?"

Andy laughed. "I wouldn't go that far, no."

"What then? What's in it for you?" Laila's words, not hers.

Andy paused to consider. "How corny would it sound if I told you I was passionate about running? I believe in the healing powers of this sport because I know how much it has helped me grow—not just fitness-wise, but as a *person*. I'm trying to help, because I *know* I can help."

Great, now she felt exposed and stupid. Mira sighed, making a mental note to kick Laila's butt when she returned. Luckily, there were enough chips left in the basket to give Mira something to do while the dust of awkwardness between them settled.

"So, are you game to train with me?" ventured Andy.

Mira breathed in. "If you're sure, then I'm sure." She smiled.

WHEN THE FOOD had been eaten and the drinks drunk, Andy and Mira decided to walk around Fremont for a bit. Mira refused to admit to herself how comfortable she felt in

Andy's company. How different it felt from her interactions with Jay. Her marriage to Jay had felt mechanical. Like the sum total of many chores: he worked, she cooked, he watched TV, she cleaned up after him. They had never really *connected*. Never just talked. They had gone to watch movies together a few times, but it had felt to Mira more like a school field trip than a romantic outing. Jay had held her back. But with Andy, she, for the first time in years, was just being herself—unguarded and free.

They laughed and chatted like old friends, as if they knew each other from another life.

"Did you always know what you wanted to do? Start a tech company?" Mira asked him as they walked by the bustling shops that had come alive under a night sky.

"Starting Cloud-9 was on my bucket list, but it's more of a means to an end. It's not really my *ultimate* goal in life."

"Oh yeah? Then what is?" Also, should she tell him what hers had morphed into these days? Getting through an entire day without self-deprecation or thinking about Jay the Jackass. Every time she did it, she gave herself a cookie.

"My dream is to own a lake house in the wilderness," said Andy.

"Huh?" she replied, her eyes wide with curiosity.

Andy's smile flooded his eyes as always, turning them into crescents. "I know, it sounds a bit unconventional."

"Mmm, not if you like solitude . . . and Sasquatch," she said, and then admired how his smile bloomed into a gorgeous laugh. *Look, but don't touch*, she warned her racing heart. "Do you have a place in mind?" she asked him.

"I do. It's in a remote part of Whidbey Island, and I've

had my eye on it since I was sixteen and used to take fishing trips with my dad."

"Oh, wow."

"But I still have a long way before I can buy my lake house," said Andy. "I need to get Cloud-9 off the ground and to do that, I need a whale investor."

"I see," Mira said thoughtfully. "Do you have anyone in mind?"

Andy nodded. "There are a few venture capitalists we've been chasing, my partners and I."

"And?"

"We haven't been able to snag anyone yet. But we'll get there . . . And believe me, the day we do, I'll celebrate with a bottle of champagne and call my real estate agent to put the down payment on that lake house."

They laughed together, their eyes occasionally colliding. And that's when Mira realized how long it had been since she'd been happy—smiling without faking it.

"It went well, then?" asked Laila as she cozied up on Mira's bed late that night. "Did he ask you out?"

Mira let out a long sigh. "Yes, it went well, and no, you were *dead* wrong. He's just really passionate about running."

Laila squinted back at her cousin. "You almost have yourself convinced."

"Think what you want. I know what I know," Mira replied.

"When do you see him next?"

"I'm going to start training with him next weekend. He has to work during the week," Mira said, ruefully slamming her laptop shut. "Unlike me, who can't seem to find a single job out of the thousands. I can't even land an interview—"

"Oh, that's why I came in. Thanks for reminding me." Laila cut in. "I got you a job interview."

"Wait, *what*?" Mira sat up. "Are you kidding? Because I'm not amused."

"Nope, it's no joke." Laila shook her head. "My audio engineer's girlfriend is a recruiter at a consulting firm, and he mentioned they're hiring for an office assistant. So, I twisted his arm and got you an interview."

"Like, how? Did you *blackmail* him?"

"Er, no," replied Laila with a casual shrug. "I literally grabbed his arm and twisted it till he caved."

Mira leapt forward and hugged her tight. "Thank you so much." For the first time since that awful night Jay left, this felt like the chance Mira needed to rebuild her life. *And I won't let it slip.*

Chapter Ten

FALL – September

IT DIDN'T FIT her. *Damn it.* Mira cursed under her breath as she stood before the full-length mirror in Laila's room, tugging on her tweed jacket—the only one she owned, back from her newly married days when she'd had dreams and a sense of self-worth. "How bad does it look?" she asked Laila, who lay sprawled on the bed.

"Well, you look like a—"

"Actually, don't answer that." Mira quickly added. The look on Laila's face said it all.

Mira sighed and closed her eyes. She knew she'd gained "some" weight. But that morning, the day of her first job interview in *many* years—essentially, the worst day to do it—Mira had decided to *weigh* herself. The scales told a sad story—of the many, *many* pounds of internalized emotions she now carried on her waist, her butt, her thighs, and every nook and cranny that could house cellulite. With her dark, diving lashes against her caramel skin, her brown eyes, and prolific lips, framed by shoulder-length black hair, Mira was an attractive woman. She had no qualms about her weight, either. Who cared how many extra pounds she carried? That was her business. But the jacket didn't fit.

"Ugh," moaned Mira, peeling the thing off before flinging it on the bed. She then checked her watch. "I'm going to be late for the interview."

Laila got up and walked over. "Right. Take this off . . ." she said, tugging at the cable sweater Mira had on.

"Wait, I need that," the latter objected, but her cousin pulled it clean off.

"Now, this," Laila said, ripping off the long T-shirt underneath.

"Why are you undressing me?" cried Mira. *What the hell was happening?* Nothing but her bra remained as Laila walked over to her closet and pulled out a black camisole. "Here," she said, flinging it at Mira.

"I can't even fit into my own clothes these days, and you're expecting me to fit into *yours*?"

"Chill, it's one-size-fits-all," said Laila. "Put it on, and then try the jacket again."

Mira obeyed, and this time, the jacket fit—at least well enough for Mira to be able to (conservatively) move her arms and breathe occasionally.

THE RAIN POURED relentlessly. Mira defogged her windshield and poked her phone for directions as she gunned her second-rate Honda down I-405. "Shit!" she cursed. She could barely see through the shower curtain of rain. Plus, she couldn't remember if she'd eaten breakfast, because her stomach appeared to think not. Mira squinted through the glass, trying to determine if she needed to take the next exit.

She still had a few miles left to go, so she decided to play it safe and fish a cereal bar out of her handbag on the passenger seat. "Yes," she said, retrieving the bar, but "God, *no*..." she'd missed her exit.

Feeling like a giant nincompoop, Mira re-circled the freeway. And because life was a cruel, cruel joke, Auntie Sharmila called just as she approached the exit a second time. By the time Mira could decide whether or not to answer it, the ringing stopped. "You have *got* to be kidding me," she cried out. Yup. She'd missed her exit again. All she needed to do now was miss it one last time, and she'd officially set a world record for most exits missed on a single trip.

Inside the Bellevue Business Center, Mira jabbed the elevator button for the top floor. Tugging on her jacket and feeling like a pumpkin in a bathing suit, Mira finally made it a minute shy of her appointed interview time. "I hope I'm not late?" she gingerly asked the receptionist as the latter handed her a visitor card to garland around her neck.

"You're fine." The young woman smiled back. "I'll let Molly know you're here. Can I get you anything to drink while you wait?"

Soda, lemonade, a pint of self-confidence? "Er, no, I'm fine, thanks."

Settling into a large leather chair in the lobby, Mira pulled out her phone. Other than the missed call from her auntie and a voicemail, Mira noticed she had a new text message. It was from Andy Fitzgerald. The sight of it invariably brought a smile to her lips. They had been texting each other since they last met, and she'd told him about the interview today. *Good luck, Mira. Go get 'em!* read the text. And that was the boost she needed. Putting her phone to her ear, she then listened to her auntie's voicemail:

"Hello, Mira? This is Mummyji. I know things did not go well when we talked last time, but we are family. Your problem is my problem, whatever you say. I actually have some good news to give you, which I think will make you happy, so I will come by Laila's apartment to see you over the weekend. Okay, I have to go now. All this tension in your life has aggravated *my* hypertension, so Papaji has booked me a massage appointment to help me relax. I told him no need, I am happy to take the stress on Mira's account, but he insisted. Anyway, I'm running late. Take care, don't forget to call your poor mother, and I will see you soon."

Fifteen minutes passed, then Molly Messner, girlfriend to audio engineer Peyton, whose arm had been physically wrenched to attain this interview, arrived. "Hi, is it Mira? Did I say that right?" she asked, reaching to shake Mira's hand. She was a tall, smiling brunette who had on a killer pantsuit and chili-red lipstick.

"Yes, you said it perfectly," replied Mira, returning the shake. She couldn't remember the last time she was in this situation—shaking someone's hand like a professional.

Molly led Mira into a conference room, and they each settled into a swivel chair around an oval desk. A row of large windows afforded a view of downtown Bellevue.

"Thanks for taking the time to come down here on such short notice," began Molly, as she opened a folder to extract Mira's resume. She then opened up her laptop and started typing. "I hope you won't mind me taking notes?" she paused to check.

"Er, no, not at all, and I really appreciate this opportunity to interview for this role. I'm pretty excited about it and I was reading about your company on your website—"

"Oh?"

"Just doing some groundwork for this interview," Mira said with a shrug as Molly continued to type away.

"So, what did you learn about our company from your research?"

Mira casually placed her arms on the table and leaned into the conversation. She'd forgotten how much she loved interviewing—she loved meeting new people and talking about new things. Along came the memory and, with it, her adrenaline rush.

"I picked up a lot about what your culture is like here at Pacific Consulting. I love that the company is employee-centric, and I also took the liberty to read reviews from your former and current employees, and I was so impressed to see how many positive things people had to say about this place. I'm guessing that's one of the reasons why some of your employees appear to have worked at Pacific for over a decade I believe?" Mira felt like she was standing on tiptoe on a surfboard, riding a giant wave.

Molly had stopped typing. "Yes, you're right, actually. And it's pretty neat you already know so much about us. I like that you went the extra mile to prepare for our meeting... it's exactly the kind of proactive thinking we're hoping for in this new hire."

"The office assistant role?"

"That's right." Molly smiled. "And I think we're off to

an excellent start."

Molly and Mira got along like peas and carrots. For the next half hour, they covered everything they could about the role, with Molly alluding to how perfect a candidate Mira appeared to be. "Of course, there are still some final decisions to be made—"

"Of course, and I respect the thoroughness," agreed Mira. *It's in the bag!*

Molly briefly studied her laptop screen. "I think I've covered most of our interview questions," she said, turning to Mira again. "You know, I have to admit, I was a bit skeptical about your candidacy when Peyton first asked if I would interview you for this role. No offense, it was just that there was a pretty big gap in your resume; you hadn't worked in *three* years."

Mira nodded. "I completely understand."

"And it's fine, really. This is an entry-level position, and we're expecting whoever fills it will require some ramping up." Molly shut her laptop with a casual shrug. "Plus, a lot of people take time off from working a nine-to-five to raise a family, or travel, or even learn a new language—"

"I didn't do it to learn a new language," interrupted Mira. "I wanted to work. I wanted to keep going." Uh-oh.

"So, then why—"

"I married Jay," Mira cut in again, her head bobbing in a rhythmic trance. Yep. It was happening. She could feel the flood of fury rising up inside her like a tsunami, with the heat from it drying the back of her throat. "I married Jay, and he cheated on me with another woman while I sat around cooking and cleaning for him. He was having sex with *another* woman while I sat wondering why he didn't want to touch me anymore... while the 'giant gap' in my resume grew, grew, and *grew*."

"L-look, I didn't mean t—"

"And you know the worst part, Molly?" Mira stuttered through her rage, and with tears welling up. "My *entire* family—my auntie and my mom too—are going about acting like none of this is Jay's fault. My auntie is even pinning her hypertension on me... *ME*. As if I screwed up my marriage... *forced* Jay to have an affair. *Was* it my fault? You tell me, Molly... YOU TELL ME!" She'd gone ballistic, pounding the table with her fists like a deranged ape. And unbeknownst to Mira, a perplexed Molly had reopened her laptop and begun typing things in it at warp speed, likely feeling proud of the recruiting skills which had prompted her to ask the deal-breaking question.

Chapter Eleven

THE PACIFIC NORTHWEST rain was unforgiving as it blew Mira's umbrella away from her head. She'd been walking in it for thirty minutes, and by the time she reached Sethi's Indian Grocery Store, she was soaked through and freezing. Mira checked her reflection in the window before entering, just in time to catch a fleeting glimpse of Jaggu Sethi himself before he disappeared into the lentils- and beans aisle. Jagdish Sethi was a short, pale man with plump jowls, betel nut-stained teeth, and the temperament of a honeybee. Threaten his stash, and he would strike.

"*Jaggu-bai*," Mira called out as she made her way to him. *Bai*, meaning brother, respectfully.

"*Arey?*" Jaggu smiled. "Welcome, Mira-ji. So, it's your first day working at this store, yes?"

A painful, unavoidable outcome of her disastrous interview. Mira nodded, trying to fake a smile.

"Okay, Shanti will give you a tour, and you can stand by her side today to learn how to work the cash register okay?"

A second nod. "Is there somewhere I can store my bag?" asked Mira, gesturing to the large tote she was carrying. Regardless of the fact that her work life was in shambles, Mira still had the half-marathon mountain to climb. She and

Andy had decided to train at the trail that weekend. Mira felt it would help if she practiced running solo before then, so she could at least minimize her embarrassment when she did train with Andy. She tried not to pay attention to how much she was looking forward to seeing him. He felt, to her, so simple and uncalculated. Like the Xanax she needed to combat her life's present challenges, a.k.a. the Sood family.

Her shift at the store ended at two, and she planned to change in the back restroom before heading out to the trail for a comeback, solo run.

"Oh yes, you can put your bag under the counter," said Jaggu.

The shift rolled on, nice and slow. After all, she was among her tribe—the incessant Bollywood music tunes, chattering cashiers who were all aunties of varying ages, the smell of mango powder and ghee, *diyas* and henna cone pyramids.

"So, how long have you lived in the U.S.?" asked Shanti Auntie, a gregarious woman in her mid-fifties, wearing a flower-printed sari and a hand-knit cardigan.

"About three years," replied Mira, as she weighed a bag of green chilies for a customer.

"Are you married?" followed Preeti, who appeared to be a little older than Mira.

Mira sighed. The question had been inevitable, and she needed to get used to answering it. "I'm . . . s-separated from my husband." The words felt foreign as she spoke them, and they silenced Preeti, Shanti auntie, and the third auntie, Manjula, who had yet to say a word.

"Oh, I am in a similar situation. My husband and I just

did not get along. Fighting all the time and he would do whatever his mother asks him to," said Preeti, breaking the ice. "But getting a divorce isn't so bad these days."

"Tch, tch, tch..." Manjula clucked her tongue. And with that, the older woman chose to abort the conversation by offering to help a customer look for whole-moong dal.

Mira cleared her throat and turned to Preeti. "So, you're divorced, too, then?"

"Nah-nah." Preeti shook her head firmly. "My family would *never* allow that. No, we sleep in separate bedrooms. After two kids, we have done our duty to the family. I let him live his life and I live mine."

Mira felt a sullen sense of pride for her fellow Indian housewife. Another quiet warrior.

AT 2:05 P.M., Mira slipped into the back restroom of the store to quickly change into a pair of loose-fitting joggers, a sweatshirt, her new shoes, and her favorite fanny pack. She then drove over to the trail, and attempted, for a second time, to become the kind of runner who could race across a half-marathon finish line without giving herself a heart attack. Mira unsteadily pushed the start button on her running app and took off down the trail.

Mmm, she thought. The shoes sure felt good to run in, and following Andy's advice, she'd stuffed them with paper towels for a couple of days to stretch them out. "You'll need to break them in, so try wearing them wherever you can," he'd added.

The rain came down incessantly, and Mira felt her lungs swiftly deflate within a few minutes of running. Pulling to a stop, she doubled over to catch her breath, shaking her head with anguish. Maybe there was something physically wrong with her. Her father was a heart patient, and so was her grandfather. Maybe it wasn't in her *genes* to be a runner? Mira sighed. If only she'd been a little less stubborn, that excuse might have actually worked for her. She breathed in a long, fresh stream of air. And then she started running again, instinctively shortening her stride and slowing her pace. That seemed to grant her a few point miles, following which she was forced to stop again.

The punishing exercise continued for a full half hour, at the end of which, Mira had run her first mile. She stopped to study the numbers recorded on the app, and while she wouldn't exactly post it on Instagram, Mira felt a sliver of pride. For the rest of that week, she continued to return to the trail. Each day, after six hours of bagging groceries and establishing the difference between Ponni and basmati rice, Mira hit the trail. Each time she did, she ran the same one-mile distance in half an hour, taking breathing breaks so she wouldn't pass out. Ironically, even with her unimpressive pace, she felt she was getting a wee bit better each time she ran.

SATURDAY ARRIVED RATHER uncoremoniously, the way all apocalyptic storms do. Mira had tossed all night and woken up looking like a bush baby, with eyes as red as hot peppers.

She reluctantly pulled herself out of bed and ate a semi-healthy breakfast of Frosted Flakes topped with a generous helping of self-doubt, afforded by an hour-long phone call with her mother. The latter confirmed her disbelief in Mira's life choices and how much she believed running, like walking, was for people who didn't have access to a vehicle.

"And running *thirteen* miles?" she'd cried. "How many Indian kilometers is it?"

"Kilometers aren't quantified by country, Ma." Mira sighed, as she did the mental math. "Twenty-one," she then said.

"*Ram, Ram*," her mother said disapprovingly. "Is that even *legal?*"

"My God, is she still talking?" asked Laila as she emerged from an adjacent room to join Mira at the kitchen counter.

The latter breathed out softly, begging for the telephonic torture to end. And it did, after sixty minutes and twenty-three seconds. "By the way, your Mummyji will be paying you a visit soon," her mother reminded Mira before signing off.

"Yes, I know, Ma," Mira muttered. "She said she had some news that will make me happy. Do you know what it is?"

A pause ensued. "She will tell you when she sees you," her mother replied evasively. If there was one thing Sood women liked more than offering up redundant news, it was withholding lifesaving news.

"So, I take it she doesn't know about your training . . . and *Andy?*" asked Laila, with a raised brow, as an exhausted Mira ended her call.

"Considering she and Mummyji still think I should get back with Jay, no."

"You've decided to lie to them, then?"

"Er, I'm not lying. I'm *withholding*," clarified Mira, and checked her watch. "I'd better get downstairs. Andy's picking me up at the curb in twenty minutes."

"Hey, put up a good fight out there," cried Laila. "Don't let Andy walk away thinking we Soods are only good for eating, drinking, and Bollywood dancing."

Mira paused to consider. "Aren't we?"

Laila shrugged. "Yeah, but he doesn't need to know that."

STANDING OVER TO one side of the trail, Mira fiddled with her fanny pack, occasionally stealing glances at her tormentor, Andrew Fitzgerald, who was a few feet away from her, standing up against a tree and taking turns pressing each foot into it with his palms flat against the trunk. The cold cloud patches that had earlier blanketed the skies had disappeared, and the warming rays of a dewy sun radiated onto Mira's caramel-peach face. Andy looked formidable as he tied his runner's knot on his shoelaces. He then showed her how to do it.

"What does it matter how I tie them?" asked Mira as he hunched over to tie her laces for her.

"A regular knot on a lace may come undone and trip you. A *runner's* knot will support your feet and keep the laces in place."

"Interesting." She nodded, as Andy stood up again.

"And there's one other thing we need to, er, take care of," he said, his eyes shifting upward from her feet to her fanny pack.

Mira glanced at her waist. "What, *this*?" she asked with surprise. "This is my favorite fanny."

"You don't need it," said Andy. "The lighter you travel, the farther you will go."

Mira frowned. "Listen, Mr. Tony Robbins, this pack has been my companion since my college days in India, okay?"

"I'm not saying throw it in the river; I'm saying leave it in your car."

"I need it for my run," she protested. The pack carried memories, and amidst the things in her life that were dissolving into nothingness, this pack had invariably become her blankie. No way she was going to admit all of that to super-hot, just-a-friend Andy, but no way was she going to leave the fanny in her car.

"Why, what's in it?" Andy asked with a raised brow.

Mira's eyes widened for a moment. "W-what's in it?"

"Actually, I've been dying to know ever since I caught you simmering in that puddle."

Mira started to protest, but then realized that maybe if he saw what was in the fanny, he would feel convinced enough to let her carry it. "Fine," she said, and unclipping it, she handed it to Andy, who promptly unzipped it and began pulling out the contents.

"A four-ounce water bottle . . ."

"A.k.a., lifesaving oxygen in liquid form," Mira added.

"Wallet, cell phone—" he looked up. "*Three* candy bars?"

"In case I get hungry on the run," explained Mira. "Unless you want me to pass out from low blood sugar?"

Andy appeared to fight back a smile. "I wouldn't want that, no." He kept going. "A reflector, a four ounce can of pepper spray—" He looked up again.

"What?" Mira asked in self-defense. "Everyone knows Washington is bear country."

"Mmm . . ." He pursed his lips. "And if the bear doesn't yield to the pepper spray, were you planning on offering him a bribe?" he then asked, pulling the last and final item out of the fanny pack—two ten-dollar rolls of quarters tied neatly together.

Mira's eyes widened. "I swear, I didn't know that was in there. That's for the laundry machine."

Andy neatly packed all the items back into the fanny. "Are you willing to risk your life, running without your fanny pack today, Mira Sood?"

How does one defend a checkmate? "Fine," she conceded and watched as Andy walked back to his car to drop off her precious fanny.

"So, how many miles are we doing today? What's my goal?" she asked him. Mira figured the best way to redeem herself would be to ask Andy thoughtful questions. At least that way she could *sound* intelligent, while possibly looking like a total fool during their run together.

"We're going to run by perceived effort," he replied briefly, as he switched a hip flexor stretch from his right leg to his left.

What the what? What did that even mean, *perceived effort*? Mira had never heard of that before, and her phone, which was inside her fanny, was now in the car, so she couldn't even look the damn term up on the internet. Or maybe it wasn't a term at all, and meant something else? Like the name of a trail? They would run up Perceived Effort, then segue into Nauseous Fear?

Mira sighed. *Super.* Now, she'd waited too long to backtrack and ask Andy what he meant by "perceived effort." Clearly, this was going to be the most mortifying run of her life.

"Try not to worry about performance. Just enjoy the run and do what your body says, okay?" he said in a reassuring voice with a warm pat on her back.

She nodded, still completely unsure of the outcome of her first training run with Andy.

He tapped his GPS watch and they started together down the gravel trail. Mira tried to breathe in deep to relax her nerves and her racing heart. As they ran down the trail, she gained control of her body. She relaxed her muscles and told herself that this was happening. *So, suck it up, Sood.* And she did what Andy had advised—not obsess over how she was doing, but instead, pay close attention to the way her body was responding, keeping it in check at all times.

At first, it was a hard thing to achieve—Mira struggled to peel her mind away from the discomfort of her off-center breathing, her clunky footwork, not to mention the anxiety caused by the fear that she was making a complete fool of herself. But a few minutes into their run, Mira consciously paid more attention to her body, keeping her running form in check, exactly the way Andy had instructed her to do before they started running.

Spine straight? Check.

Weight balanced between both feet? Check.

Arms slightly swinging, forearms parallel to the ground? Check.

Arms swinging from shoulder, not elbow? *Whoops...* and check.

They ran in perfect coordination, their feet striking the ground alternatingly. Mira soon established her momentum, and her breathing was steady and rhythmic. Andy didn't push her, but neither did she relent and slacken her pace. She kept up with him and he paced her. She wasn't sure whether it was her new shoes or the man who'd helped her buy them, but she was doing way better this time than the last. Andy explained to her as they ran that runners should always ration their stamina. "If you take off at antelope speed at the very start, you'll have an empty fuel tank by mile three or four—"

"Or *one*, in my case," Mira said dryly, remembering her last run.

She wasn't keeping track, but it felt to her as if they were making pretty good progress in terms of distance. It wasn't easy, and she could begin to feel the shortness of her breath along with her aching limbs. Within the next five-to-ten minutes, Mira was visibly uncomfortable, and Andy turned briefly to check in. "Are you doing okay?"

She nodded but didn't dare speak, knowing if she did, she'd drain herself of the last few ounces of oxygen. By the time they ran past another mile marker, Mira could no longer ignore her body's cry for a break. But Andy kept going, and his gaze was strapped to the horizon, which could mean anything, from him wanting to run another mile, to him wanting to run all the way to Idaho. There were a few moments when Mira almost opened her mouth to ask if they were ever going to stop. But she didn't, for some reason. Or maybe the reason was that in her typical pushover style, Mira secretly preferred to pass out from a lack of oxygen to her brain than ask someone to change their plans for her sake. She just hoped she'd pass out sooner rather than later, so the pain would end.

They hit a slight incline on the trail. Basically, a-nightmare-come-true for Mira. She knew for a fact that if this hill didn't take her down, nothing would. Andy turned briefly to her and said, "Make sure when you run up a hill, you lean your upper body forward to maintain balance as you ascend . . . swing your arms just enough to generate momentum. Take shorter strides and steady breaths to recycle your energy."

"'Kay," panted Mira. *Wait, do what with what again?* Too late. They had begun their ascent. Mira breathed in, trying to brace for impact. She didn't realize it, but her arms instinctively began to swing just the way Andy had instructed. Mira's thighs were on fire, as were her glutes, and neither one was willing to work with her anymore. She was at her breaking point. Her head was bent low, and she smuggled in the last few breaths of oxygen as she wondered how much longer she could fake it. And then something incredible happened—Mira looked up. They had made it up and over the incline and were now on their way down again. She'd *conquered* the hill. Mira smiled as she felt the blood rush to her brain and provide an elastic-band feeling to her limbs.

"Okay, Mira, the hard part is done. Go ahead, and kick back through the descent. Drop your weight onto your heels and lean back a bit as you run, or you might lose your footing," Andy said, keeping his eyes firmly on the trail.

Mira obeyed and tried to refocus herself from admiring how calm and steady his voice sounded. Ironically, after enduring the height of her pain—the burning muscles in her thighs, her wailing calves, the breathless fatigue—her body did something amazing, which surprised Mira. It rose from the ashes. And this time with a new vigor and drive. It was as if her body needed to hit rock bottom in order to sail once more. Her limbs felt reinforced, and her lungs were no longer tugging on her sleeves for a recovery break. She and Andy ran a few more meters, following which he pulled to a stop along the dense vegetation on the side of the trail. When Mira stopped, she realized how hard she'd pushed herself. She was whipped but *pumped*. She tried to speak, but ended up doubling over to cup her knees with her hands so she could breathe. The effect was dizzying, and she almost thought she'd fall sideways. But she immediately felt Andy's reassuringly firm hand reach for her to hold her body in place. "That's the blood rushing to your brain," he said with a warm laugh.

She looked up for a moment to smile up at him. "Good, because I thought I was having an aneurysm."

"Do you want to know how incredibly well you did today?" he then asked her, with the kind of endearing look that almost brought her to tears. No one had cared so much about how or what she'd done in a very long time. The fact that this amazing man cared wasn't lost on Mira. In fact, it was almost too much for her to bear.

She nodded, sniffing in the tears.

"Three miles in thirty-seven minutes," Andy said, smiling.

Mira straightened up. "That's not possible. Are you sure?"

"You should give yourself a little more credit, Mira..." he replied and showed her the watch he'd used to track her performance. Yup. It was three miles. *Oh Krishna!*

"But the last time I tried, I could barely manage a mile. How could I go from that to running three miles?"

Andy pursed his lips thoughtfully. "It could've been any number of things—the shoes, the time of day you chose to run... for example, if you were running after a long day of work, sometimes that can impact performance. Or maybe it was because you hadn't fueled properly before your run?"

"I ate a pretty decent breakfast today."

Andy nodded. "There you go."

"Wow," Mira sighed. "I know I'm miles away from the thirteen-mile half-marathon distance, but today was amazing, Andy. Thank you."

"You're very welcome." He smiled back, his eyes gripping hers for a fleeting second. But before Mira could decode it, he unlocked his gaze and turned away.

Chapter Twelve

FOLLOWING THEIR RUN, Andy and Mira decided to hike up the trail. After a few miles of walking, they paused at a scenic viewpoint overlooking a lake. "The Pacific Northwest is so beautiful," said Mira, facing the view.

"Yup, I've lived here all my life and still can't seem to get enough."

"So, you grew up in Seattle, then?"

"Whidbey Island," said Andy. "Do you ever miss India?"

Mira considered the question with a pout. "I miss what I had back then—a sweet, uncomplicated life," she said. "My separation has been hard on my family. My mom and my auntie are constantly trying to 'fix' my life."

"You mean fix *you*?" asked Andy.

"Wait, do you know them?" Mira asked, coughing up a sarcastic laugh.

"If I were you, I'd tell them to back off. It's your life. You should be allowed to live it the way you want, Mira." He frowned.

"That's easier said than done. My auntie is a . . ." *Gosh, so many words to choose from.* Mira preferred to let it slide. They turned back to the trail to continue on their hike, with the words between them flowing like a summer stream.

"I think I'm beginning to get the general idea," Andy said with a soft look in his eyes. "But don't let it get to you."

"If only." Mira shrugged. "Do you remember that interview I took last week?"

"Of course. Did you hear from them yet?"

Mira gurgled a sigh and told Andy from top to bottom about her ghastly meeting with Molly Mesnik.

Andy clenched his teeth and offered up a comforting pat on her back. "Did it at least feel therapeutic to let it all out?"

Mira shot him a sardonic glance. "It did, actually, thanks for asking."

THE RUN COMBINED with their heart-to-heart chat had left both Mira and Andy with one heck of an appetite. They grabbed lunch at Naan Ya Business—an Indian food truck in Fremont run by two college guys. "We'll have two of the #3 Special, and a side order of the tikka sauce," Andy said to one of them. He then arched low to whisper into Mira's ear. "You'll *love* their side-sauce."

"At this point, I will eat *anything*," she promised.

With their appetites bursting and plates piled high with food, they settled into some chairs by the truck. "Do you like it?" Andy asked Mira with eager anticipation.

"I want to *live* in this sauce," she replied with a fist covering her stuffed mouth. She watched how Andy tore the naan bread with two hands instead of one (like she did). "Here," she said. "Let me show you how we Punjabis do it." She then showed him how to hold one end of the bread with his ring and pinky while tearing off a piece with the remaining three fingers. He attempted to do it a couple times, but reverted to his old method. "Looks like there's not enough 'Punjab' in me," he conceded with a shrug.

Mira smiled at him. "I like that about Americans, though. You're always so open to learning about new cultures."

"Yes, we're experts at being interested in everyone else's business but our own," Andy replied with a dry grin.

It was while they were at Wally's Chocolate Co. for free samples that Mira's brother, Manoj, called. "Hi, *Bhaiya*," answered Mira.

Manoj pretended to ask some preliminary questions, following which he got right down to business. "Have you tried calling Jay?"

Mira breathed in as she watched Andy taste a chili-peppermint bark with a mild frown on his face. "No, why would I?"

She could sense Manoj's disappointment over the phone. "So, you're going to go ahead with this divorce business, then?"

Mira felt the start of another anxiety episode. She'd been struggling with it even more since the separation, and all it took to trigger it was the word, "Jay." "I've decided not to contest the divorce. I want this chapter of my life to end."

"Unbelievable, Mira. You're making all the decisions while your family suffers the consequences. Ma is so upset about your situation, her blood pressure has dropped, and Papa . . . well, I'm sure he is feeling the pain, even if he can't express it. I hate seeing them this way. We are all getting dragged through the mud along with you."

What was she supposed to say? "I'm sorry you're all being put through this." Mira could feel the anxiety welling up inside her. Her heart was racing, and her throat dried up. She was dizzy and nauseous, and by the time her call with Manoj ended, she was ready to curl up into a ball right there on the floor of the chocolate shop. She absently watched Andy, who was standing a few feet away from her, inspecting a piece of ginger-latte dark chocolate. Instinctively, she wanted to go to him. But she was careful not to let him sense her pain. "Is that your fiftieth sample?" she asked, faking a smile.

"It certainly *feels* like my fiftieth," he replied, wrinkling his brow.

Mira let out a dry chuckle. They tasted a few more samples together before walking out of Wally's (without actually buying a thing). They walked side by side back to his car, and Mira leaned against Andy's shoulder.

He drove her back to her apartment. When he pulled to a stop, Mira turned to him. "Andy, thanks for today. I feel so much better about myself after today's run than I did when I trained solo, you know."

"I promise, you'll feel more confident running solo, over time. All it's going to take is grit, and I know you have *tons* of grit."

Mira's eyes softened as she produced a skeptical smile. "How do you know?"

"Considering you're still here? After *everything* you've been through, and with no support from your family, as I understand it—you're still here, sitting, talking to me in coherent sentences. If that's not grit, I don't know what is." Andy's eyes stayed attached to Mira's a few seconds longer than she was used to. His words were ringing in her ears. *So, this is what being supported feels like*, she told herself. *Amazing.*

"By the way," Andy said, popping her bubble of thoughts. "I'm throwing a little get together at my apartment next Friday. Just a few friends, no big deal. And I was wondering if you'd like to come?"

"Oh."

"Plus, this will give you a chance to meet my business partners, Joe and Rama," he added cheerfully.

There didn't appear to be any evidence of risk in accepting the invitation. "Sure, that sounds great." She smiled.

⁓

WAVING GOODBYE TO Andy from the sidewalk, Mira ascended the stairway to her apartment. But even before she could pull her keys out to unlock the door, Laila opened it. "Where the hell have you been? It's about time you showed up," she snapped, pulling Mira in.

"Why? Showed up for what?" asked Mira as Laila nudged her into the living room.

"She's gone to use the damn potty, but the moment she's back, I want you to keep her far, far away from me, you got that? Or I'm going to kick her to the curb, and I don't *care* if she's family."

Mira squinted back at Laila. "Have you been smoking again? She who?"

"Mira," Auntie Sharmila cried, bursting into the room with outstretched arms.

"Mummyji?" exclaimed Mira, turning briefly to eye Laila before walking over to touch her auntie's feet. The latter pulled her back up to kiss her forehead.

"I'm going to get going," Laila cut in. "I have to take care of the t-thing that needs taking care of . . ."

Auntie Sharmila frowned. "But Mira just got here? Won't you join us for some chai and samosa?"

Laila shook her head. "I wish I could, but maybe next time, Mummyji." And without another word, she exited the apartment, slamming the door shut behind her.

Mira made a batch of chai for herself and Auntie Sharmila. The latter had brought over some homemade samosas, and they settled into the sofa to enjoy it along with their tea.

"So, Mira?" began Auntie Sharmila, audibly sipping out of her teacup. "How's everything?"

Mira watched her auntie take another sip of tea before trading in her teacup for a samosa. "Everything's fine, why?"

Auntie Sharmila appeared suspicious as she folded in her lips. "Living with that hippie? How can you be fine?"

"Laila's not a hippie, Mummyji."

"She's more modern than is good for her. She's forgotten our culture . . . our *values*." cried her auntie. "She won't even touch my feet anymore, you know? But I still give my blessings. I do my part."

It was nine o'clock, and Mira had run her first three miles that day. She couldn't wait to cook something spectacular for dinner that night and hit the sack. Did she want to hear Auntie Sharmila's discourse on the overall shortcomings of Laila Sood? No, thank you.

"Mummyji, didn't you say you had something to tell me? Ma said so too."

Her auntie repositioned her body weight, looking eager. "Yes, I do, in fact. That's why I came here. I had to invite myself in because Laila wouldn't even do that. She's never invited me to her house—"

"So, what was the news?" nudged Mira.

Auntie Sharmila breathed in. "I know you are feeling a bit upset over this whole divorce business, Mira. We *all* are. But I have spoken to Mohan-ji and—" she paused. "Do you remember Mohan-ji?"

Mira groaned inwardly. "Yes." The perv who'd apparently run away with his wife's sister only to worm his way into becoming the trusted Sood family astrologer? The guy who'd sworn that Jay and Mira were a match made in heaven? Yeah, she'd heard of him.

"You'll be glad to know that your mother and I video-chatted with him last week, and we have some news from him that will fill you with joy, Mira," said her auntie, beaming. "Mohan-ji studied your birth chart, and he's assured us that you are indeed going through a horrendous time. He said your moon is in the house ruled by an opposing planet. But listen to this . . ." she said, pulling a sheet of paper out of her purse to read to Mira. "'Her moon is resting in the twelfth house, and this is a time of turmoil. Both love and happiness are on the horizon, but she will have to overcome great barriers and cross great lengths to find it. If she can persist in overcoming the hurdles that her opposing planet will set in her path, she will succeed. If not, she will remain a spinster for ten more years until her moon is in the seventh house again,'" Auntie Sharmila concluded with a smile.

"What?" cried Mira. It was as if someone had blown a handful of glitter into her eyes. And when was the "joy" part supposed to kick in? "This is *awful*. I hate that Mohan-ji."

Her auntie patted her knee. "Now, now, Mira. The man is merely reporting what he's seeing."

"How's this supposed to make me feel joyous, Mummyji?"

"But—"

"I feel *nauseous*, not joyous."

"But you heard what he said, didn't you? If you overcome your future hurdles, you will find love and happiness . . . and maybe *children*, even." That last ingredient felt more like Auntie Sharmila's than Mohan-ji's. "You don't have to give up hope. Things might still turn around for you and Jay, but you should be willing to fight for it, is what Mohan-ji's saying."

"Jay?" asked Mira, looking incredulous. "You honestly believe Jay and I might still get back together?"

"My dear, marriages are made in heaven. *Especially* Indian marriages, and a signed piece of paper is not strong enough to change that."

Mira pressed her fingertips into her temples to stop herself from imploding. She now wished she'd stayed in Andy's car and never gotten out. Her auntie continued to talk, and at some point, her mother called, which felt scripted to Mira. Auntie Sharmila and Mira's mother spent the rest of the evening chatting in Mira's apartment, *about* Mira, while she sat back and imagined the sound of Andy's comforting voice inside her head: "You have grit, you have grit, *you have grit* . . ."

Chapter Thirteen

THAT WEEK, MIRA went to the trail each evening after work. She'd been thinking about Andy's party all week—her first grown-up playdate since her divorce. Plus, she couldn't wait to be in the company of someone she wasn't biologically related to. The Soods were great—in small, sporadic doses. But Mira had clearly overdosed. The party at Andy's was exactly the tonic she needed to reboot herself.

As she ran down the trail on Friday afternoon, Mira paced herself, continually checking her running form to ensure she wasn't slouching—it was one of the biggest challenges she was facing, and according to Andy, one of the most common mistakes runners made when they were fatigued. She felt steady, and the fact that she'd turned running into a habit was helping her cause. Plus, she was eating a much healthier diet now. She refused to skimp on the things she loved, but she'd begun to eat them in moderation. Mira had also managed to perfect a few smoothie recipes and drank a batch before she set out running each day. She was pretty proud of her little inventions, because they were something she'd come up with all on her own, instead of simply acting on Andy's imparted wisdom. She respected everything that he'd shared with her, but it mattered to her equally that she had her own "ingredients" to add to her half-marathon training recipe—like her Sunburst-in-Sumatra smoothie, which called for a mix of grapefruit, tomato, and orange juice, a hint of ginger, a sprig of mint, and a splash of coconut water. And to that, her body responded with a big, fat, "YES, MA'AM!"

However, there was something else Mira had discovered about herself—she wasn't very fast. Her new shoes helped boost her performance, but she felt she had a better handle on the endurance aspect of running than the speedwork. Half-marathons demanded both, as Mira had come to know. Which meant she needed to push harder and work on building her pace.

For now, she allowed herself to bask in the sweaty wind of other runners on the trail, as they blazed past her. Some of them almost appeared apologetic about passing her at such great speed. The moms were especially sympathetic as they pushed their thirty-pound strollers at a sweatless, ten-minute-mile pace, right past Mira. Their mommy instincts caused them to say encouraging things to her as they passed like, "You *go*, girl!" or "Nice job, hon." Which only left Mira feeling even more inadequate as she fake-smiled back at them. Mira worked hard to push herself, putting "mind over body," which Andy had said would change the way she ran. But each run pumped her with self-confidence and added a layer of grit to the next time she ran. She was now able to run three miles, at a beginner's pace, at each run. So, she'd essentially gone from running zero miles in thirty years, to running three miles in one day. Pretty good comeback for a formerly heartbroken housewife.

Following her run, Mira stopped by the local grocery store. She wasn't sure how the system worked in America, but visiting a friend's home for the very first time in India usually entailed something home baked—and given that she loved to bake, and Andy loved Indian samosas, she knew exactly what she wanted to take to his house party that night.

With her brain fully charged from her run, and a load of grocery bags brimming with possibilities, Mira burst into her apartment, almost throwing Laila off-balance as the latter did a headstand on the floor. "Damn it, Mira! What the hell?"

"Sorry, sorry," Mira quickly said, hurling her bags onto the kitchen counter to pull out her recipe book so she could write down her ideas before they left her brain. "Why are you doing that, anyway?" Mira asked her cousin absently as Laila repositioned her legs over her head against the wall.

"I'm channeling my lyrical ideas."

Mira smiled to herself. "You should try running." She turned on the oven to preheat, then began to unload her grocery bags.

Laila studied her cousin from her upside-down stance. "Your mother called six times on your cell while you were out running. I don't know why you left that thing behind. The woman is relentless."

The words caused Mira to lose her grip on a bag of Yukon potatoes. Talking to her mother was, by far, the best antidote for any of her highs. "I'll call her back later tonight," she replied, opening the bag up.

Laila came off the wall and crashed onto the ground. She then studied Mira in silence as the latter began smashing room temperature butter to layer into sheets of dough.

"Why're you beating the shit out of that butter?" she asked.

Mira paused the culinary flogging to look up at Laila. "I'm making a short crust pastry."

Laila continued to look confused.

"I'm baking a samosa pie to take to Andy's tonight," Mira explained, as she carefully laminated the flattened butter into the dough.

"A samosa *what*?"

"Oh, and a mango rice pudding dessert pie," Mira added with a smile. Regardless of how life was treating her on any given day, cooking for other people was all Mira needed to stay positive.

"Argh, I forgot that was tonight," groaned Laila.

"You're still coming, right?" Mira asked. Yes, she'd had enough of Sood company, but she couldn't be expected to give it up cold turkey—not when Andy had been kind enough to extend the invitation to Laila.

Laila nodded. "Yeah, I'll go. But it's mostly to investigate your 'friendship' with this guy."

Mira rolled her eyes. "Give me a break," she said, and threw her pie dough into the freezer so she could start working on her fillings. "Look, whether or not you believe it, Andy has no interest in me whatsoever beyond friendship, I swear." Mira felt an unsettling tug at that thought.

Laila raised a brow at her cousin. "How about I give you my final verdict tonight after the party, huh?"

Chapter Fourteen

ANDY LIVED IN a modern, newly built condo in Ballard overlooking the water. Standing outside his door, Mira couldn't understand the butterflies in her stomach. They had no business being there because Andy was *just a friend*. Had she spent a few extra minutes selecting her outfit for the night—a velvet, long-sleeved LBD with a pair of maroon fishnet tights? Maybe. And what about her decision to go the extra mile to generate those waves in her flowing hair? Mmm, she liked waves. No biggie. "And why are you wearing mascara? You hardly ever wear mascara," Laila had interrogated her before they had left their apartment.

"What are you saying?" Mira had frowned. "I *love* mascara."

"You made it." Andy smiled as he opened the door to them. His eyes darted from Mira to Laila and back to Mira again. Her heart was racing like Seabiscuit's on steroids. And now she genuinely wished she hadn't taken all this effort in getting ready because all of a sudden, she felt *way* more beautiful than she was used to feeling. "Moderately attractive" would have sufficed.

"Come on in, you guys," Andy said in his warm voice as he opened the door. As Mira passed his six-foot frame, she invariably inhaled some of his scent—that warm musk cologne that reminded her of a great calm ocean. Considering she smelled like a samosa pie, she thought their auras meshed quite nicely—like eating a samosa by an ocean.

"This is a really nice shack you have here," said Laila as she took her coat off.

Andy reached out. "Thanks. Here, let me take that for you, and . . ." he immediately turned to Mira. "Do you want me to take those?" he asked her, referring to the two pie boxes she was carrying, stacked one on top of the other.

"Yes, please." She smiled, as she felt his fingers come for the pies, overlapping her grip on them for a millisecond.

It truly was a lovely condo, with a fluid, open-concept design, complete with a beautifully embellished kitchen and an adjoining living room with a gorgeous electric fireplace. A balcony neighbored the space, overlooking the incomparable views of the lake and downtown Seattle. Breezy lounge music wafted from the home-theater speakers, adding a touch of serene luxury to the atmosphere.

A group of people stood scattered around the room, drinking beer and wine, and snacking on finger food. "What can I get you guys to drink?" asked Andy.

"Vodka martini, thanks," Laila called back.

Andy nodded. "And you, Miss Sood?" he asked, turning to Mira.

"Er . . ." She couldn't think what to drink, as her brain chose that very moment to erase its whiteboard. "Maybe some wine?" she said meekly.

"Coming right up." Andy smiled, and dashed away with the pie boxes, returning a few moments later with their drinks. "Let me introduce you to the rest of the gang," he offered, leading Laila and Mira toward the others. He walked them over to a tall brunette with a pixie haircut. "This is my sister, Brooklyn," said Andy. "This is Mira, and her cousin, Laila."

"Brook," said the woman, extending her hand along with the most gorgeous smile Mira had ever seen—one that bore a striking resemblance to Andy's. "So, *you're* Mira Sood." Brook nodded, as if with realization. "Andy's told me a *lot* about you and your half-marathon challenge."

"Well, I hope he lied a little if only to save my face?" Mira smiled back, shaking Brook's hand.

"Andy's convinced you have what it takes to nail it," Brook assured her. "And if he's your trainer, you're in good hands."

Mira turned just in time to catch Andy looking away from her. "Are you a runner like your brother?" she asked, turning back to his sister.

"*Yikes*, no," Brook said, eyes wide. "I'm all about hot yoga."

"Oh, I love that stuff," Laila chimed in.

"And I know you'll say thundering through the trees, getting splattered with dirt while eating gnats on the way to your twentieth mile helps clear your head," said Brook, glancing over at Andy as he raised a brow at her. "But nothing relaxes me more than lying in *Savasana* in a hundred-degree room."

"Where've you been all my life?" Laila cried out as she and Brook laughed and began chatting more about the benefits of eating a yogi diet.

Andy leaned in briefly to whisper into Mira's ear. "Now do you understand why I insisted you bring Laila?"

Mira laughed softly. "Was it to get Brook off your back?"

"And just look how happy they are . . . talking about eating out of a banana leaf and . . . what the hell is Sutra-paste?" he asked with a frown, catching the tail end of Laila and Brook's conversation.

Mira laughed and led Andy away by his arm. "Come on, you don't want to know."

"By the way, your hair looks great today," he said in a casual tone of voice, as if he were commenting on the thermostat setting.

Mira's heart skipped at the sound of his words. "Thanks, I decided to go wavy tonight."

"Wavy works for you," he said with a smile. "Let me introduce you to the others," he added, leading them toward another small group of people—more of Andy's friends and a couple of colleagues who worked for his company.

"These are my business partners, Joe and Rama," said Andy. "Guys, this is Mira Sood."

"Nice to meet you, Mira," said Joe, extending his arm to her. As one might have guessed right away, Joe was a mustached, Indian American software developer whose real name was Jyothiganeshawara Muthu. He'd shortened it to "Joe" shortly after his feet touched American soil, when he could no longer bear for his name to be butchered by his otherwise well-meaning, non-Indian friends.

"Glad to finally meet you, Mira," said Rama, elbowing Joe's hand out of the way to extend his own to her. Contrary to Joe, Rama Harrington was a six-foot-tall, two-hundred-pound Caucasian deer-hunter from Aberdeen, and one of the best cloud security analysts on the West Coast. Back in the '60s, Rama's pot-smoking hippie parents had had a particular fetish for Indian mythology and thought it would be cute to name their three sons Rama, Vishnu, and Shiva.

"It's nice to meet you both, but I'm wondering why everyone seems to already know who I am?" asked Mira.

"Well, Andy here's been talking our ears off about you—"

"Hey, quit exaggerating, man," Andy cut in.

"Oh, I never exaggerate," Rama replied, and turned to Mira. "He won't even come out drinking with us on the weekends anymore because he says he's training with you."

Mira tried not to overanalyze the fact that Andy had turned a deep shade of pink. Sensing his embarrassment, she turned to her natural instincts. "Listen, would you mind helping me get those pies out?" she asked him.

The question appeared to ease him, and he nodded. "Yeah, let's do it."

Walking over to the kitchen, Andy pulled the lids off the pie boxes. "Oh, wow," he cried. "This smells incredible."

"And hopefully it'll taste just as good as it smells."

"This is reminding me of something... something I love, but I can't put my finger on it—"

"It's a samosa pie." Mira smiled. "And this one's a dessert pie—mango rice-pudding."

Andy bent low to breathe in the warm pie smell. "*Damn.*"

Mira looked around the kitchen counter. "You wouldn't happen to have a pizza cutter, would you?"

"Behind you, top drawer."

Mira opened the one closest to her.

"No, not that one—" Andy tried to say. But by then, Mira was staring down at the drawer's contents, with part disbelief and part confusion. "What the—?"

Andy moved in closer and stood by her side in silence.

"Medals?" Mira asked, puzzled. The drawer was filled to the brim with medals.

"Finisher medals, actually," Andy explained, picking one up for her to inspect up close. "It's all the races I've run in my life."

Mira numbly turned her gaze from Andy back to the drawer. She then peered in and reached for one (of the *many*) gold medals. "This one says 'Champion' on it . . ."

Andy nodded bashfully. "That race, I won."

There were several champion gold medals in the drawer, with names of various marathons embossed on them, along with the year Andy had run them.

Mira picked up another medal that caught her eye. "Oh, my Lord. You've run the Boston Marathon?" she cried out. Even *she'd* heard of that one.

"Many years ago," he replied, and pulled open another drawer to retrieve a pizza cutter, which he handed to Mira.

"Thanks," she said, accepting the cutter. She was slowly beginning to understand why Seth, the guy at the shoe store, had called Andy a "marathon star." And why Brook thought Mira was in good hands if Andy was her trainer. Double yikes. This realization suddenly caused Mira to become very (*very*) self-conscious. How could she have trained with this guy? A marathon champion? How could she have run with him, and that, too, a ridiculous three-mile distance at snail-speed, and then celebrated afterward? Mira cringed at the memory and closed the drawer gently, to avoid exposing herself to further humiliation.

"Here, let me refill your glass," Andy offered as Mira gulped down the last of her wine. Grabbing the bottle on the counter, he poured some into her glass and then some into his own, while Mira began slicing up the pies. Andy then reached for a slice of the samosa pie. "May I?" he asked, as Mira nodded. "Wa-ow," He groaned, fist to his mouth. "Where on earth did you learn to cook like that?"

Mira shrugged casually. "I don't know. I've just always loved to cook," she replied, cutting into the dessert pie.

Andy reached for a slice of the second pie and rolled his eyes with his first bite. "I never could have imagined rice pudding in a *pie*." He laughed. "It's brilliant."

Mira joined his laughter. "Okay, clearly, you have not tasted good Indian food, because I'm not even that good."

"Man, if I were half as talented as you, I wouldn't need to survive on takeout from the Taj Mahal Cafe."

"I *love* that place." Mira smiled with recognition.

"Oh? Then you'll be glad to know that that's Cloud-9's official world headquarters," Andy said with pride.

"You're kidding."

"Yup, it's a lot cheaper than having to rent an office at the Seattle Business Center, downtown."

"Wow, I'd love to visit your official world headquarters sometime, Andrew." Mira smiled as she instinctively felt the distance between them shrink. Was it the wine freestyling through her bloodstream, or had Andy inched closer? She sipped her wine and wondered how "non-friendly" it would be if she reached out and touched his face. If not to kill the nagging desire in her head, then just to remind herself of the sensation of a man's skin.

THE PIES WERE a smashing success, vaporizing within the first ten minutes of being served. Mira grabbed a slice of the rice pudding for herself, just as the final slice vanished into the tiny opening on Rama's flaming-red-bearded face. "Man, oh *man*." He smacked his lips. "This stuff's a knockout."

"Thanks." She smiled back.

"It's Mira's silver bullet." Laila winked. "Her culinary skills."

"Not mine," said Brook, throwing her hands up like a white flag. Mira watched Brook with a half-smile, but her gaze invariably shifted to her brother, who was sitting on a barstool a few feet away, watching them all in silence. "Although, I'm crazy enough to try baking a pie and have it explode in the oven."

"You want to try something *really* crazy?" began Joe. "Try going elk hunting with a maniac."

"Hey, you signed up for it. I never asked you to," Rama cried out. "And all you did was scare the elk away with your constant yipping. I should've just taken Andy."

"The mosquitoes were as big as bees out there," Joe tried to argue.

"Oh, mosquitoes as big as bees are nothing compared to skydiving off a cliff in Bhutan," Laila cut in.

"You *didn't*..." Brook's jaw dropped open.

"Did too, and I was just sixteen. Ask Mira, she was there."

The audience instinctively turned to her for confirmation. "Y-yeah, I was there, but I didn't jump," Mira replied with a quiver of regret. So far, she'd contributed nothing to the story pool.

"Why not?" asked Brook. "I would've loved that."

"That's because you're insane," said Andy, diving into cold water to offer Mira a hand. "I'm glad you didn't jump," he said, turning to Mira with a reassuring wink. "That sounds pretty crazy even to me."

"Oh, *pah-lease*." Brook rolled her eyes at her brother. "Nothing's as crazy as what you do, running those crazy distances, Andy . . . and how about The Huntsman, huh?"

"What's that?" Mira asked, leaning in with a curious squint.

"Let me tell you about *real* insanity," Brook began, turning to Mira and the others. "This guy, here," she said, pointing to Andy, who was looking stern as ever, "decided, at age twenty-four, to run The Huntsman Marathon in Utah, right in the middle of the state's worst heatwave. Can you imagine, this Pacific-Northwest-bred, samosa-eating vegetarian maniac, did it while the rest of us—his support team . . . which was like me, and a couple of runner friends of his—couldn't even stand under a shade longer than ten minutes. It was like standing on freakin' hot coals."

Mira's gaze drifted from Brook to Andy. His eyes were already on her, deep and unflinching. "Did you really do that?"

Andy shrugged. "Everyone does something crazy at some

point in their life."

"Well, in that case," Rama grinned. "I think you should get the last slice of Mira's excellent samosa pie, you *maniac*."

Andy sported a soft smile as he stood up to claim his prize. "Thank you."

The others were still talking when Mira quietly slipped away to the open balcony. She found a cozy spot in a cushioned chair close to an outdoor heater. Pulling her legs toward her chest, she huddled in it, watching the lights of the city as they flickered in the distance.

Andy's comforting voice reached for her. "You okay, Mira?" he asked, standing at the door. He hadn't known her as long as her auntie or mother, and yet he knew her better than they did—he sensed her frustrations, gauged her emotions better than they did. And unlike them, he always seemed to want to fix things *for* her, as opposed to wanting to fix *her*.

"I'm fine," she lied, hoping he'd let her get away with it.

"Mind if I join you?" he asked softly.

To her surprise, she felt her heart lifting at the sound of his offer, and she nodded.

Andy pulled up a chair next to her and sat down. They didn't speak for the first few minutes and instead watched the lights together. To Mira, it was as if he knew she didn't want to talk. At least not until she was ready to address the question that was drumming against her brain. When she finally did speak, he appeared to listen with an earnest interest.

"How come I didn't jump?" she asked, dropping the words one by one.

"Jump?" asked Andy with a puzzled frown.

"In Bhutan, all four of my cousins jumped off that cliff, but I didn't," she admitted slowly.

"Could it be because you were the only sane one in the group?"

"Then how come I'm the only one who didn't have a craziest-thing-I-ever-did story to tell tonight? Even Joe, who's *way* more subdued than I am, had a story to tell. But me? *Nothing*. I've done absolutely nothing exciting in my life... nothing crazy. All I ever did was spend my time making *rotis* and doing laundry for an ungrateful jerk."

"But Mira—"

"And you? Oh my Lord..." Mira cradled her head in her palms as the image of his drawer full of race medals came to mind. "You're a running champion, and you've completed all these extreme races. Laila's a rockstar... like, *literally*, and also because she's always been a trailblazer in our family, to the point where my auntie's convinced she isn't even a Sood."

"And that's a compliment?" Andy tried to clarify.

"The *greatest* compliment, from where I stand," said Mira, her shoulders drooping and her heart weighing a ton. "It's like the rest of my generation—you, Laila, your sister and... pretty much everyone whose anywhere near my age, are all living your lives, and I'm just... I don't know, living in a cave, using stones to light a fire." Mira bowed her head. It was embarrassing to admit, but Andy was such a good listener—so absorbed—it felt easy, spilling her heart out to him. "I'm sorry, I don't mean to dump all my emotions on you... and, right in the middle of your party."

A NEW MANTRA

"I just wish I could take you out of it," he replied softly.

"Well, thanks for listening, anyway," she smiled, and allowed herself to be held by his comforting gaze without counting the seconds on propriety.

Chapter Fifteen

WHEN THE DOORBELL rang at 2:00 a.m., Mira was cocooned inside her REM cycle. They had gotten back late that night from Andy's party, and while Mira preferred to go straight to bed, Laila decided to sit up and work on some lyrics for an upcoming single. In the end, it was her thundering knock on Mira's room door that joggled her awake.

"W-what the hell?" she gasped, her eyes still closed and refusing to open. Tumbling out of bed, Mira wobbled over to open the door to find Laila staring back with a deep-set frown on her face and a guitar held upright against her torso like a shield.

"He's here for you," she said sardonically. "Your 'just-a-friend,' Andy."

That was enough to whack any remaining sleep out of Mira's eyes. "What? Where, *here?* Why?"

"All great questions you should ask him. Now get moving."

Stepping out of her room, Mira found Andy waiting for her in the living room, a smile dazzling across his gorgeous face. "Hey," he said, as if this whole dropping by unannounced at two in the morning was in no way psychotic.

"Hello..." replied Mira, feeling extremely unsteady. Could she be dreaming?

"Okay, Mira, I need you to go back into your room and get changed into your running clothes, got it? Lots of layers, it's a bit nippy out," he said, in his most centered voice, but with eyes twinkling.

Mira frowned back. "Pardon?"

"You'd better hurry, or I think Laila's head's going to explode," he added with a laugh.

"Damn right it is. You kids are out of your mind." Laila frowned. "Will you please do as he says and leave me to songwriter in peace?"

"Wait, I don't understand, Andy? Why are we—?"

"Just do it. You won't be sorry," he promised her.

WEARING A BUNCH of sweat-wicking layers, along with a look of confusion, Mira walked alongside Andy to his car. "I'm afraid to ask, but where are we going?"

"You'll see." He smiled, opening the door for her. "In exactly forty-five minutes."

"Oh Lord," Mira muttered to herself, only to hear Andy laugh softly.

They drove out to nowhere Mira recognized, but it was clearly some kind of state park perched all the way up on a mountain. Pulling to a stop, Andy turned off his ignition but left his headlights on so they could see through the pitch blackness.

Mira peered through her window. "Where *are* we?"

"Cougar Mountain Park," Andy replied calmly.

Should she be concerned that the park's name featured a large carnivore? Stepping out of the car, Mira surveyed the deathly quiet of the park. "Er, this place is closed," she said, in a voice that came out sounding like Minnie Mouse's.

Andy nodded. "Yup, I know." He walked over to pull a bag out of the backseat. From it, he extracted two neon headlamps, giving one to Mira, and strapping the other to his own forehead.

Oh shit, no way. "Wait a minute, you're not thinking of going running through *there*, are you?" cried Mira, as the realization whipped her brain.

"Not 'I,' 'we,'" he gently corrected, and then proceeded to take the headlamp out of Mira's lifeless grasp to strap around her head. "That's not too tight, is it?" he asked casually.

"Andy, you're not seriously considering doing this."

"'We,' not 'I'—"

"Will you stop that?" cried Mira, her stomach in a knot. "First of all, the park's closed, we'd be breaking the law . . . and I've never done anything illegal in my *life*. Not to mention this place has a serious post-apocalyptic vibe to it, and I'm a hundred percent sure if we go in there, we're never coming out, and—" *Oh.* She'd just noticed the sign. "Em, why's there a Polaroid of a black bear pinned to the park notice board?"

"Relax, Mira," came Andy's yogi voice. "Breathe and stop thinking about all the things that could go wrong. I promise, you will be fine."

Mira breathed in deep, continuing to stare at the bear-sighting notice, while Andy pulled out a couple of spare batteries, a flashlight, and . . .

"What's that for?" she asked, trying to retain a calm voice. "Those bells?"

"To tie around your ankles," replied Andy.

Mira cleared her throat. "Why?"

"You don't want to know." He smiled. "It'll only freak you out more if I tell you."

"Okay, Andy, is this really necessary? Training for a half-marathon this way?"

"It's not part of your training, although it could be," he said with a shrug.

"Then why are we doing this illegal, midnight, hey-bear-come-get-me run through a closed state park?" sobbed Mira.

"Because you told me at the party it bothered you that you'd never done anything crazy in your life, and everyone else had a story to tell but you."

Ugh, the perils of honesty. "Okay, but this isn't crazy. This is *suicidal*," she cried.

"Even better than what I was going for." He winked. "You ready?"

"No, no, and I'll never be ready." Mira began to pace. "Look, in case you haven't noticed, I'm not really cut out for things like this . . . Laila, maybe, or my other cousin, Sahana. But me? *No*. I'm just an ordinary person, with very, *very* low expectations of life . . . *and* myself, and—"

Andy reached out and held Mira by the shoulders. His grip on her remained gentle, yet firm. "That's *exactly* it," he said. "I feel like everyone who's ever met you knows how incredible you are . . . everyone except you."

Mira watched her reflection in Andy's eyes as a sliver of confidence returned to her pounding chest. "Fine," she conceded. "Let's do the damn thing."

THE COUGAR CLAW Trail was a six-mile-long unpaved path that looped around a quarter of the entire state park. Despite the pep talk, Mira was on pins and needles as she gently hustled through the woods, close on Andy's heels as he led the way at a comforting pace. No way she could run six full miles yet, so the plan was to stop at the halfway point and hike the rest of the way. With bells jingling on her feet, and her heart pounding inside her ribcage, Mira kept turning to ensure there wasn't a wild animal jogging along with her—or behind her, ready to take a bite out of the most promising part of her body. *Dear Lord Krishna, save me*, she chanted to herself, praying this would all end swiftly and painlessly—jaws or no jaws.

Andy said absolutely nothing as the pathway broadened, allowing them to run side by side. He kept his eyes focused on the trail, occasionally stealing glances at Mira. She, on the other hand, continued to pitch a fit inwardly. What was the point of this insane exercise, anyway? What was Andy thinking? He'd got it way wrong this time. She'd feel much better about herself if she were back home curled up in her sheets than out here in the cold, waiting to be bear food.

When the fussing tapered away, Mira turned her attention to the quiet around her. At first, she tried to split hairs with anything and everything she heard—a twig snapping, leaves rustling, wind fluting through leaves, the falling sound of rain. Her imagination had a field day with all of it. But then, after the first ten minutes of running through the darkness, with nothing but a small light to lead her way, Mira found an odd sense of comfort in the quiet darkness. It felt like the very blanket she'd craved, and she allowed herself to be wrapped in it as her body swayed to the gentle rhythm of her own stride. It was as if the run was rocking her to sleep, with the night creating that perfect mix of solitude and self-awareness—the sounds of her breathing, the soft thud of their feet pattering down the trail, the way the raindrops felt on the tip of her nose, the gentle percussion of her racing heart, and Andy's body next to hers.

For the first time since the start of her running journey, Mira didn't count the final minutes to the halfway point. She didn't check her watch or ask Andy how much farther they would go. She ran, as if for the sake of running. As if running were the end and not the means anymore. She no longer noticed nor cared as she passed milestones on the way. When she did finally run out of steam, Andy, quick to sense her discomfort, slowed down along with her as they continued to hike up the steep slopes toward the viewpoint at the very top of the mountain, just before the trail began to loop back downward.

Recycling her last ounces of oxygen, Mira teetered across the viewpoint behind Andy. They hadn't spoken a word to each other through their entire run, and yet she felt connected to him at every step. "Come take a look at what you've earned," he finally said, with a smile bursting across his lips. It was only then that Mira noticed—the horizon had split open to make room for a faint grapefruit light. Everything else around them still lay engulfed by darkness, except for the growing light in the distance.

"Wait, i-is that the sunrise?"

Andy nodded as he, too, watched it.

"I can't believe it," whispered Mira, as the light grew brighter, lighting up everything it touched. "This is so beautiful."

"Isn't it?" sighed Andy, turning to look at her.

They continued to watch the sunrise for a few minutes longer, and although she was unsure exactly when or how, Mira felt tears roll down her face. And for once, she didn't attempt to hold back.

"Mira, what's wrong?" Andy asked, appearing startled. "W-what is it?"

She shook her head at him, sniffing and wiping tears off her face only to make room for new ones that came rushing out. Andy reached for her, and she instinctively buried her face in his chest, allowing herself to melt into his arms. His warm clasp around her provided an undeniable sense of solace—as if nothing bad in the world could ever touch her so long as he was there.

She allowed herself to be held in Andy's arms, even as her Indian-bred instincts screamed for her to peel away. What would Auntie Sharmila say, and her mother? But in this one and only instance, Mira didn't care. She stood there, unabashedly tucked into his musky bear hug, for the next five minutes. Andy allowed her the time she needed, and when her tears had finally receded, she decided to emerge again, only to dive right into his gorgeous eyes as his held hers. She then felt his hazel gaze slide down to her lips for the shortest second in the world before returning to her eyes again. "Clearly, you're not a morning person," he said, causing Mira to let out a dry chuckle. Snuffling, and suddenly very aware of herself, she pulled away from him as the carriage turned back into a pumpkin.

"God," she said, taking a few steps back and wiping off the remaining tears. "You know, I was thinking... I should've got that last slice of pie, not you."

A gentle frown emerged on Andy's face. "Oh yeah? Why's that?"

"Because I did the craziest thing of all. I was the biggest maniac in the group... I married a man I didn't know," Mira said, allowing the words to spill out.

"That *is* pretty wild," admitted Andy with a small smile. "Did you and Jay never date before you married?"

Mira shook her head. Every American she'd befriended had asked her that. "I never dated him. He and I met *once* in my parents' house. He arrived with his entire extended family—his parents, his two older brothers, his auntie and uncle, and grandmother—and then the two of us spoke a little while I gave him a tour of our paddy fields." Mira coughed up a laugh. "And even *that* was too progressive for his grandmother, who had insisted we stay in the room and chat, with them watching us the entire time." Mira paused to consider. "But my dad insisted we be given some privacy."

"Are you close to your dad?" asked Andy with a tilt of his head.

Mira walked over to rest herself against a bench. "I love him more than anything in the world. But he suffered a stroke a little while ago which partially paralyzed him. Since it happened, he and I haven't really been able to interact the way we used to," she said, swallowing the serrated knot in her throat.

"I'm really sorry to hear that," said Andy, inching forward to lean up against a tree. "So, what happened after you and Jay spoke?"

Mira glanced over to smile at Andy. "He went home, my mom began planning the wedding, and I was asked to quit my job so I could begin training . . . to be a perfect housewife."

"You didn't love him, then?" Andy asked, sporting a bewildered frown.

"It's how arranged marriages work in traditional families like mine," Mira said, with a shrug. Somehow, saying it out loud made the whole thing sound even more ludicrous.

"You must really love your family to be willing to do that to keep them happy."

"I suppose I do," Mira said softly. "They're a large, noisy, archaic bunch, but I love them very much." She turned to look sideways at Andy. "What about you? Your family?" she asked him, almost as if to distract herself from the tears that threatened to make a comeback appearance.

"Er, we're kind of close . . . my parents, Brook, and I. But I would never in a million years marry someone they chose, just to keep them happy."

"That's because you're not as brave as I am, Andrew." Mira laughed.

He joined her in her laugh. "That is true."

"But how come a guy like you is still single?" she asked.

Andy raised a brow at her. "You mean, am I a psychopath?"

Mira held a fist against her mouth. "Are you?"

"You'll have to *date* me to find out. I don't like to give away all my secrets."

"Yeah, right," Mira said, narrowing her eyes at Andy.

"I haven't found the right girl yet," he said with a shrug. "And I'm not the kind of guy who can walk down the aisle half-heartedly."

Mira nodded as she got ready to ask her next question—one she'd been dying to ask for a while now. "Is that why you and Savannah broke up?"

Andy's eyes immediately pivoted from her to the horizon. "We were together almost two years, Savannah and me. But we grew apart, fighting a lot more . . . I didn't necessarily want to break up with her, but I knew I had to."

"I don't understand."

"I was at a point in the relationship where I felt like I'd come too far to give up, but at the same time, it was getting too painful to go on . . . similar to what one might feel during a race, you know?"

"What helped you decide in the end?"

Andy shrugged. "I asked myself the million-dollar question—how bad do I want this? And I realized not enough to want to go on."

"And that's why you're still single?"

"I guess. I'd rather wait and find the right woman than rush into something I might regret later."

"That makes sense." She nodded.

They continued to watch the sunrise a bit longer. And as

she did, Mira felt a serene, inward calm. When Andy spoke next, his voice was clear but soft. "Do you think you'll ever marry again?"

Mira's brows furrowed as she squinted against the sun's rays. Would she? Considering her broken marriage had destroyed the peace within the Sood family, fractured her relationship with her auntie, and left an open wound on her mother's heart that was refusing to heal itself? "Highly unlikely," she replied in a firm voice.

Chapter Sixteen

FALL – November

IT WAS A second chance, and potentially her last one. But as Mira inwardly swayed against her growing anxiety, she watched her interviewer smile at her resume. "This looks great," said Chantelle Kempler, the owner of Sound Consulting, a thriving boutique wealth-management firm on Mercer Island. "The only trouble is, Mira, I think you're a bit overqualified for this role. I see you have a college degree from India? And you worked for a few years there, and—"

"And I don't need sponsorship or a visa. I have a *green card*," Mira cut in.

"Well, that does help. This is an entry-level role which is a backfill for our office assistant, who recently accepted another job. As you can imagine, we're eager to fill this position . . . with the right candidate, of course."

"Oh, of course." Mira nodded.

"I'm not sure how much time this will give you to transition out of your current role at . . ." Chantelle momentarily squinted at Mira's resume for reference. "The . . . er, Say-tee Store?"

"Yes." Mira smiled. "And it's not a problem since I know the store owner. Well, I was a store patron before I became employed there, and well, he's understanding that way, Jaggu-bai. I mean, he already knows that bagging drumsticks and stacking jackfruit isn't really my dream job, and . . ." *Please stop talking, please stop talking, please stop talking.* Mira quickly pulled it together with a heaven-sent belly breath.

"Great," Chantelle said, and extended her hand. "In that case, Mira, we'd love to make you an offer."

"Oh, wow, thank you," cried Mira, reaching out to return the shake.

WHEN SHE RETURNED to her apartment after her interview, Mira noticed a bottle of port with a tag hanging around its neck. It was a note from Laila: "Port wine—can be drunk happy or sad, depending on how your interview went. I'll see you Tuesday. XX"

In all the excitement that came with prepping for her interview that morning, Mira had completely forgotten Laila's travel plans with the band. They were performing at a corporate event in San Francisco, and she'd left early that morning and wasn't going to be back until the next night.

Breathing in, Mira eyed the bottle of wine, trying not to pay attention to the anxiety triggering inside her—the last time she'd found herself alone was after Jay had left her. And the thought was making her sick to her stomach. The idea of once again being alone in an apartment felt threatening. All of a sudden, Mira could feel her heart beating faster; her airways seemed to be tightening, and the room appeared darker and almost too quiet to bear. While she'd left the interview feeling sky-high and ravenous, she had no semblance of an appetite now. Settling down into the couch, Mira tried hard to breathe in deep and think happy thoughts, despite her throbbing head. How was she supposed to sleep alone here tonight? Would she leave the light on? What if she had those dreams again—the ones that had bombarded her the night Jay left? *Ugh*. Mira's happy thoughts didn't stand a chance against the emotional baggage of her past. Breaking into a cold sweat, she felt herself doubling over as her anxiety transformed into a full-blown panic attack.

Mira instinctively curled up into the fetal position on the couch, knees pulled tight to her chin and eyes closed against the feeling of being alone again. The mere tinkle of an incoming text message on her phone caused her to jump out of her skin.

How'd it go??? The message was from Andy, and the sight of his name flashing across her screen caused the tension in Mira's neck to suddenly dissipate.

I got the job! she texted back and then waited for a response. Nothing. For the next twenty minutes, Mira remained a prisoner to her anxiety as the latter grew in intensity. And then her phone rang. It was Andy.

"Hey, you did it," he cried out. "Sorry, I was just wrapping up a client meeting in Seattle, so I couldn't text you right back. I managed to slip that first message in from under the table," he said with a laugh.

Mira tried to laugh, but it sounded more like a cough. "Thanks. I'm happy about it," she replied, swallowing hard to try to reopen her anxiety-clogged airways. If only she could have Andy on the phone with her for the rest of the night.

"Well, I would've loved to celebrate with you tonight, but I've got to work on some financial reports for an upcoming investor meeting next week," he said ruefully.

"S-so, you'll be at your condo then? Working?"

"Yeah, I'm driving back now," he said. "Why do you ask?"

"Oh, no reason, just curious," Mira quickly said. But her mind had already begun to race.

When she hung up the phone, she grabbed the bottle of port wine and headed straight toward her pots and pans. The next two hours included a few pantry ingredients—eggs, milk, flour, sugar, sour cream, and five-spice—all combined with a judicious helping of wine. Then Mira was out the door.

STANDING OUTSIDE ANDY'S condo, Mira couldn't bring herself to ring the doorbell. Every time her heart asked her to, her brain contradicted the move. Andy had made it pretty clear he was working, and for all she knew, he'd decided to work out of another location and wasn't even home. Either way, dropping in on him uninvited wasn't an ideal scenario—very, *very* Sood—but not ideal, no. Besides, Mira was embarrassed she needed to resort to *this* to avoid passing out from another anxiety attack. She felt pathetic, and childish, and foolish, and a great many things, which were all standing in the way of her ringing that doorbell.

In the end, she couldn't bring herself to do it. Turning around, she walked back down the stairs and got in her car. She seemed fine so long as she wasn't in that house alone. Anywhere seemed better—sitting in her car, walking down a street. She pressed her fingertips into her forehead.

The sudden knock on her window caught Mira completely off guard and she squealed. "ANDY!" she cried out, feeling the weight lift off her chest at the mere sight of him outside her car window.

"Where do you think you're going?" he asked her, as she sheepishly opened the door.

"I-er—I was just listening to the radio . . ."

"Right. See, that's what I thought you were doing, except your radio's off." Andy smiled back.

Oops. This was easily more embarrassing than the time she'd RSVPed to a wedding that had already happened, and the bride had called her out on social media.

"You know you're the world's worst liar, right?" he asked, helping her out of the car.

"Yeah. I know," Mira said, handing him the bottle of port and the cake box she'd brought along.

Andy looked down with eager eyes. "What's all this?"

"Laila's travelling with the band until tomorrow night, and she left me a bottle of Port to drink all by myself, so I thought I'd stop by and share some of it with you," Mira said with a casual tip of her head. Maybe she wasn't the *worst* liar in the world.

Andy nodded. "And what's this?" he asked, referring to the box.

"I figured the best thing to eat with port wine was a port-wine cake." Mira shrugged.

"Wow." Andy smiled. "It's a good thing I caught up with you before you drove off."

Mira cringed inwardly. "It's just that, the idea sounded good as I drove here, but I wasn't so sure you wanted to be disturbed tonight, since you said you had to work, and plus this whole dropping by unannounced isn't a very American thing to do, so I didn't know how you'd feel about—"

"What say we chat more about our cultural differences upstairs? With some wine?" asked Andy, cutting in.

Mira laughed and shook her head. "How did you know I was here?" she asked, as she followed him back up the stairs.

"I was out on the balcony working when I thought I saw your car, and a few minutes later I saw you getting back in, so I ran down to catch up, and lucky I did, 'cause this cake smells like port-wine heaven."

IT WAS A chilly night, so regardless of the romantic ambience it created, it was necessary to light a fire. That's what Mira told herself as she sank into the comforting arms of the couch, a wineglass in her hand. Andy sat a few feet away with his feet up on the coffee table. The wine, along with the earthy warmth of the burning firewood, soothed her from the inside out. They had small dessert plates out with a slice each of Mira's port-wine cake which had turned out even better than she'd hoped.

"I'm really sorry I ruined your work night, Andy," Mira slowly said.

Andy forked a big piece of cake and rolled his eyes. "My *God*, this is good," he cried out. "And you didn't ruin anything. I'd mostly finished what I needed to do for now."

"How's it coming with finding those investors?" she asked, sipping her wine. It rolled down her gullet, leaving a warm trail behind.

Andy ate another bite. "It's coming along, and we're working on some minor improvements like our website and things like that, before our next big investment pitch—" he paused for a moment. "Hey, you should take a look at our website. Maybe you'll have some ideas for improvement."

Mira laughed. "I am the least technical person you will ever meet, Andy."

"That's exactly the point," he said. "We want our website to feel accessible to the average user ... you know, potential clients who aren't necessarily tech nerds and geeks ... a school principal, for instance."

"Are you calling me average?" asked Mira with a raised brow.

Andy smiled. "You're *anything* but average. But believe it or not, you represent a good percentage of our site users."

"And you think I might be able to provide some valuable insight?" asked Mira, letting her head slump against a large cushion. Andy's phone rang at that very moment, and he turned to pick it up.

"I sense your sarcasm there," he said with a smile. "But I'd actually love your opinion." He then turned his attention to his phone. "It's Joe calling. Do you mind if I take this, Mira?" he asked her.

"Oh God, yeah," she replied. "Should I leave?" she asked.

But Andy waved for her to stay as he answered the call.

"Hey, what's up, Joe?" he said, and then followed with a grim pause. "Cancelled? Why? What reason did they give?" he cried into the phone, involuntarily running his fingers through his majestic brown hair. He walked over to his laptop to open it and placed the call on speaker as he logged into his email. Mira cowered into her spot on the couch, as embarrassed as if she were taking an unwarranted shortcut through a neighbor's front lawn—not that she'd ever done that or anything.

"They didn't give a reason, man," came Rama's voice. He appeared to be on the call along with Joe. "His assistant called me just now and said we needed to reschedule this meeting."

"Unbelievable... *fu*—" Andy stopped short, gazing briefly over at Mira before pressing the tips of his fingers into his temple.

Rama sighed at the other end of the line. "Do you still want to meet at six tomorrow morning?"

Andy paused to align his glasses then went back to vigorously tapping the keyboard.

"Andy?" came Joe's voice.

"Let's regroup at Taj Mahal Cafe tomorrow morning around nine. That'll give me a chance to reach out to Paul's assistant and find out why they chose to waste our time—"

"Oh, not that place again," Rama immediately protested.

"You know I can't think straight without a samosa and chai tea. We need this meeting to be productive, guys," Andy said firmly. Mira listened, quiet as a church mouse. She'd known Andy a little while now, and she'd never seen him this frazzled before. It was almost *comforting* to know he wasn't porcelain-perfect, after all.

Rama sighed. "Okay, fine."

The men talked a few minutes longer, which gave Mira the time she needed to transport their wine glasses and cake plates to the kitchen sink. She then gathered her coat and purse, just as Andy signed off the call. He poked around his laptop a couple minutes longer and then turned to face her with a flummoxed look. "Don't tell me I scared you and now you're leaving?"

Mira fake laughed. "No, I just realized the time . . . I should get going," she said slowly. Of course, the mere thought of entering her empty apartment was chilling, but Mira realized that was her problem, not Andy's.

"Listen, Mira, I'm really sorry about . . . *that*," he said, vaguely pointing to his laptop. "It's just that we'd spent weeks trying to set this meeting up with this guy, Paul, who's a potential investor and he—"

"Cancelled on you?"

Andy shrugged and pocketed his hands. "It happens, and we'll get back on the horse. I'm sorry, I didn't mean to lose it like that."

"You don't have to apologize. You should be able to lose your temper in your own home."

A brief smile touched Andy's lips. "Anyway, you don't have to go."

"I don't want to, but I need to face this."

"Face what?" Andy's eyes zeroed in on her.

Shit. The words had inevitably slipped out, now warranting an explanation. "Nothing, it's—I was a bit overwhelmed by the idea of spending the night alone in the apartment, that's all," explained Mira. The notion sounded even more embarrassing outside her head than inside. "I haven't been alone since I moved in with Laila, and I've had some . . . a-anxiety issues, but it's nothing that I can't handle, and I'm going to go now and drown myself in a bathtub because I feel so stupid." She meant every word of that.

"Wait a minute. You shouldn't have to handle it alone," Andy said, gently reaching for her arm as she tried to leave. "Listen, I don't know how you're going to take this, but I'm probably going to be working all night anyway. Why don't you just take my bedroom and spend the night here?"

Mira's eyes widened as she felt herself equally divided between a feeling of cheer and horror. Sleeping over at Andy's house was the perfect solution to her problem. However, no Sood woman, alive or dead, had ever spent the night with a man she wasn't married to—alone in his one-bedroom condo, and, oh, had he mentioned something about sleeping in his bed? Mira shook her head. "I can't do that."

Andy nodded. "Okay, I think I know why you feel it's a bad idea . . . I can't imagine how it would go down with your family if they found out, but if you're not comfortable spending the night alone, then you shouldn't have to, Mira. Look, I promise I will stay far, far away from you . . . I'll sleep on the couch." Andy paused to consider for a moment. "And I know I said I wouldn't reveal *all* of my secrets, but guess what? I'm no psychopath. I'm just a techie trying to launch a goddamn startup so I can buy that goddamn dream lake house."

A smile burst across Mira's face despite her furrowed brow. "I-if you're sure, then I wouldn't mind taking you up on the offer," she replied meekly.

"Excellent," Andy said with a nod. "Give me a couple of minutes and I'll get your room ready for you." He disappeared into the bedroom. Mira settled back into the couch, still feeling unsure of her decision to spend the night at Andy's. It felt both humiliating and reassuring, and for now, she preferred to cling to the latter emotion.

Andy emerged ten minutes later with a broad smile across his face. "Ready to see your room for the night?"

Mira nodded and followed him in. It was a lovely master bedroom with an ensuite bathroom. Andy had put clean sheets on the bed and laid out a couple of clean towels for her. "Oh, and here," he said, handing her a pair of pj's. "These are Brook's and I know she won't mind."

"Thanks," smiled Mira, accepting the clothes. "Andy, I really appreciate this, you know that right?"

His eyes felt soft as they collided with hers and lingered long afterward. "You're very welcome."

Comfortably tucked into her borrowed pajamas, sitting on her borrowed bed, and with the imaginary smell of musk all around her, Mira opened a browser on her phone to check out the Cloud-9 website. Her mind felt a post-spa surge and her body relaxed against the softness of Andy's bed. It was as if he was right there, wrapped up with her in those sheets. She tried not to focus on the sweet ache she felt inside her that begged for a man's touch. It had been a while since she'd felt it, and she was grateful the woman inside her hadn't died along with her marriage. Although her body was ready for a second chance, her heart vetoed the idea. No way in her right mind could she put her family in harm's way again. Trust was now a luxury she couldn't afford, which meant love didn't stand a chance in her world. Regardless of whether or not Andy was the most amazing, sweet, thoughtful, and yeah, sure, incredibly handsome man she'd ever met.

Chapter Seventeen

MIRA COULD HEAR the ring of her phone in the distance. But her arm lay paralyzed, unable to reach across to answer it, as dreamless sleep still flooded her eyelids. It was the best sleep she'd had since that awful night Jay left her. "Ugh," grunted Mira as she forced herself to roll over and reach for the device so she could silence it. When she picked it up, however, the caller's name, "Ma," caused her opaque vision to suddenly turn lucid. *Oh Lord.* She was suddenly very aware of where she was—cocooned inside Andy's comfort-excellence sheets, in his house, and wearing his sister's clothes. *Yikes.* She decided to let the call slide to her voicemail. But she knew there was a sixty-forty chance that maneuver wouldn't work with her mother. The woman was fluent in misreading cues. To her, a voicemail was merely an automated signal to let the caller know they needed to keep trying a few hundred times more. To Mira's relief, her mother conceded.

Setting her phone down, Mira tiptoed over to the bedroom door to peek outside. She found a neon Post-It stuck on the door: "Out running. Coffee is in the kitchen.—Andy"

Mira decided to test the authenticity of the note by sticking her head out of the bedroom. She couldn't sense any form of life, so she stepped out. The moment she did, she caught sight of Andy in the kitchen. And before she could dive back into the room for cover (and possibly to check her reflection in the bathroom mirror), he spotted her.

"Are you up or just sleepwalking?" he called out.

"Er, sleepwalking," Mira called back. She heard him laugh as she slowly inched forward. "I thought you were out running?" she asked. *Which is why I stepped out of the room.*

He was standing, facing the gas range, making what appeared to be pancakes. "I actually wrote that note four hours ago." He smiled.

"Oh," Mira said, scratching her forehead. "What can say? I really liked your bed—super comfy." She shrugged, peering in the direction of the smoke that was actively rising from Andy's frying pan. "Are you making pancakes?"

"My *world-famous* pancakes, yes," Andy said, trying to flip one. It landed half-in and half-out of the pan. "I'm getting better at this every day," he added cheerfully.

Mira laughed, wrapping her arms around herself as she admired him. He had on an unassuming white T-shirt, jeans, and his spectacles and yet, he looked like the imaginings of a romance novelist. "Very impressive," she said when he finally managed to flip the sucker back into the pan.

"Well, yeah. I didn't want you to think you were the only one with cooking skills," he replied with a playful frown.

Mira leaned into the pan for a closer look at the charred edges of Andy's pancake. "Clearly I am not, Barefoot Count."

"*Who?*" asked Andy, which caused her to laugh.

"Never mind. Is it done? I'm starving."

Andy studied the pan. "I guess it's done. Although, typically, I would've waited for it to get a darker crust—"

"Oh, my Lord," cried Mira, pushing him out of the way so she could rescue what was left of the poor pancake. "It's crusted enough, trust me."

They ate their pancakes at the breakfast nook by the kitchen. "Yup, tastes like shit," reported Andy, following his first bite. "How're you eating this?" he asked Mira as he got up and walked over to pull something out of the oven.

"I'm being polite."

Andy laughed, returning with a plate filled with warm pastries. "It's a good thing I had Plan B ready to go."

"Wow. When did you get all this?"

"I picked it up from the bakery down the street on the way back from my run this morning."

Mira bit into a croissant and moaned. "*Mmm-mm.* This tastes so good."

"Yup, my pancakes usually make everything else taste really good," Andy admitted with a shrug.

They laughed and talked some more, eating pastries and sipping coffee.

"Oh," Mira said as she remembered something. "You know how you told me to look over your website and tell you what I think?" she said, trailing her words along as she stood up and walked back into the bedroom only to return again with a sheet of paper in her hand. "Here," she said triumphantly, extending the paper to Andy. "These are a few things I thought would help make it better."

Taking hold of the page, Andy studied it closely while sporting an expression that Mira found frighteningly blank.

"Maybe I shouldn't have?" she wondered aloud.

"These are *excellent* ideas for improvement," Andy said. "Like the one about including a live chat feature?" He looked up from the paper at her and smiled. "Thank you, Mira."

"Sure," she replied as she returned to eating her croissant.

"How's the rest of your day looking?" he asked, as he refilled first her coffee and then his out of the warm carafe.

"I'm going to let my store manager know today that I got a new job. He's not going to love it, but hopefully he'll still let me buy my plantains there," said Mira with a tilt of her head. "What about you? You still meeting Joe and Rama this morning at Taj Mahal Cafe?"

Andy nodded, looking grim all of a sudden. He continued to sip his coffee in silence.

"Andy?" began Mira, watching him closely. "How's Cloud-9 doing? Really?" She watched as he drew in a deep breath and sipped more coffee. "If you don't want to tell me—"

"Not great," he replied. "There's nothing wrong with our revenue streams, but our consumer base is growing way faster than we can support it right now. Every penny is being redirected to support overhead costs. We need more money and fast. That's the bottom line."

Mira frowned back. "You mean your growing success is actually the problem?"

Andy coughed up a laugh. "That's exactly it. Classic growth pains."

"And this Paul guy you're trying to meet . . . what's his deal? Can he really help Cloud-9?"

"Paul McMahon? He's a leading venture capitalist . . .

founder and CEO of Maritime Ventures LLC, one of the top venture capital firms on the West Coast, if not in the country. He's the whale investor we need to save our company."

"He's got deep pockets, huh?"

"Yes, but more importantly, he knows the tech biz better than anyone in the industry, which means he could provide not just the capital we need to scale, but also valuable guidance all around."

Mira watched Andy as he reclined into his chair, netting his fingers behind his head as he stared out the large window at the mountains in the distance. She wanted so badly to ask one final question, but she knew it would put Andy on the spot. She cleared her throat and decided to do it anyway. "And er, what happens if you can't get him? Mr. McDeep Pockets?"

Andy's gaze stayed fixed to the window, but his voice came through loud and clear. "If things don't start looking up by the end of next quarter, we'll be forced to declare bankruptcy, pack our shit up, and go home."

Mira bit down on her lower lip as the grimness of Andy's predicament sank in. And to think he'd offered her a hand in her training, appeared calm, pleasant, and so supportive toward her, while all the while his own world was slowly burning to the ground. It was almost too unbearable to think about.

"Don't worry," Andy said, slicing into Mira's quiet musings. "I won't let that happen. A *lot* would have to go down before Cloud-9 does," he said, a smile reappearing on his face.

Mira envied his ability to rise up out of the ashes like that. Where did he find that kind of spirit, anyway? The ability to forage and find a silver lining even in the darkest of clouds? If only she had that, her life would be twice as beautiful. "You're the most optimistic person I know, that's for sure," she said, looking into his eyes.

"Well, I have to be, don't I? If I throw in the towel without a fight, I'll end up taking my employees and my customers, and Joe and Rama—pretty much anyone and everyone who's ever put their trust in me—down with me. I can't do that."

"Okay, now you're also the most principled person I know. Well done." Mira laughed. Andy laughed with her, his eyes darting from her lips to her eyes to her hair as he did. Mira could oddly sense his desire to want to say something more. But he never did.

STANDING AT HER car door, with Andy a few feet away from her on the sidewalk, Mira said her goodbyes. "Thanks again for letting me stay the night."

"Anytime."

"Oh, are you still up to meet me at the trail this weekend?" she asked as she started to open the passenger door to throw in her bag.

"Actually, Mira, instead of the trail, could you meet me here Saturday?"

"Your condo?" frowned Mira.

"Yeah, I want to up the ante on your training, so we're

going to do something different than our usual trail run."

"Up the ante? You mean, make my life even harder?"

Andy laughed. "I promise it's for the greater good."

"But can you at least tell me what you've planned?"

Andy shook his head. "Nah, I prefer not to kill the element of surprise."

"Ah-haha." Mira shivered a laugh. "You don't want to spook me?"

"Yup, exactly," Andy said with a nod. "Just be prepared, and you'll do great."

"Be prepared?" repeated Mira. *What on earth did that mean, anyway?*

Chapter Eighteen

WINTER – December

THROUGH HER LAST week of working at the Indian grocery store, Mira kept the nervous excitement of her Saturday training with Andy within her sights. She had no idea what he had in store for her, so she chose to bolster her self-confidence by tenaciously following through on her running goal each week—run thirty minutes Monday through Friday, rain or shine.

With her new job at Sound Consulting on the horizon, and a substantial increase in her monthly income, Mira allowed herself a wardrobe upgrade. She ditched her clunky sweatpants and shirt and bought herself some running gear. She never would have imagined her closet would ever welcome such a category of clothing, but such was life's sweet unpredictability.

The winter chill was disheartening, so Mira countered it with layers. And in her running tights and sweat-wicking tees, Mira "felt" like a runner, which forced her to run like a runner. Unbeknownst to her, Mira's body responded with equal fervor. She still wore her curves with pride, but running began to highlight her curves in a way that made them appear more structured, less like Jell-O. The dresses that had draped her like a tarp over a dirt mound now hugged her in the right places. Suddenly, she had a waist.

Running wasn't changing her, but bringing out the best in her. She felt better about herself after each run and felt a desire to chase happiness rather than focus on her past.

With three months left to train, Mira knew she had a mountain to climb still. But the good news was, the mountain didn't scare her anymore.

Jogging swiftly down her trail, Mira stopped to check her app at the halfway point. *Perfect.* She'd run 1.5 miles in fifteen minutes—better than her record from last year, which was zero miles in zero minutes.

Snapping a quick picture of herself with the lake behind her, Mira continued down the trail. In the oddest possible way, she'd become something of a celebrity in her family these days—what with the impending divorce and now the half-marathon. Maybe not the kind of celebrity one would idolize, but the kind one would follow online just to see if they'd fallen off their horse yet. She still liked to post pictures of her running journey on social media. For one, she could track her progress, and also because her dad checked social media on his tablet, using the only two mobile fingers he had. It was Mira's way of keeping him updated on her life.

As she neared the two-mile mark, her body responded the usual way—by beginning to fall apart. Regardless of how well she paced herself, how perfectly she maintained her running form, how well-balanced her weight was between her feet, Mira always ended up suffering through her last mile. Always. She wasn't sure if her body would ever get used to the feeling of running three miles. And if it didn't, how was she ever expected to run 13.1?

She could feel her shins tugging as they continued to drag the growing weight of her body. The latter felt like a ten-pound bag of russet potatoes as she chugged down the trail toward the 2.4-mile mark. God, this was agony. Every step she took caused pain. Her arms were tired and slumped on either side, she was hunching over, and although she could hear Andy's voice in her head, "Back straight, check your form." She just couldn't do it. She continued to tow her weight as her feet now began to cramp. Mira switched modes and tried a strategy that she'd started to use the past few runs. She began counting down the minutes in her head. She set her eye on a tree a few feet away. All she needed to do was run to that tree. Pushing herself, Mira got to the tree and then changed her target—a park bench a few feet away. *That's it*, she consoled herself. *All you have to do is run to that park bench. Breathe, you've got this.*

When the park bench had been reached, Mira continued to trick her brain with smaller, more achievable, less scary targets. Strategy or no strategy, her lungs continued to feel like they were on fire. Her airways were so tight she could barely breathe, so she instinctively tipped her head backward, toward the sky. *Just a few more steps. You can do this.*

As she huffed and puffed her way across the final mile point, Mira doubled over to catch her breath. She pushed the Stop button on her running app and sat down on a bench a few feet away from the parking lot. It was rather frustrating the way Mira saw it—since she'd first started training for her half-marathon, her abilities as a runner had improved by leaps and bounds; however, when she compared where she was as a runner within the greater scheme of actually running a half-marathon, she still had a long way to go. Drawing oxygen in through her mouth, Mira's thoughts slowly drifted to her Saturday training with Andy, wondering what he'd meant by asking her to be prepared. *Be prepared?* What an incredibly subjective, vague command that was to Mira. And how did her Sood brain do word-math? Not very well. To her, subjective plus vague, equaled mortified.

When Saturday did finally arrive, Mira was outside Andy's condo at 9:00 a.m. which is when they usually met at the trailhead. "You made it right on time," said Andy as he led her into his home. When she stepped in, she froze. Andy had transformed his living room into a workout zone with all kinds of equipment—free-weights, exercise balls, jump ropes, a goddamn weight bench, and . . . "What's that?" asked Mira, pointing to a bag filled with an odd, disc-shaped object that looked like a giant purple coaster.

"Those are gliding discs," Andy explained, with eyes twinkling "We're going to do mountain climbers with them."

Mira stared back at him, puzzled. "Mountain *what?*"

"Climbers."

"Wait, but why do I need to do all of this? I'm running a half-marathon, not a half-mountain climb-athon."

Andy raised a brow at her. "Okay, tell me, how's your pace right now? Your runtime?"

Mira's face turned to stone. "Not great."

"Strength training is a key aspect of endurance running . . . such as for a half-marathon. Stronger muscles create more horsepower for a runner. Mixing in a little strength training into your regime will help you run faster, and better. Make sense?"

"Mmm . . ." Brilliant, actually. Why hadn't she thought of that? It seemed so obvious when Andy said it so simply, but it had never occurred to Mira that maybe what she needed to improve her runtime was some of that mountain-climber stuff.

"Right, let's start with a quick warm-up," he suggested, and using a remote, he turned on the stereo to play some workout music. They started with some jumps and stretches, then moved on to lunges and plyometrics. The burpees made Mira want to curl up into the fetal position, and the sumo squats made her want her mommy. Andy then got Mira into crunch position and made her play pass between her feet and her hands, using a giant exercise ball.

"This amounts to doing traditional crunches," Andy tried to explain, hunching down behind her.

"Argh...Bah-han," Mira replied. Translation: "Lovely. Thanks for clarifying.

The free-weights routine, Mira loved. She was, after all, a former Indian housewife. Which, incidentally, entailed strong arms—owing to all that dough-kneading and ladle-stirring.

"You like these, huh?" said Andy with a smile.

"These are my favorite so far."

Andy was an incredible spotter, watching Mira closely every step of the way. And she, in turn, loved how he always managed to correct her without ever patronizing her—considering he had a drawer full of race medals, and she had yet to earn her first one.

"Push your belly button into your spine when you bench-press," Andy said. He was kneeling on the floor right above Mira's head as she lay flat on her back, on the weight bench, lifting up a barbell.

"Like this?" she asked, arching her neck up at Andy.

"Yes, exactly. Pressing your ab muscles inward will take the pressure off your back during bench presses."

Mira breathed out as she pushed the barbell up and away from her chest. "Heavy..." she said, coughing up the words.

"About sixteen pounds without the added weights," Andy acknowledged with a nod.

"Feels c-closer to a h-hundred pounds..."

Andy let out a warm laugh. "We have three sets of climbers, and then we're done, I promise."

"Sounds just lovely," Mira said between pants as she hauled the barbell up in the air again. She cried inwardly because she'd completely forgotten about those stupid mountain-climber discs. "Looking forward to it," she added, trying to overcompensate for her lack of genuine enthusiasm.

But Andy had her figured out. "You don't like the idea of the gliders, do you?" he asked. Where was he getting this access to her brain from? It was beginning to freak her out just a wee bit.

"Not excited, b-but intrigued." The barbell was killing her.

Andy tried to pump her up. "Just three more sets of eight with the barbells, you've got this."

"Yeah, I can't hear you, I'm brain-dead right now."

Andy smiled and momentarily boosted the barbell off Mira as she sat up to catch her breath.

"You can do this, Mira," he said to her, looking firmly into her eyes.

"I'd like to see *you* try?" she shot back and immediately bit her lip. The lack of oxygen to her brain was making her say things she'd normally only *think*. "Sorry, I didn't mean—"

"Alright, I'll make a deal with you," Andy cut in, in his I-mean-business voice. He was kneeling down on one knee before a panting, red-faced Mira.

"You get through three sets of presses for me *and* the mountain climbers, and I'll bench-press you fifty times, just for kicks."

This made Mira laugh. "That's crazy because you don't know how much I weigh." Andy wouldn't make it past his tenth one, as far as she was concerned.

"What if we call it a challenge?"

Mira felt the goosebumps rising on her skin. "You're on, mister."

"Okay. Now, back to those bench presses," he said, gently handing Mira the barbell again. She pushed hard and completed the remaining sets. And following that, she endured the gliders to complete the mountain-climber exercise. The latter was as tough as it sounded—getting into a push-up position, with a purple glider disc under the ball of each foot, Mira continued to alternatingly bring each knee to her chest, until she finally begged for a meteor to strike the earth and end her pain. Her thighs and glutes were on fire; her calves cramped so hard she wanted to cry out. But she pushed through the pain, and not just because she wanted to experience the feeling of being bench-pressed by Andy, but . . . okay, maybe it was just for that reason that she did it.

Following four sets of mountain climbers, Mira was done with her training for the day. It was odd how there were muscles in her body that felt sweetly sore that Mira didn't even know *existed*. "Man, that feels good," she cried with an incredible feeling of satisfaction.

"Are you ready to be bench-pressed?" Andy asked her.

She was still out of breath when the question emptied the remaining oxygen from her lungs.

"Yeah, I'm ready," she said meekly. Her heart began to pound as she watched Andy ceremoniously flex his forearms before lying flat on his back on the weight bench, with his feet resting firmly on the ground. "Alright, I'm ready for you, Ms. Sood."

Gulp.

Mira's body was tingling inside and out. She obeyed, inching close enough that he could hoist her up with the palms of his hands, supporting her back and thighs. Mira lay facing the ceiling, feeling Andy's hands on her body; her skin felt as bubbly as champagne, and her heart had turned to pudding.

"Okay, now hold as steady as you can. Don't try and escape or anything."

"Er-okay . . ." Mira closed her eyes so she could absorb the feeling—the feeling of being driven up into the air by a pair of powerful arms. He made it appear effortless as he hoisted her up and let her cascade down again. It felt electric to Mira, the way Andy softly grunted when he crossed thirty. But he continued to bench-press her, his arms unwavering. He made her feel oddly secure even as he held her up in that precarious way, horizontal to his vertical body.

It came as no surprise that Andy bench-pressed Mira fifty times, and he'd done it as easily as she could have eaten a box of fifty bonbons in bed. When he was done, he carefully placed her back on the floor again and sat up on the bench.

"Well?" he asked her, resting his elbows on his knees. "How'd I do?"

Mira blushed, but tried to hide it with a mere shrug of a shoulder. "Pretty cool, if not completely out of this world, and unlike anything I've ever experienced in my life before," she replied calmly, as if she were reporting the weather.

They laughed, their eyes locked.

"I really loved today's training. I didn't think I would, but I did," she added. "Maybe we could do it again tomorrow?"

"Actually, I meant to tell you, I can't train with you tomorrow—I have a race."

"A race? Wait, you mean, you're *in* it?"

Andy nodded almost apologetically.

"Oh wow," cried Mira. "Can I watch?"

This caused his brows to shoot up. "You want to come watch the race?"

"If it's okay? If you don't mind?"

Andy's face lit up. "I'd *love* that, Mira. That would be . . . just so great to have you there, but are you sure? These things take a few hours from start to finish, but if you have a friend along with you—"

"I could bring Laila?"

"That'll work," he fired back with a look of enthusiasm. "It's the Bear Back Mountain Marathon, and it's a big one for me because it's a qualifier for the L.A. Marathon I'm running next year."

"There are qualifier races, too?" asked Mira, eyes widening. So, so far away from her Sood world, this all sounded.

"Yeah, and it's going to be so great to have you there," he said again. "Plus, you'll get a taste of how it will feel when you run your own half-marathon in three months."

"Yeah, that too," she said, warily.

Chapter Nineteen

THE BEAR BACK Marathon was already in full swing when Laila and Mira pulled into the Bear Back State Park's parking lot. The race, as Mira had discovered on their website, was a 26.2-mile, rugged, uneven trail loop around the inner park. As Mira exited the car, the December morning air on her skin felt frigid, and the rays of warm sunlight remained lost in the thick 7:00 a.m. fog. The morning light was just breaking through the blanket of navy-black sky, but even with the low lights, Mira noticed Andy in the distance. He appeared to have spotted her instantly as he began walking toward them, past the crowd of volunteers and park rangers, a smile sweeping across his face. "Mira, you made it." He smiled. He looked formidable in his long-sleeved running tee, gloves, and shorts; he'd forgone his glasses for the occasion.

"Damn it, it's freezing out here," growled Laila, stepping out of the car. "When does this thing start, anyway?"

"In about fifteen minutes," replied Andy, his eyes still fixed on Mira as she cupped her gloved palms to her face against the cold. "You don't have to stay for the whole thing—"

"Oh, I want to," insisted Mira. "I know you said I

should just meet you at the end, but I wanted to catch you as you started off. I've never seen a race before," she added with a shrug.

"Come on, I'll show you," said Andy, and led them closer to the gathered crowd of racers.

There was a sea of racers panting and warming up, from the starting point all the way down to a few feet shy of the parking lot.

"Where will you be?" asked Mira.

Andy pointed in the direction of the starting line. "I've got an assigned corral, so I'll be right up front."

"What's an assigned corral?"

"It's a spot you can request, which the race organizers will proactively assign to you based on your past performance. It's to ensure a smoother flow of race traffic."

"You mean the fast ones are up front, and the slower guys are the caboose?" Laila asked, raising a brow.

"Something like that." Andy shrugged.

"And you're up front?" Mira tried to confirm, just as the racers got ready for the countdown.

Andy nodded. "I'd better get going," he said, smiling straight at Mira.

"I'll see you on the other side—good luck!" she cried, feeling that inexplicable tingle under her skin. She watched Andy melt away into the sea of runners, so she decided to move farther into the crowd of spectators to catch sight of him. She spotted him, right up front and center as he jiggled his limbs in preparation for the start. The race countdown had already begun, and with the final digits down, the racers took off. Mira could no longer spot Andy, even as she arched her neck and stood on tippy-toes.

Laila let out a groan. "Great, he's gone. Can we go home now?"

"Of course not. We need to wait till it ends. Why do you think we're here?"

Laila opened her mouth to say something but was cut short by another voice. "Hey there." They both turned toward it and Mira instantly smiled with recognition. "Seth? From Sporting Goods?"

"In the flesh." He smiled as his eyes glanced at Laila for an introduction.

"Oh, this my cousin, Laila Sood," Mira said as Laila produced a dry smile and shook Seth's hand.

"It's a pleasure to meet you, Laila."

"Yeah, likewise, although it would've been more pleasurable with the sun high up in the twelve o'clock position."

Seth nodded cheerfully. "Are you guys out here to support the defending champion?"

Mira sported a frown. "Er, no, we're here for Andy . . . I mean, we're here to cheer him on."

"He's our defending champion." Seth nodded with a smile.

This caused Mira's eyes to widen. "Huh?"

"Andy's won this race two years in a row and is defending his title today. If he manages it, he'll end up setting a pretty unbeatable record for the old books."

"No kidding?" Laila said with a pout. "And where's the coffee at?"

Mira rolled her eyes at her cousin as she turned back to Seth. "I had no idea. He never told me."

"Yeah, Andy doesn't like to toot his own horn."

Mira nodded as her thoughts drifted to him. "Oh, I know well enough."

"But it's a sticky wicket for Andy this year," Seth was saying. "He may be the defending champion, but he's got to have his fight face on if he wants to win today."

Mira leaned in. "Why's that?"

"Mark Melrose." Seth nodded, as if the name were self-explanatory.

"What's that? Runner code for 'potholes on the trail'?" Laila frowned.

"Mark's the new guy on the block," Seth replied with a look of foreboding. "And he's twenty-six-years old, which means he's got less mileage on those muscles than Andy, who's been running, what, fourteen years?"

"Sixteen," corrected Mira softly. "And has Mark ever won this race?"

"He's never run this one before," Seth said, upturning his lips. "Which means, he'll be hungry for a podium finish."

"Great." Mira sighed. A jagged shudder ran down her spine.

"But every other race the guy ran this year, he's won," Seth concluded with a shrug.

His words caused Mira's lips to stiffen, although Laila appeared hopeful. "Great, it sounds like Andy doesn't stand a chance, so maybe we should just leave now, and you can bake him a condolence cake later, okay?" she proposed.

Mira shot her cousin a sharp look of disapproval, despite Seth's echoey laugh. "I'm not leaving until I watch the finish," she replied firmly.

"Oh, I don't think you should leave," added Seth, looking squarely at Laila. "Mark may be young and feisty, but Andy is . . . well, *Andy*."

"What do you mean?" asked Mira, a flicker of hope emerging inside her.

Seth breathed in slowly. "Let's just say, stealing the win from Andy is going to be as hard as pulling a salmon out of a bear's mouth."

"That's very lyrical." Laila frowned. "What are you, a writer?"

"Just on the weekends. But right now, I'm the guy who knows where to find the coffee." Seth smiled back.

Laila pivoted to Mira. "I'll see you at the finish line in a little bit," she declared, then turned back to Seth. "Are you gonna show me or what?"

Mira watched as Seth and Laila disappeared into the crowd. She fidgeted with her jacket hood just as the rain began to fall. She checked her watch and made her way closer to the finish line. Considering the racecourse was a loop, it took her no time to find a good spot on the sidelines to watch the epic finish. A little while later, both Seth and Laila joined Mira with an extra cup of steaming joe and fries. The three of them chatted and ate—although it was mostly Laila and Seth who did the talking, while Mira contributed a polite laugh every once in a while. Before she knew it, a wave of cheers erupted in the crowd of spectators. It caught Mira's attention, and her eyes darted in the direction of the oncoming racers. She couldn't exactly see through the screen of rain and mist, but it was clear they were fast approaching the finish line. There were at least ten runners of varying attributes heading their way, and none of them was Andy. "Where is he?" Mira wondered aloud. Her heart pounded with a mild fury. It was as if she were out there running along with them and not on the sidelines eating fries.

"There," pointed Seth, using a long-cut fry to aid him. "Right behind bib 1557..."

Mira had noticed the bib on Andy when she waved him off at the starting line. He was bib number 2731 and presently in fifth place.

"Better start planning that condolence cake," Laila muttered to Mira, who shriveled with disappointment on the inside. Why she cared so much about Andy's potential loss, Mira had no clue. But the feeling of her heart sinking down to the pit of her stomach was felt in real time.

The racers were now less than half a mile from the finish line. And that's when it happened. As if by sheer will, Andy picked up the pace. His eyes remained at ground level, as if he didn't care about the finish line, just his next step. *Five, four, three...* Mira watched, awestruck, as Andy moved up in place, picking the lead runners off one by one.

"He looks so rejuvenated all of a sudden," Mira said with a flickering smile.

"He's an *excellent* actor," Seth replied. "The man is in extreme physical pain, not to mention fatigue. He's pushing all the buttons on his LT right now—"

"What's LT? That sounds bad," Mira cut in, her brow re-curling.

"Lactate threshold... it's how hard you can physically push yourself before you feel like you're about to throw up, or pass out... or both," explained Seth, dunking some fries in ketchup. "Andy's definitely beginning to infringe on his LT. His VO2 Max is probably at, what, seventy percent, right now?"

"English, please. What's VO2 Max?" asked Laila.

"VO2 Max is how much oxygen your body can get to your muscles per minute. The higher the number, the better your performance—"

"But what's happening with Andy right now?" Mira cut in, leaning up in time to catch a glimpse as he thundered into third place, with just a few hundred yards left to go.

"Notice how he's picked up the pace? He likely has about five minutes to go before he hits his LT, which will probably be at about 85 percent of his VO2 Max."

Mira's head was spinning. Seth could have said it all in French and she'd have understood just about the same as she did now. She decided to rely on her own analysis, which was based on the old-fashioned method—using her own eyes. Looking past the crowd, Mira watched Andy in motion. He looked formidable, the way he thrashed the gravel under his feet. She noticed, even with her relatively inexperienced eyes, his perfect running form—fluid yet strong, with his feet sharing the onus of each foot strike. The latter appeared deliberate and calculated across the uneven terrain of the trail. Andy continued to sprint with an unwavering drive as he charged forward to quickly swap spots with the second-place runner. Which meant it was now down to Andy and Mark Melrose, both of whom were an arm's length apart, with Mark leading the race.

Just a few more yards remained as they approached the finish line.

Seth began shaking his head at the two racers, who were now running neck and neck. "Yup, he's close to full horsepower now. They're feeding off their adrenaline . . . that, and pure *grit*. But Andy needs to move quickly because pretty soon he'll experience the dreaded 'dead leg.'" Seth paused to turn to Mira. "D'you know what that is?"

She cocked her head. "Dead leg? Yeah, I think I can figure that one out, thanks." The words stuck to her throat, as she felt parched from all the nervous excitement.

Mira bit her lip as the crowd roared in unison. Mark Melrose was still a couple of feet ahead of Andy, and the finish line was less than a couple of feet away from Mark.

Maybe I could do a plum cake? Mira solemnly mused to herself. *Something warm and comforting to help Andy cope with the loss.*

"Holy shit," cried Seth, as the crowd of spectators suddenly began to cheer wildly.

Mira turned just in time to watch the epic race finish—like a lightning flash out of a stormy sky, Andy, in a trice, went full throttle, which caused the crowd to bellow with excitement. Mark looked like he didn't realize what was happening as Andy dashed past him. Swooping into first place, Andy ran clear across the finish line with a fiery Mark, huffing close on his heels, looking extremely unnerved.

"NO, SHIT! Andy's just set a new personal record time for himself. Man, he's a warrior."

"WOO HOO!" Mira clapped, finally letting all her pent-up emotions loose. She whipped around and ran through the crowd in search of him, only to realize he was already hunting for her.

"Andy, you did it," she cried out and before her brain could hit the big flashy, "DON'T, MIRA" button, she'd leapt up and into his eager, flailing arms. He hugged her tight, and she coiled her arms around his neck and held on as tight as the pride she felt for him would allow. That was the easy part. Forcing herself to pull away and then pretending his touch hadn't triggered a sweet ache inside her? That was the hard part.

His arms appeared reluctant to leave her waist, lingering a bit before slipping off. Mira tried to appear nonchalant, hoping her flushed cheeks weren't spilling the beans on how she really felt.

"Y-you were so great," she tried to say.

His eyes lay focused on her as he continued to pant from the effort of winning the marathon. "I'm just glad you could be here," he replied softly. He opened his mouth to speak again, but just as he did, Seth and Laila burst out of the crowd to congratulate him, followed by Mark Melrose, who came up to shake his hand.

"They did warn me about you," Mark said with a gracious smile as the two men shook hands. "Congratulations, man," he added.

"Thanks, and you gave me a good chase." Andy winked back, slapping Mark on the back. A few other racers walked up to chat with Andy, as did the race organizers to inform him they would be giving out the podium placing medals in the next half-hour.

"You don't have to stay if you don't want to," Andy said, turning to Mira.

"Oh, no way. I want to watch you get the gold medal,"

she said, but then paused to consider. "Unless you don't want me to stay and prefer to do it alone?"

"No, I *want* you," Andy blurted and almost instantly appeared to catch himself. He cleared his throat. "Er, I mean, I want you guys to stay. Maybe we can all go grab a bite to eat after?"

Mira nodded, despite the pressing questions floating inside her head: Had Andy almost said what she thought he did? Was the precinct of their friendship beginning to crack under the weight of the undeniable chemistry between them? They were compatible, sure, but there was more, wasn't there? Under the layer of casual laughs and drinking chai teas, there was a palpable source of oxygen that Mira had discovered whenever she was with Andy. And when he wasn't around, she felt his presence constantly. No single touch ever occurred between them that didn't cause Mira's skin to tingle. But now, was he feeling it too? Or was her imagination determined to run amuck? Because all it was going to take for Mira to run for the hills was a clear sign from Andy that his feelings for her were beyond just friendship. Heartless as it sounded inside her head, she was determined to protect her family from a second shock wave—a condition which she knew, in all likelihood, they would neither forgive nor survive.

"Mira, you okay?" Laila whispered. "Why're you frowning so hard?"

"Er, i-it's nothing. I'm fine, thanks," said Mira as she watched Andy and the other two winners, silver and bronze, gather close to the podium.

Chapter Twenty

STANDING INSIDE SOUND Consulting Inc.'s supply closet, Mira kicked the industry copier a few more times. This was the second time the stupid machine had copped out on her in the two weeks that she'd been employed here. When she was back at her desk, which was located in the far back end of the bullpen, Mira checked her phone. There were three missed calls from her mother, and one from Auntie Sharmila, who had bothered to leave behind a voicemail.

"Mira, it's Mummyji here. Hope you're doing well? It feels like ages since I saw your face, so I hope you and Laila will be coming to our holiday party tonight? I know you confirmed it already, but Papaji and I have some exciting news to share, so I wanted to make sure I'll be seeing you. Bye, and God bless."

Staring down at her phone, Mira tried to picture various scenarios that would entail exciting news for a Sood. Let's see . . . marriage, childbirth, second childbirth—that's it. Now all that remained for her and Laila was to uncover which one of these three possibilities was the lucky winner.

For a moment, Mira surveyed the floor. It was alive with 10 a.m. office activity—employees typing, some chatting, brewing fresh espresso by the snack nook, or toasting a bagel.

Breathing in, Mira soaked in the coffee-bagel "office smell." It felt good. *Satisfying.* Naturally, there was a limit to how much one could love sitting in a chair all day, answering the telephone for a few dollars above minimum wage. Yet, to Mira, this felt liberating—like a step in the right direction.

The tinkle of an incoming text broke Mira away from her musings. It was from Laila. *Tonight's a no-go for me. Band practice.*

Mira raised a brow at her phone before typing back. *Nice try. NO.*

So, you don't care about my happiness, then? came Laila's response.

Mira sighed inwardly as she typed her reply. *Not tonight.* Going to Auntie Sharmila's house wasn't a task Mira was willing to perform solo. At least, not since her separation.

Placing her phone to one side, she shifted her focus back to her computer screen and the dozen or so emails—everything from purchase requests to timecard submissions were waiting for her response. *Better than making rotis for a jerk,* she reminded herself as her eyes scanned the overflowing inbox.

"IF I KILL a Sood tonight, it's your fault," Laila fumed, unbuckling her seatbelt.

Mira sighed and silently followed suit.

"By the way," said Laila as the cousins began walking down the cobbled driveway of their auntie's home. "Did I tell you I have a date with Seth this weekend?"

"What? Andy's runner friend?"

"The same." Laila nodded.

"I didn't even think you liked him that much."

Laila shrugged casually. "I thought he was cute. Anyway, we're going to Rocko's for a cozy dinner, and from there, we're hitting a nightclub."

"Are you going to tell them?" asked Mira, gesturing to her auntie's front door.

Laila punched the doorbell. "*Absolutely*. Nothing would make me happier than to watch their chickpea faces when I tell them I'm going *hybrid*."

Mira shuddered at the thought. The night was still young, and already she couldn't wait for it to end.

Mummyji's living room hadn't looked this lively since her Diwali party a few months ago. Trays of samosas and kachoris were passed around by aunties who were both friends and relations. The women were dressed in their finest shimmering saris and chunky jewelry, while the men wore traditional silk kurtas.

A group of aunties soon walked up to Mira, who instinctively reached down to touch their feet. "It's nice to see you looking well, Mira," began Geeta Khurana, a podgy second auntie whose lipstick had bled over her lip line from a recent samosa bite.

"We all heard about Jay's affair," Pritam Kaur added with a perfunctory look of worry.

"And no children?" Rinki Batra shook her head. She was

Auntie Sharmila's best friend.

Breathing in, Mira tried to gain perspective. *If I can push through running three miles, I can push through having this conversation.* "No, we didn't have kids. But I'm glad, because the separation would have been hard on a child."

Pritam auntie seemed appalled. "Huh? But without a child, Mira, how are you coping emotionally?"

Mira needed to nail the interrogating aunties with a single response. "I'm coping by running a half-marathon," she said with a smile. But the aunties only appeared confused.

Rinki Batra let out a gasp. "Eh?"

"*Running?*" Pritam auntie tried to confirm.

Feeling perfectly satisfied with herself, Mira excused herself from the auntie-group and made her way over to Laila, who had found a cozy spot on a couch. She watched Mira approach with an all-knowing grin.

"How did that go?" she asked.

"Shut up, Laila."

"Hello everyone. I'm so glad to see all of you here today," came Auntie Sharmila's voice. She was standing at the center of her living room, holding up a flute of champagne. "Please make sure you all have a glass to toast, because Vinod and I would like to welcome the New Year with a special announcement, which is that our youngest daughter, Samira, is getting married to our very own Ronit Kapadia." An immense cheer and hooting ensued, following which Ronit's parents rose out of the audience to embrace their future in-laws. "*Badhai-ho, ji. Badhai-ho,*" cheered the aunties and uncles in the crowd to the two lucky sets of parents. Congratulations on checking the box.

The older guests in the crowd took turns embracing the parents, feeding them customary pieces of *mithai* (sweets) from an open box. Ronit and Samira turned themselves into cuddly bears, knitting arms and rubbing noses to prove the legitimacy of the announcement. Essentially, they could go ahead and make out right there, and it would all still be legit because Ronit was a nice Hindu boy from a traditional Punjabi family, a cherished family friend of the Soods and, wait for it . . . an *orthodontist*. Boom, mic drop.

"This is so typical," Laila muttered under her breath. "God forbid someone should think outside the box for once."

"I take it you don't approve the match?" asked Mira, leaning in.

"I disapprove and I promise to do the exact opposite to spite every living Sood *if* I ever decide to get married."

Mira pouted. "I'll remember you said that."

"Go ahead. And I can't believe they stole my thunder. How am I supposed to follow now, with the news of me and Seth?"

Mira inhaled deeply, trying to find a happy place inside her head which, at the moment, felt like a fog room.

Laila stood up from the couch. "I'm gonna get a soda," she said and walked away. It only took a moment for Auntie Sharmila to spot the vacancy. Walking over, she sat down next to Mira.

"Congratulations, Mummyji," Mira said and gave her auntie a hug.

"Thank you, my dear." Auntie Sharmila smiled back. "Of course, tonight's announcement was just a formality.

We all knew this was coming, and even Mohan-ji had blessed their union a few months ago, saying their *kundlis* were a nine-out-of-ten match."

"Oh wow," replied Mira. A slam dunk in the world of astrological matchmaking.

"What about you, Mira?" her auntie asked. "Now, even your younger sister is getting married. And your Ma says these days you don't even answer your phone?"

"I answer my phone," Mira replied with a frown. "And I'm doing fine."

Her auntie squinted back. "*Are* you?" she wondered out loud as she studied Mira in her emerald-green sari. "You do look pretty toned these days . . ."

"Yes, my half-marathon training's helping me stay fit."

"Uff..." Her aunt's brows curled with worry. "You're still doing that running business?"

"I am, and it's going well," insisted Mira. Why this was a problem, she had no idea. Thankfully, at that very moment, Laila returned to the scene, sporting a look of irritation at the sight of Auntie Sharmila.

"Hey, Mummyji. How's it going?" she asked, flinging herself onto the other side of Mira.

Her auntie grunted and served up an ice-cold nod. "Nice that you could make time for our family holiday party."

"Hell, yeah. Wouldn't miss it for a night with Randy Rhoads."

Pursing her lips, Auntie Sharmila turned her gaze back to Mira. "By the way, I've been following Jay on social media. Do you know he's been travelling with that woman?"

"That's okay, Mummyji, I don't need to kn—"

"Paris, Istanbul . . . I saw pictures of him snorkeling, cycling, and there was one of him *skydiving*, shameless man."

Mira was lost for words as she pictured Jay under the Eiffel Tower with his arm around the other woman. She wanted her auntie to stop and was grateful when Laila's voice came to her aid.

"Forget Jay, Mummyji. Guess what? I'm dating a white hippie dude of Bahai faith." Laila said with a cheerful wink. "And there's a sixty-forty chance it's true love, so stay tuned. I may have an announcement of my own soon."

Auntie Sharmila sported an intense frown as she dropped her jaw and rose from her seat. "None of this will be funny when you're eighty and all alone with no grandchildren, and no husband to comfort you."

"Who says I'll live to be eighty?" replied Laila, swatting the idea.

To that, Auntie Sharmila turned her back and stomped off.

"I don't know whether to laugh or cry," Mira said, turning to her cousin.

The two of them walked into the large dining room where a catered dinner had been laid out, buffet-style—large chafing dishes with steaming food that smelled like Indian heaven.

"Why do you let Mummyji bully you like that?" asked Laila, sipping from a soda can, and watching Mira scoop up some koftas to top over her cumin rice.

"I can't ask her to shut up."

Laila tossed her empty can in the trash and picked a plate up for herself. "You know your problem? You care more about what other people think than you do about yourself."

"What? Just because I care about my family doesn't mean I don't care about myself."

Laila shrugged, plating some tandoori paneer tikka and peppers. "You're always putting them ahead of yourself."

"What nonsense," Mira fired back.

"Then how come you haven't told them about Andy?"

The sound of his name (always, but especially in this context) caused Mira to flush inwardly. "I-er, there's nothing to tell. We're friends."

This only made Laila laugh out loud. "You spent the night in his condo the week I was touring."

"I spent the night at his condo because I had no choice," Mira whispered back, suddenly aware of all the nosey relatives in the buffet line. "You know very well I've been struggling with anxiety issues . . . I felt sick at the thought of spending the night alone in our apartment. And to be completely fair, it was *his* idea."

"Yeah, okay," Laila said, waving a papadum at Mira. "But the guy is helping you train for your half-marathon."

"So what?"

"And you went to support him at *his* race."

"Again, so *what?*" volleyed Mira. "That's what friends do—support each other."

"Right, right . . . *friends* do," Laila nodded, holding back a smile. "So, you don't love him, then? Your 'friend,' Andy?"

"No, of course not," Mira shot back. She felt blindsided by the question, only because she'd never stopped to ask herself the same thing, always preferring to tiptoe around it instead.

Laila laughed some more. "Wow, you love this guy... it's *so* obvious."

"Okay, nothing's obvious."

"Please," Laila said, placing a palm on her chest. "I'm an *artist*. I know love when I see it, so don't treat me like a six-year-old who's beginning to have doubts about Santa Claus."

Mira rolled her eyes at Laila. "I don't love him. I would know if I'm feeling the love *feeling*, okay?"

Laila raised a skeptical brow. "You're running out of words just trying to describe it. Look, I may not know Andy. But I know *you*, Mira. And I've watched you with him. You're falling for him, baby. *Hard.*"

"You're crazy," Mira snapped back. She felt irritated. Why? Because this was a fairly pointless discussion. Why would Mira want to put her family through another test of endurance, when they had barely survived the shock (and humiliation) of her separation from Jay? She couldn't let their expectations bite the dust again. Therefore, she saw no point in doing an emotional pat-down on herself to check for any feeling she might have for Andy beyond friendship.

Chapter Twenty-One

WINTER – *January*

SHE WAS SCARED to admit it, mostly because she wasn't sure if it was true or just her wishful thinking. But Mira's life felt like it had finally come back on track again. Regardless of Auntie Sharmila's badgering and her mother's incessant taunts, things felt better than they did a few months ago. The six-foot-deep trench Jay had dug in her heart was slowly filling in. Her career felt more solid than . . . well, four weeks ago; her half-marathon training was chugging along, and running had given her a lifeline she never expected. She felt more energetic, more alive, more upbeat and optimistic than ever before. Sure, things weren't perfect. Sure, there were many, *many* pieces in her life's puzzle that were still missing, but compared to a few months ago, at least now, she had a life.

Making her way down the narrow trail, Mira drew breath through her mouth as she recalled Andy's advice to her "Pace yourself." So, she did just that, controlling the initial urge to run faster. She pushed her body just enough to pick up her heartbeat, but not to the point where she'd become breathless. Her phone with the mile-tracker app was strapped to her upper arm, and it spoke to her as she ran.

"Total distance . . . 2 miles." Mira smiled as she remembered how there was a time when she could barely manage a half mile.

When Mira reached the three-mile mark, she stopped for a breath of air. She was still not at the point where she could just make a stylish U-turn at the halfway milepost and run the homestretch. So, she decided to engage in some active recovery. She walked close to the bluff adjoining the trail that overlooked Puget Sound. The weather was as perfect as a Pacific Northwest winter day could be—cold but dry, with a gentle blanket of gray clouds for added comfort. Mira instinctively pulled her phone out of her armband and snapped a selfie. She smiled at it—at how far she'd come since that nasty night Jay left her. She took a few more seconds and posted the photo on social media. *Why not?* She thought to herself. She looked cute in the photo, too, with her metallic-navy tights and powder-pink, long-sleeved running tee. The shy Indian woman inside her hated to admit it, but she looked *hot*.

With the confidence that comes with posting a picture of one's newly resuscitated life on social media, Mira ran back the remaining miles to her car. It felt so much easier these days for her to run five to six miles. Thinking back to when she first started, this was good progress.

As she approached the last mile of trail, her app spoke to her again. "Total distance: 5.0 miles."

It was time for Mira to pick up the pace. The homestretch was the time to sprint and use up all that reserved energy. She ran faster. She had a mile to go to complete the run, so she needed to go full throttle. However, she also needed to do it carefully so she wouldn't prematurely burnout. By now, she knew not to underestimate the power of a mile.

Mira pushed onward as the app threw some statistics at her. "Average pace: 11:10 minutes per mile." The pain in her calves was tugging at her pace, but she pushed through it. She tried to find a happy place—the baking aisle in the grocery store; a book with a steaming cup of chai tea... Andy's "world-famous" pancakes? *That'll work.* Mira chuckled inwardly. She proceeded to dash across the imaginary finish line, a.k.a. the entrance to the trail parking lot. Hunching over, she cupped her knees and devoured breaths of air through her mouth. Oxygen-rich blood surged into her head, causing the ground under her to sway gently. When she'd gained control, Mira checked her app to see how she'd done—she had run a total of six miles in an hour and five minutes. Not envious, but still pride-worthy for a woman who had never run in her life before.

On her way home, Mira stopped by the grocery store and picked up some ingredients. She was going to make biryani that night—slow-cooked basmati rice with vegetables, onions, ginger-garlic, and a range of Indian spices. It was a recipe that had been passed down through generations of Soods. And it was downright the best comfort food for any occasion, be it heartbreak, celebration, or just plain old hunger pangs like hers.

She was in the ethnic foods aisle, grabbing a bottle of garam masala when her mom called. "Hi, Ma." Mira wedged her phone between her shoulder and ear as she dropped the spice bottle into her grocery basket.

"Why don't you call anymore?" asked the older woman.

Mira frowned at her basket. She'd forgotten to get scallions. *Damn it.* "Er, I-what do you mean? I called just two days ago, and we spoke for an hour." *Ooh, and fresh peas . . .*

"Do you know, today I spoke to Mrs. Lulla, our next-door neighbor. Her daughter is visiting from America next week with her husband and *two* kids. Mrs. Lulla couldn't stop talking about all the things she is planning to do with them," Mira's mother said, sounding disappointed.

"Mrs. Lulla is doing *what*?" Mira tried to clarify. She'd lost her mother's voice somewhere between Mrs. Lulla and the price of scallions. The stillness at the end of the phone line meant she'd let her mother down—again. Mira clutched her basket and walked out of the fresh produce section, scallions and peas in hand.

"Hey *Ram*," her mother sighed. This was a popular Sood parenting strategy—using the name of an influential Indian God to drive home a point with one's child. "Do you know Jay is posting kissing pictures on Instant-gram with that new girlfriend of his?"

"*Insta*gram," corrected Mira with a sigh. Of course she knew. "Ma, I'm sorry I can't give you grandchildren. I'm sorry my marriage fell apart. This wasn't part of my plan. Look, maybe after my divorce is finalized, I can come see you and Papa in India?"

Her mother began to sniff, which meant it was still Mira's turn to talk. She decided to sit down at the market's in-house cafe. If she was going to do this, she needed caffeine in her bloodstream.

And also, maybe a slice of chocolate cake.

A NEW MANTRA

IT WAS LATE that evening when a text came in from Andy; Mira was getting ready to tuck herself into bed with a book. *Mira, you awake?*

Yeah, why? she texted back, propping herself up on a pillow. She and Andy had planned to meet at their usual trail that Saturday, so she wondered if maybe he needed to cancel. She stared back at the phone screen, and the latter stared right back, looking blank as ever. A few minutes passed in silence, then her phone rang.

"Andy?"

"Hey, I'm really sorry to call this late," he apologized. "But I wanted to share some news."

"Why, what is it?" asked Mira, feeling a wave of excitement.

"Do you remember Paul? The investor I told you about?"

"McMillionaire guy?"

Andy laughed. "That's the one. We've got a meeting with him at 2:00 p.m. tomorrow."

"No, way. When did this happen?"

"Over the week. His secretary had been giving us the runaround, but in the end, we got the appointment."

"Andy, that's so great."

"And there's one more thing," he said softly. "I took your suggestion and added a live chat feature to our site. Joe hooked us up with top-notch software, and our metrics indicate it's boosted our site traffic by about three percent . . . and our customers *love* it."

"I'm so glad to hear that. It was a completely random suggestion, though, no analysis of metrics was involved on my end." She laughed and pulled her laptop closer to open the Cloud-9 website. It looked better than ever with a brand-new header and graphics. Mira clicked the live chat button in an attempt to socialize with the software. "Hey, your chat thing is really cool," she cried. "I'm going to spend the next hour asking it *really* stupid questions."

Andy laughed at the other end. "Knock yourself out. And if you run into trouble, call Joe. He loves nothing more than troubleshooting in the middle of the night."

"Really?"

"Nope, he hates that." Andy laughed, with Mira joining in.

"So, when will you know the outcome of your meeting with Paul?"

"I expect it will last a couple of hours at least . . . if he's interested, that is."

"So, the longer the better?" Mira tried to confirm.

"Yup. But I'll call you when it's done," replied Andy. "Regardless of the outcome."

Mira shuddered. "Yeah, okay."

Chapter Twenty-Two

TIME WAS OFFICIALLY frozen. Mira was sure of it as she wishfully gazed at the digital clock on the floor, just inches away from her nose. She was presently holding (or trying to hold) her perfect plank position—one of the most grueling, yet most rewarding, core-strengthening exercises on the planet. Mira winced as she consciously re-tightened her stomach muscles, clenched her butt cheeks together, and stabilized her legs. All this would ensure she wasn't dumping her body weight onto her back. Her body begged for her to stop; her muscles kept slipping their hold, trying to throw the weight of her body back onto her spine—which was, essentially, her body trying to find the easy way out. But Mira resisted. She knew the importance of her strength exercises in the grand scheme of her half-marathon training. Nope, she wasn't going to cave.

Glancing up at the clock again, Mira promised herself she was almost there—she had been holding her plank for a minute, and she had another minute to go. She could do this. She refused to be defeated by sixty seconds. Why? Because it was *sixty seconds*. The time it takes to microwave popcorn. *Mira Sood, you may have been cheated on by your husband, but no way you're letting yourself be conquered by popcorn-popping time.* She grunted inwardly.

Clenching her teeth, she counted the seconds off in her head. Twenty seconds down. Just forty more to go. Drops of sweat fell to the ground, dripping off her forehead. Thirty-five... Mira tried to distract herself with random thoughts—*Hmm, I wonder what the weather forecast says today? Probably rain... Rain... Pain—I feel pain... SUMMER. Such a lovely season. Best time for mangoes. Mango... Let-go... Wow. I want to let go of this hold so bad.* Mira winced as she felt her stomach muscles beginning to cramp. *Shit.* That wasn't good. But at that very moment, her timer began to chirp. She'd done it—held her perfect plank for two whole minutes. It was in the bag. Mira stretched her arms out above her head. She then folded her legs, sinking her belly between her thighs with her forehead to the ground, and collapsed into child's pose to stretch out her aching muscles. And of course, at that very moment, her cell phone began to ring. It was right there a few inches from her, and Mira opened her eyes and grabbed it to see who was calling. *Damn it.* A number she didn't recognize. Not Andy, whom she'd been waiting to hear from all day. She knew his meeting with Paul wasn't until that afternoon, but it was close to five in the evening, and yet she'd heard nothing from him. Mira silenced the ring and flopped forward, exiting her child's pose in *not* the most graceful manner. But who cared about that when she'd nailed her two-minute plank?

She stood up and wiped the sweat beads off her face with a towel. Picking up her phone, she studied the missed call again. No voicemail, meaning it was probably one of those bogus calls. Crashing into her couch, she debated whether or not to text Andy and ask how the meeting had gone.

"Still waiting to hear from him?" asked Laila, walking in from behind Mira and causing the latter to spring out of her skin.

"Oh my God," cried Mira. "Stop sneaking up on me like that."

But Laila was watching her closely. "Well?"

"Well, what?" challenged Mira. She had nothing to hide. "I was hoping Andy would've called with some news by now, so I was checking my phone."

"Right." Laila nodded. "Because he's your 'friend.'"

"Yes, and I care about his well-being and—" The sound of the doorbell caused Mira to pause mid-sentence.

"Saved by the bell, huh?" Laila laughed, walking to open the door. "A-ha, the man of the hour," she announced, stepping sideways to make way for Andy to enter the apartment.

"Andy?" cried Mira, leaping forward to greet him. "I thought you'd call?"

"She's been plastered to the phone all day," said Laila, grabbing her handbag.

"Not *plastered*," protested Mira, blushing to a tone of pink.

"Whatever," Laila replied, exiting the apartment.

Mira watched as Andy ripped his coat off to reveal a navy suit, paired with a sky-blue button-down shirt and tie. And although she would never admit it to herself, she couldn't help but notice how handsome he looked in it, with his characteristic glasses, chiseled features, and deep-set eyes. She watched in silence as he loosened his tie and walked toward her. "Andy, you okay?"

He smiled feebly. "Yeah, I'm just tired."

"Let me make some chai tea," she then offered, and quickly disappeared into the kitchen as she watched him sink into her couch. She returned a few minutes later with two cups of steaming hot chai and some homemade samosas. "So, how did it go with Paul this afternoon?" she then asked, landing the question fair and square between them.

Andy sipped his tea and watched her across the brim of his cup. "It went well," he replied.

"Really? You mean he was interested in Cloud-9?"

Andy nodded. "Paul loved our presentation, our solutions . . . he was *very* interested."

"Oh, wow," cried Mira, although her smile remained short-lived. "But why aren't *you* excited? I thought you'd be over the moon about this?"

Andy hunched over and gently massaged his forehead with his hand. "He proposed an acquisition," he said and dug his hand into his coat pocket to pull out a piece of paper for Mira to look at. "For that much."

Her jaw dropped when she read the numbers. "A-are those zeros after the three?"

Andy nodded. "But I couldn't agree to that."

"What? Why not?"

Breathing in, Andy reclined into his seat again. "He wanted to buy us out, Mira. I can't allow that."

"But this could save your company," she contested softly.

Andy shook his head. "It's not that simple. This acquisition would entail a complete overhaul of our core business strategy. Their plan is to shift the entire focus away from what we've always valued—move from customer satisfaction to profits."

"But why's that bad? Profits are good, aren't they?" Mira asked meekly.

Andy produced a soft smile. "Cloud-9 was built on certain principles. Our focus has always been quality, not quantity. The reason we've resisted scaling the company in the past is because we don't want to become just another corporation with its head stuck in an obsession to make profits. We want to make money, but we value our product, and we value the *people* who're buying our product and trusting us with their needs. This has always been the soul of our company. No way I'm selling it... even for *that*," he declared, and began ripping the piece of paper into teeny, tiny pieces.

Mira watched him in silence—this tired-looking man hauling the weight of his principles, willing to sink to save them. A man who held his principles closer to his heart than all the money in the world. *How lucky would the woman be, who he chooses to love?*

When he turned to look at her, she was still watching him. And when he reached to stroke her cheek, she did not resist. Nor did she pull away when he leaned in to kiss her lips—gently, almost carefully, as if not to override her choice. Mira's skin was on fire as their lips collided and fused together, more deliberate now than before. Never before in her life had she felt so electrified, as if her body had just been shocked by ten thousand volts of pure passion. She placed her palm on his broad chest and melted into his kiss, allowing her heart to take charge even as her brain raised the fire alarm. *Are you crazy, Mira Sood?* When that didn't work, her brain projected a life-size image of her mother, followed by her father, then Auntie Sharmila. *Lord, how will you face them now?* "I can't," Mira gasped, suddenly peeling her lips away from Andy's. The sound of her words caused him to pull back.

"I-I'm sorry . . ." she said again.

He shook his head, as if trying to shake off the aftereffects of the kiss. "I don't understand. Why not?"

Mira shook her head and stood up. "I can't do this to them." She was dizzy, nauseous, and so angry with herself.

"Them?"

She began pacing. "Andy, you have no idea how hard this whole thing has been on them—Jay's affair, the separation, and my soon-to-be-final divorce. It's been nothing short of a nightmare for my family. I was raised in an orthodox Hindu home. Sure, we like to drink and dance to Bollywood music, and have a good time, but divorce is a line that can't be crossed among my kind of people. And I did it, I crossed the line. And now, am I going to go back and tell them I'm dating a white man? It would kill them."

"Okay, but do you realize you're forgetting yourself in the process?"

"I don't care about that. I've got to protect my family from any more scandal and gossip. My mother and I haven't had a normal conversation in *months* since it all started, and I know she's hurting, and my dad—" Mira paused to catch her breath. "I can't, I'm sorry."

"Do you know what I think?" asked Andy, his eyes grabbing hers. "Your family might be traditional and antidivorce, and ... anti-*me*—a non-Indian white guy from Whidbey Island. But they're not the ones standing in your way, Mira. You are."

"What?" Mira cried out. "What are you talking about?"

"You're using your family as an excuse to push me away."

Mira threw her hands up. "Why would I do that?"

"Only you can answer that, I'm afraid," Andy conceded with a shrug.

"Look, I'm not ashamed to admit I'm closely attached to my family. I'm a Punjabi-Indian girl, for God's sake, it goes with the territory. And it's hard for someone to understand the concept from the outside, looking in."

"Even so," Andy said, biting his lower lip as if to stop his next words from spilling out. "It's crazy to let that closeness ruin your life, don't you think?"

"Ruin my life?" Mira cried, trying to blink away the anger. "Listen, *Maharishi* Andrew, I really don't think you know enough about me or my family to pass that kind of judgment."

"I know you well enough, Mira," said Andy. "And I'm not passing judgment here. I'm being honest, and I'm sorry if that offends you."

Mira shook her head. "Well, sometimes honesty does nothing for anyone." Considering this was the last thing she'd expected from Andy tonight—the kiss, followed by the most absurd insinuation, Mira had nothing left to say to him.

Andy considered her silence for what seemed like the longest minute in the world. "You know what, today's just not my day," he said with a dry chuckle. Standing up, he walked straight out the door without another word, and without Mira trying to stop him.

That night, Mira was only half herself as she spoke to her mother on the phone at their usual chat hour. And when the call ended, she lay back in bed, staring blankly as shadows danced on her bedroom wall with the wind. Why, oh why, did it all have to go down this way, and right when her life was beginning to reshape itself? She couldn't understand it. Just when she thought she'd plucked all the needles out of her butt, she found herself sitting on yet another cactus. If only Andy hadn't kissed her, she could have gone on as usual, pretending to herself and to him that the tingles she felt every time he touched her, or when their eyes met, were just her imagination. After all, she was nothing if not an excellent actress. Her Oscar-worthy performance from her three-year marriage to Jay was proof of that—she had managed to uphold the aura of a happy wife, despite living in a loveless marriage. As she lay back on her pillow, Mira noodled Andy's words as they floated quietly inside her head like lost soap bubbles in a park. She didn't know what to make of them. They confused and infuriated her, only because she couldn't tell with certainty if he was right. *Was* she hiding behind the veil of tradition? Everything she'd done, every choice she'd ever made—was that her, hiding? And from what, exactly? As she locked eyes with the question, the answer peeked out. Mira could see it from the corner of her mind's eye. For a while, she tried to ignore it. She tried to stay angry. In the end, though, she knew she couldn't fight the truth. Breathing in, Mira knew what she needed to do—finish the unfinished business. Stripping the sheets off herself, she put her coat on and blasted out the front door, unfettered by the lateness of the hour.

ANDY WAS AWAKE; she knew it because he answered the door at the first ring.

"Mira?" he cried out at the sight of her standing outside. He immediately opened the door to her, gesturing for her to come in. But she shook her head.

"You're right," she said. "Well, at least you're not wrong," she then amended.

"Mira, look I—"

"I *am* hiding. I *am* using my family, but not as an excuse, you know. I'm using them . . . as a shield to protect myself," she explained with a soft smile. "Jay almost succeeded in breaking my spirit. And I alone know how close I came to losing myself. So, yes, I'm scared to trust my heart again. I don't ever again want to test my survival skills."

"You know, today was supposed to be the worst day of my life, considering we lost the one investor that could've saved Cloud-9. Yet, I felt like I had something to live for the minute I saw you tonight." Andy's eyes softened as he smiled back at her. "I'd never hurt you, Mira, and I'd never let anyone, or anything, hurt you."

Mira shrugged and wiped away a stray tear. "That's a blank check. You can't promise that."

"And you can't live your life without ever taking a chance."

"I know." She nodded. "And I will take the chance, if something . . . *someone* is worth the risk." Mira's eyes settled on Andy.

He remained still as he watched her in silence for the next few seconds. His next words stumbled out, quiet yet conclusive. "And I'm not worth the risk."

Mira stood with her arms firmly crossed over her chest. At the sound of his words, however, she broke the casing of emotion, and, lunging forward, she sank her lips into his. Andy didn't let a microsecond slide as he collected Mira into his arms, holding her like she'd never been held before—as if nothing could ever make him let go. She melted into him like a sun-kissed popsicle—as his hands moved down to the small of her back only to gently surf back up again, taking the pathways around the sides of her breasts, all the way back up to cradle her face. His thumbs grazed her cheekbones as he paused to consider her. "You're beautiful, Mira," he whispered to her lips, which completely surprised her. *Beautiful?* Who, her? She'd never thought that about herself. Presentable, sure. Moderately above average on a good day? Right on. But, beautiful? She didn't know what to say to that.

"Thank you," she replied, as polite as a freshly trained grade-schooler. This only made Andy laugh, and then he kissed her again.

Chapter Twenty-Three

MIRA COULD HARDLY see where they were going, but she didn't care. The feeling of being locked in Andy's firm arms provided all the assurance she needed. With lips latched, they kissed their way into the living room, crashing into the couch like a couple of happy, conjoined spring butterflies.

Layers were purged in the order of priority—her jacket, his glasses, her shoes, his sweatshirt.

It was painfully clear to Mira how unprepared she was for this moment. Her penguin-printed pj's, for instance, should never have left the house that night. But in the midst of her emotional epiphany, she hadn't exactly thought things through before leaving home. And now, here she was, lying under the world's sexiest IT guy, wondering whether or not she was wearing her one and only super-sassy underwear that read "Can't Touch This."

Well, it's too late now, she scolded herself. As she watched Andy peel his shirt off, she realized (with contented glee) that she didn't care anymore. *WO-AOW*. For a moment, Mira was awestruck. Was a woman like herself—a slightly rounded, nearly divorced, modest Hindu girl, allowed to touch, or even look at such a man? What did the Bhagavad Gita have to say about all this? And would it be fair to all her other high-achieving, better-looking, overly righteous cousins who had succumbed to the Sood way of life only because they were expecting her to do the same? Would it be right to dupe them this way? Mira sighed. *HELL YEAH.*

In fact, she thought, it was high time she put her imagination to rest and feel those abs she'd been dreaming of touching since the day she first saw him topless. Reaching her hand out, she touched topless-Andy for the very first time—with just one finger. WOAH. It was even better than she'd imagined, so she let all her fingers touch topless-Andy.

Gorgeous. Firm, yet smooth. From Mira's culinary point of view? Andy's bare torso was like a giant slab of pink Himalayan rock salt. *Beautiful.* And she could hardly stop herself from letting both hands glide up and down it, getting a kick out of feeling the bumps and troughs of his taut ab muscles as they brushed against her skin. She sighed to herself as she dreamily looked up to find Andy's smile in full bloom. He was watching her very intently and seemed slightly amused.

"Having fun?" he asked her.

"Mm-hmm." Mira nodded unabashedly as Andy kissed the curve of her neck and began unbuttoning her pajama top. "I thought you said you weren't interested in dating me?" she asked him, trying to distract herself from the exploding mix of eager intentions and mild nervousness she was feeling inside.

"I was lying," he whispered back, kissing her between her breasts and causing the sweetness of the ache inside her to spread like wildfire through her limbs. "I've been wanting to do this to you forever."

"Even when we were out shoe shopping? When you were telling me about foot pronation?" she tried to ask, giggling as she felt his trail of butterfly kisses all the way down her stomach.

"*Especially* then." Andy laughed and kissed her softly as his hand captured one of her breasts. Mira gasped, feeling an electric wave seize her body as his lips soon traded places with his hand.

"Unbelievable man . . ." She winced as her skin broke into bumps, as his hand began to explore between her legs. It was like hot yoga for her soul, really. A complete and total expulsion of all the pent-up desire inside her, since . . . well, puberty. Considering Jay had remained mostly uninspired in the bedroom, and sex before marriage was taboo where she grew up, this was Mira's first official trip to Disneyland. Before long, Mira had eagerly surrendered her bra, then her pajama bottom, followed by every other piece of clothing that separated her body from Andy's. Desire and imagination continued to roil between them, powered by that magnetic pull of mutual attraction and respect. In the end, it culminated in Andy throwing Mira over his shoulder and marching straight into the bedroom where they feverishly summited their respective peaks in perfect unison, collapsing into each other at their journey's end. "Thank you," Mira blurted out, heart-happy and head-dizzy, with their bodies still sandwiched together.

This appeared to amuse Andy. "Wow, no one's ever thanked me after sex. You're welcome." He laughed.

Mira joined in the laugh, curling up into his side. He

instinctively wrapped a protective arm around her and kissed her forehead with his eyes closed. "You're amazing, Mira," he said, opening his eyes to look at her again.

"Really?" she asked. Clearly, he was on a post-sex high.

Andy nodded firmly. "In fact, you're the most perfect woman I've ever met."

Mira felt her cheeks flush. She'd never been any good at receiving compliments—she needed to change that about herself. For now, she decided to change the subject. "By the way, I'm really sorry it didn't work out with Paul," she said softly, arching her neck to look up at Andy. He was watching her intently.

"It'll be alright," he replied, his voice calm and steady like a battleship. "I'll fix it."

"How?"

"I don't know at the moment." He shrugged. "And I won't sugarcoat the fact that my company is in trouble. But I will fix it."

That kind of fighter talk made Mira's skin tingle. She smiled and kissed Andy on the cheek and tucked herself back under his arm. "I know you will."

Of course, she couldn't predict the future, and maybe it would ultimately contradict her. But tonight, Mira felt like the luckiest woman in the world.

WHEN SHE OPENED her eyes the next morning, Mira found Andy lying on his side with his head propped up on an elbow, smiling at her. "Morning, beautiful." The sheets on his end were pulled down to his waist, exposing the best parts of him. *Beautiful morning*, Mira thought inwardly. It took her a minute to realize it was a Saturday too. Doubly beautiful that she could languish in the giddy aftereffects of her euphoric night with Andy, which had been interrupted only by delivery pizza and midnight ice cream.

Leaning forward, Mira kissed Andy's lips. He responded by pulling her directly under him. They remained entwined in the sheets, in each other, for the better part of that morning. They eventually entered the kitchen, starving and euphoric, wanting to make frittatas for breakfast. Instead, they broke a ceramic bowl and burned three eggs in a pan as hunger soon gave way to passion, and the kitchen counter became their muse.

"I thought you said you were an orthodox Hindu?" Andy softly remarked as Mira reached between his legs.

"Shh. Don't tell anyone," she whispered back, squeezing him hard and pulling him into her.

Because Mira had left home in pajamas the night before, Andy drove her back to her apartment so she could grab a change of clothes and a night bag. They intended to spend every minute of that weekend together. They walked hand in hand around University Village, toured a local winery, and took a picnic out to Carkeek Park despite the chilly weather. They talked, kissed, and laughed, drowning in each other while drowning the rest of the world out. Back at Andy's condo, he and Mira drank wine and ate slices of cheese pizza by a crackling fireplace, which was witness to some of the most epic lovemaking in history. It was just Mira and Andy, encapsulated in the moment, body and soul. To Mira, it was as if she'd stumbled into paradise, with time standing still. She absorbed every minute, wishing that the minute would last a lifetime.

With fingers knit tight, Mira sat leaning up against Andy on his balcony, with the outdoor heater on full blast and nothing but a down comforter wrapped around their bodies. "This is paradise," whispered Mira and felt Andy's lips kiss the peak of her exposed shoulder.

"Can I ask you something?" came his voice. It was his serious-subject voice, so she turned to face him.

"Sure."

Andy appeared to pause and then laid his words out one by one. "If I hadn't kissed you the other night, would you have ever told me how you really felt? Would *this* have happened?"

It was a loaded question with no straight answer. Mira bit her lower lip. "I'm not sure . . ." she began. "I'm not sure if I would've made the first move. I'm not good at showing my feelings. I'm working on it, but I'm not good at it. And I'm still not sure how all this will impact my family. I'm not even sure how to bring it up with them . . . I'm not sure about *any* of it." Mira shook her head. "But now that this has happened and we're here, together, I am sure of one thing—I'm sure about us . . . about *you*. This feels right," Mira said softly.

A smile broke loose across Andy's lips, and Mira felt his arms tighten around her. "It's all I needed to hear," he said, kissing her forehead.

MONDAY MORNING, AFTER an entire weekend together, Andy drove Mira back to her apartment early so she could change for work. She may very well have cartwheeled into the office that morning. She felt like she was on cloud nine (no pun intended). Nothing, including the treacherous traffic on the drive in to work, could hose down Mira's happy heart. "Nothing's Gonna Stop Us Now" by Starship was stuck in her head, and she sang the chorus over and over again until a polite request from a coworker forced her to switch to humming the tune inside her head.

Close to quitting time, Mira began clearing the mounds of files on her desk while putting sticky notes on the ones that needed her attention the following morning. She walked over to the supply closet so she could review her inventory chart to ensure everything looked shipshape. She stopped by the restroom to check her reflection, and just as she grabbed her bag to leave, her cell phone began to ring. Mira smiled even before she looked at the screen, knowing it was probably Andy calling. "Hello?" she answered in a singsong voice. Nothing. She pulled the device from her ear to check the screen. It was an unknown number, faintly resembling the bogus call from the other day. She shrugged and disconnected the line.

Walking to her parked car, Mira dissolved into the sun-warmed driver's seat. It was a gorgeous, sunny day with temperatures teetering around fifty degrees—a rather unusual thing to happen on a Seattle winter's day. Mira soaked in the greenhouse effect with eyes closed. A second later, her cell rang again. This time, it was Andy.

"Mira, do you have a minute?" he asked, panting.

"Yeah, I'm just headed home from work. What is it?"

"He wants in!" cried Andy "He wants to invest."

"Who? Who does?" Mira asked, only to realize for herself. "Wait, Paul?"

"He just called me on my cell . . . the richest man on the West Coast dialed my goddamn number."

"Oh, my Lord," gasped Mira, exiting her vehicle so she wouldn't fog up the windows. "What happened? Why did he change his mind?"

"I don't know exactly. But he called me and said he thought about our discussion and realized an acquisition would destroy the inherent DNA of our company and along with it, our loyal customer base, including the people who've been with us since the conception of the company, blah, blah, blah . . ." Andy appeared to catch his breath for a moment. "He just sent over the contract and Joe, Rama, and I are looking over it this evening."

Before Mira could rein in her impulses, she was jumping up and down in the parking lot. "This is so great, Andy. You can save Cloud-9 . . . and buy your dream lake house and—"

"Can I still see you tonight?" he cut in gleefully. "It might be a bit later than we planned, but I want to see you."

"You can come over anytime you want," she replied cheerily. This was shaping up to be the best day of Mira's life. She could *feel* it.

Chapter Twenty-Four

MIRA RAN UP the stairs to her apartment and burst through the door. Laila was out recording with the band, so Mira dove straight in to take the best five-minute shower in the world—including shampoo and conditioner. She then slid into her new favorite outfit—one that sweetly complimented her newfound runner's body—a seafoam-colored, long-sleeved baby doll dress and black leggings. Standing before the full-length mirror in her bedroom, Mira studied her reflection. "Mmm . . . not bad." She smiled. At that very moment, the loud shriek of the doorbell startled her. It looked like Andy had changed his mind and decided to stop by her apartment sooner rather than later. Smiling to herself, Mira hurried over to the front door, released the lock, and flung it open.

"JAY?" Her blood turned to ice as he smiled back at her.

"Mira . . ." he sighed and leaned in to hug her. "I've missed you so much."

Dizzy, confused, and out of breath, Mira was unable to put two thoughts together. She wanted to release herself from Jay's embrace, but she was shock-frozen in his arms. Peeling herself away from him, she backed up a few steps, although the correct thing to do would have been to push *him* away a few steps.

"Jay..." Mira shook her head with disbelief. "What the hell are you doing here? How did you even know where I was?"

Jay shrugged. "Look, I knew you wouldn't welcome me back with open arms, okay? But I realize now, I made a mistake. I'm sorry..." he dropped his voice. "I'm really, really sorry I cheated on you. But I'm a changed man. I want you back in my life so I can prove to you how sorry I am. Please, Mira." Jay reached out and held her hand, drawing her closer to him. "Give me another chance."

Her heart was pounding, and her head was in a fog of mixed emotions. Jay had come back to her. If this had happened a few months ago, she'd have been doing cartwheels (or died trying). But just like Jay, *she* had changed. She wasn't the same woman anymore. Mira closed her eyes to try and gain some clarity. "Jay, I can't do this—"

"Please, Mira. Look, I said I'm sorry, haven't I?" Jay held her hands firmly in his. "I've missed you so much. I've been thinking about you for some time now... and then a few months ago, I saw a picture of you on social media and you looked so... *hot*—"

"Wait, you've been stalking me on Instagram?"

"It's not stalking if it's your own wife."

"Yes, it *is* stalking, and I'm not your wife anymore," corrected Mira. This man was unbelievable. And then she suddenly realized something with mute horror. "Were you the one making all those calls? Not saying anything when I answered and then hanging up?"

Jay considered the question and then shrugged. "I love

you, Mira. I've always loved you, and—"

"Mira?" The sound of Andy's voice sent a wave of panic through her nerves. *Oh my God.* Mira pulled her hands out of Jay's clasp and turned to find Andy standing at the top of the stairs, a few feet away from her and Jay. A deep-set frown furrowed his brow. He wasn't smiling... or blinking. He just stood there, motionless, looking straight at Jay, who appeared confused and irritated.

"Who's this guy, Mira?" asked Jay, breaking away from Andy's gaze.

"Hey, he stole my question," declared Andy, his voice dense as an echo.

Mira's eyes darted frantically from Jay to Andy as the latter slowly closed the distance. Man, was he tall. And while this was the worst possible time for it, Mira couldn't help but notice how handsome he looked—with his glasses, khaki pants, and a black crewneck sweater.

"Mira?" Andy asked again. He was now standing close enough that she could see herself in his eyes.

"This is my—"

"Husband," interjected Jay. "I'm her husband, and you are?"

Andy considered Jay for a moment, as if he were a flyer offering a redundant service.

"I think you mean *ex*-husband," he replied.

"Well, nothing's official yet," Jay replied, turning to Mira for support.

"You're the guy who cheated on Mira," Andy said slowly. Deliberately. He lodged himself right in front of Jay, inches away from his nose.

Mira's heart pounded and pleaded for her to take immediate action. Andy looked like he could knock Jay unconscious with a single head butt. And Mira had never seen Andy like this before.

"Listen, I don't know who you are, but you're intruding on a private conversation," Jay said, fumbling. "Mira, say something," he added, when Andy refused to budge an inch.

Andy took charge again. "Mira doesn't need to say anything. She's told me everything I need to know about you. And since then, I've dreamed of knocking your lights out, you selfish son of a bitch!"

Mira watched in silence, half-enthralled and half-mortified at what was unfolding before her eyes. She knew she had to do something to stop Andy from punching Jay. Because if it went down that way, and if Jay called the police, then everything Andy had ever worked for—his company, his dream lake house—*everything* would turn to ashes. Jay had a remarkable talent for that—turning people's lives to ashes.

Mira's voice escaped her lips softly. "Andy, you'd better go."

For the first time, Andy's eyes switched subjects as he turned from Jay to look at Mira. "What?"

His frown was replaced by a look of . . . disbelief? Disappointment? Or was it anger? For the first time, Mira was unable to decode the expression on Andy's face. There was so much she wanted to say to him—and she would later. But right now, Mira didn't want to give Jay even the slightest peek into her relationship with Andy—it was too precious and too special to share with a person like him.

Mira moved closer to Andy and forced herself to say the opposite of what she really wanted. "Andy, it's really complicated... a-and I need to think straight. I can't have you here right now. You should go. Please?" she added with a whisper.

Looking down into her face, Andy's gorgeous eyes continued to speak a language Mira didn't understand. "You said you were sure..." he then said softly, as if conclusively—in a way that sent a cold shudder down her spine. And with that, he turned around and walked away without another word, his back cold against her, and his feet thundering down the apartment stairs with an echo of finality. Mira's instincts were screaming for her to run after him. Something had gone very wrong in that moment. In an effort to save Andy from a fistfight, something told Mira she'd caused a more serious outcome.

"You did the right thing, Mira. I knew you would." The sound of Jay's voice nauseated Mira. She turned to face him.

"You know, Jay, the day you left, I wished so hard you'd come back. My mental compass was broken back then... I was an *idiot* to want you back. The good news is, I've grown since then. Running has helped me find myself—"

"*Running?*" frowned Jay. "What are you talking about?"

"I started running. Right after you left me, I was so lost and heartbroken, and when you sent me freakin' divorce papers, I needed an outlet. So, I signed up for a half-marathon and it's while I was training for it that Andy and I became friends and we've gotten..." Mira searched her mental dictionary. "Close."

Jay's jaw dropped. "Y-you and that *white* guy?"

Mira pouted back. "I don't think you have the right to

be mad at me."

"I have every right," shouted Jay. "Mira, I'm here to rebuild our marriage, and you're telling me you're with another man? How can you say that? And how do you plan to explain this to your family? Your poor mother?"

Acknowledging his question with a nod, Mira replied, "I didn't know you cared about my poor mother."

Jay coughed up a sarcastic laugh. "At least I'm not the one who's about to break her heart. Mira, your mother was so happy when I called her and told her you and I were getting back together, and—"

"Wait, what? You called my mother?" cried Mira, wild with rage.

Jay shrugged casually. "I didn't know where you were."

"You told her we were getting back together?"

"Unlike you, she was thrilled."

With a hundred percent intention and zero technique, Mira swung her arm, powered by a fist full of rage, and punched Jay in the face. "YOU ASSHOLE!"

"*ARGHH!*" Jay howled like a madman as he cupped his hands against his nose, which appeared to have absorbed the majority of Mira's punch. "Oh God, you broke my nose. You broke it, you bitch!"

"I hope I did. Otherwise, I'll have to punch you again," replied Mira as she gently massaged her throbbing hand with the other.

Jay uncupped his face and stuck his pointer finger straight at Mira. "You just wait. You haven't seen the last of this . . . I'll have you arrested."

Mira clucked her tongue back at Jay. "Be my guest. And

in turn, I'll sue you for emotional damages."

"What *emotional* damages?"

"For everything you put me through while we were married—you made me polish your damn shoes, cook for you three times a day, you didn't let me work. Heck, you didn't even let me go out and have friends. Not to mention you kept all our finances under your name and forced my parents to pay you a *dowry* when we got married." Mira frowned at the list. "All in all, I'd say my case looks pretty solid, wouldn't you? Of course, I don't want to get ahead of myself, so we'll just let a judge decide, okay?"

Jay wiped the tiny trickle of blood that had run down from one of his nostrils. "You think you're so smart, don't you?"

"Hmm. At least I know I'm not as stupid as you, Jay."

For a moment, Jay stood there, probably wondering what to say that would make him look, well, less stupid. But when he could come up with nothing, he turned and walked away.

As soon as she was inside her apartment, Mira picked up her cell and called Andy. It went straight to voicemail. She disconnected and called him again. Voicemail. She rammed her sore hand, which she'd used to deliver her first and last punch, into a bowl of ice cubes. Andy had probably turned off his phone. She knew he was upset—he *had* to be. But she'd catch up with him. Plus, Mira guessed she had a better shot at setting things right with Andy if he had some time to cool off.

"Ah-ouch . . ." She groaned and pulled her hand out of the ice bath to examine it. It appeared slightly swollen, but she could move all her fingers, which meant nothing was broken, hopefully. Mira put her fist back on ice and picked her phone up again. She breathed in and then called her parents in India. She dreaded every ring until her mother answered.

"Ma? It's me, Mira," she said, her voice cracking under pressure.

"OH KRISHNA! Mira, I'm so happy. Is Jay with you now? Are you together? Oh, I knew you would ultimately save our family from humiliation. You won't believe it, but we haven't been able to set foot in our temple since the news of your split with Jay. Not a single wedding I have attended, and—"

"Ma, Jay and I aren't back together."

There was complete silence at the other end.

"Ma?" Had her mother hung up on her? There was no telling.

Mira heard a soft sigh. "Yes, I'm here. Where else would I be?"

"Look, Ma, I know it's hard for you to understand, but—"

"I understand everything. You have forgotten your roots . . . your *culture*. We don't get divorces in our family, Mira, we just stay together till we die."

Or die, staying together. Mira breathed in. "There's something else I called to tell you—something you may not approve . . ."

"What are you going to say *now*?" cried the older woman.

"I have a . . . There's a man I like. His name's Andy . . .

Andrew Fitzgerald—"

"An-drew?" quivered her mother's voice. "That doesn't sound like a Hindu name?"

"He's. . ." *Three, two, one.* "A *white* American," she laid down gently, at which the older woman began to sob uncontrollably.

"What sin have your father and I committed in our past life, I don't know. But we have been given a daughter who doesn't want us to be happy."

Mira sat down with the ice-bowl in her lap and her hand soaking in it. At this point, there was really nothing she could say to help, so she decided to listen instead.

"And what do we say to our people back home? How will we explain it to them? Do you even care about that . . . about your papa and me? How are you ever going to face your Mummyji and Papaji?"

It was all Mira needed to hear to transfer the throbbing pain from her hand to her head.

The conversation lasted three hours and ended with Mira's mother telling her she'd let her down, but if this was what Mira was sure she wanted—an American boyfriend and a divorce-stained life, then there was nothing that anyone (not even Dear Lord Krishna) could do. Mira signed off, feeling unsupported and alone, yet at peace with herself. If nothing else, she was glad of that fact. The truth was out now, and she no longer had anything to hide from her family—well, minus Auntie Sharmila. But that was another mountain, for another day.

MIRA TRIED CALLING Andy a few more times that night. Each time, her call went to voicemail. She drove over to his condo the next morning, hoping the night had given him some downtime to cool off. She knocked on the door as her heart pounded in her chest. When the door finally opened, she almost leapt up with delight, only to be disappointed again.

"Rama?" cried Mira with a look of somber recognition. "Is Andy home? I need to talk to him."

But the man shook his head of fiery red hair. "I'm sorry, Mira. He's not here and I honestly don't know where he is . . . the man just called me to house-sit for him and took off somewhere." Rama paused to frown. "I mean, he didn't even give me a courtesy tour, and now I can't make my fried eggs because I don't know where the bastard hides his frying pans—"

"W-When? When did he take off?" Mira tried to refocus the conversation.

"Last night." Rama shrugged.

Mira nodded absently and breathed out. Her reservations were now morphing into mild panic. Andy was more upset than she'd realized. In all the time they had known each other, they'd never once had a fight. Arguments and friendly banter, sure. But never a full-blown fight like this one. But even so, the fact that Andy had left his condo to the care of someone else and gone off somewhere worried her to no end. And why was he not taking any of her calls? If he picked up the phone just once, they could fight it out and make up.

"Is there anything else you needed?" asked Rama. "I'm sorry I wasn't much help."

Mira forced a smile. "No, it's no problem and I should probably get going." She turned to leave, but paused briefly. "Andy keeps his pans in the oven . . . because he never uses it," she said softly. The memory of them cooking and laughing together in his condo, sent a dull ache through Mira's gut and she retreated quickly, for the last thing she wanted was to break down before Rama. Back at her apartment, Mira tried Andy's phone all night. Better to appear maniacal than indifferent, she thought to herself as she dialed his number for the fiftieth time. But every time. Voicemail.

Chapter Twenty-Five

WINTER – February

WHEN MIRA WAS younger, back in her early twenties, when she was filled with gusto and life was filled with endless possibilities, if anyone had told her she'd end up a divorced, childless, thirty-something runner, she'd have laughed in their face. But this is who she was now, as she tucked herself into bed and turned the light out on another day.

A month had slipped by since she'd last seen Andy—since that night when Jay had managed to ruin her life a second time. Her divorce had come through. But that provided Mira closure, not pain. What was painful was Andy's absence from her life. Things hurt inside her—emotions she hadn't even known were there. But there was something else—something different in the way her heart broke for the second time. Unlike before, Mira was still standing. Still emotionally upright. It was as if her journey as a runner had caused her mind to grow stronger and more able to cushion her heartache. Of course, the tears still fell, because runner or not, the fact that she was human hadn't changed. However, instead of crumbling like a pie crust and sobbing into a family-sized tub of peanut butter, Mira began to redirect her pain by driving it straight into her runs. Her heart was able to find peace in pushing her body beyond its usual limits. Following Andy's departure, she continued training each week, her schedule unwavering. Three days a week after work, she hit the trail, alternating between long endurance runs to build stamina, and short tempo runs to build those muscles and her lactic acid threshold, both of which (she hoped) would ultimately carry her over the half-marathon finish line. On days she didn't run, Mira cross-trained, giving her that extra layer of strength. It surprised her at first, but her pace had improved dramatically in the past month. She was comfortably holding a ten-minute-mile pace across her six-mile runs on average. Not bad for a woman who used to run out of breath kneading *naan* dough.

SITTING ON HER bed, squinting at her handwritten race-training schedule, Mira counted down the days to race day—the day of the Lake Union Half-Marathon. Three weeks separated Mira from her moment of truth. "I've got this," she said to herself, her voice firm as concrete.

"Got what?" Laila asked, entering Mira's room through the wide-open door. She plopped herself on the bed. However, as she held two cups of steaming coffee, and presuming one of them was for her, Mira decided not to kick her cousin out.

"Is that for me?" Mira asked.

Laila extended one of the mugs to her. "Can I ask you something?"

Mira sipped the warm liquid and closed her eyes to savor its descent down her throat. "Does 'something' have anything to do with Andy?" she asked, eyes still closed.

"Probably..."

"Then, no. You may not ask." She stood up and tried to leave, but Laila yanked her arm and sat her back down on the bed. "What happened between you and Andy that night?"

Mira exhaled softly as she considered her options. "Can I get you to drop the subject for... twenty dollars?" she proposed and began reaching for her handbag.

"No." Laila shook her head. "But I will give you an 'A' for your cheapskate effort."

Sighing, Mira placed her coffee mug on the side table and pulled a pillow closer to her chest for comfort. "There's nothing more to say, Laila."

"What you've told me so far does not add up," her cousin protested. "You said you and Andy had a fight the other night when I was out recording... and then he left. What did you fight about that caused him to leave? Where the hell did he go? It's been weeks since you've spoken to him, Mira—"

"Jay showed up." Mira's words sliced right through her cousin's, like a knife through a cake.

Laila's mouth stayed open midway through her sentence. "J-Jay?"

"Yup."

"Like, your ex-husband?"

"Yup."

Laila threw her hands up in the air. "What the heck?

Who the fuck does that man think he is? And what the hell did he come for? And don't you dare tell me he wanted you back, because that's going to make me want to swallow my tongue."

"He wanted me back," said Mira.

"Unbelievable," Laila cried, covering her mouth. "He has no shame, and no conscience. He's the most uncool dude I've ever met, and I've met a lot of uncool dudes." She paused and stared blankly at Mira. "Oh, please don't tell me Andy ran into Jay?"

Mira nodded. "He showed up just as Jay and I were, well . . . holding hands—"

"Oh, shit."

Mira closed her eyes against the memory. "God, Laila. I was sure Andy would punch Jay, so I asked him to leave . . ."

Laila nodded. "Well, that was good thinking, asking Jay to leave."

"No," Mira interjected. "I asked *Andy* to leave, not Jay."

Laila sported a quizzical frown. "Jay's a gigantic prick who cheated on you for years and broke your heart. Andy's the man who stayed put in your life and has basically been your own personal, super-hot trainer for your half-marathon, and you chose Jay over him? Why would you act like an idiot when you're not one?"

Mira clutched the pillow tighter against her chest. Laila's words were bursting with truth and causing her head to spin. "I-I didn't choose Jay over Andy. I had to think on my feet."

"Sounds more like you were thinking *with* your feet," Laila replied.

Mira scoped her cousin's expressionless face. "So, you're

saying I made a mistake?"

Laila raised a brow. "Today, I added kefir to my morning coffee instead of milk. *That* was a mistake. What you did was a howler."

The words were deafening, and Mira remained silent. Her cousin watched her for a few minutes and then said, "You know, I've always been the rebel in the family—the one lone Sood who openly stands up to tradition. But you? I never would've imagined you doing something like that . . . deciding to sleep with a guy like Andy. It's so *unlike* you to break with tradition and follow your heart." Laila's eyes softened. "Regardless of how it turned out with him, I'm proud of you for standing up for yourself."

Mira shrugged and felt the sting as she held back the tears. "Thanks."

Laila studied Mira closely. "So, er, are you still planning on carrying out your crazy mission today? Talking it out with Mummyji?"

This caused Mira to look up and she breathed in slowly. "Yes."

"Is it really necessary?" asked Laila, sporting a look of concern.

"I need to have this heart-to-heart with Mummyji." Mira nodded firmly. "I've made the decision, and I'm sticking with it."

"Why don't you sleep on it? Do it tomorrow morning?"

Mira stood up and walked over to slip on her boots. "I've put it off long enough, Laila. It has to be tonight."

IT HAD BEEN forty-five minutes since she arrived, and yet, Mira couldn't bring herself to step out of her car. She watched Auntie Sharmila's front door through the driver's side window and checked her watched again. Fifty minutes. *Great.*

Dragging her weight out of the car, Mira forced herself up the cobbled walkway to ring Auntie Sharmila's doorbell. They hadn't spoken since the night Mira punched Jay's nose in—the same night she'd told her mother about Andy. In all the time Mira had known Auntie Sharmila, the woman had stood by her prerogative—call at least once a week, if not twice. Leave behind at least one voicemail, if not two. If nothing works, just show up. But in the four weeks that had passed since that night, Mira hadn't heard once from the older woman. Not one call. Not one text.

To Mira, the chances of Auntie Sharmila opening the door to her that night appeared very slim indeed. Which is why it surprised her when the door did open.

"Mummyji," Mira acknowledged, bending over to touch her aunt's feet. The latter had nothing to offer besides a deadpan expression. "I'm sure you've heard from Ma what happened between me and Jay? And about Andy?" began Mira.

Her auntie crossed her arms about her chest. "Is that why you're here? To tell me yourself? Because if so, then you shouldn't have bothered."

"I know you don't approve, and I'm not expecting you to understand, Mummyji—"

"No, I don't understand," her auntie cut in, shaking her head. "Instead of fixing your broken marriage, you say you're dating a white man? Jay made a mistake, but he came back to right the wrong he did, and you *slapped* him?"

"Punched," Mira recollected, with a flicker of inward glee. "I punched him. Because what he did was unforgivable."

"And what would have happened if I, or your mother, or *Chachi*, or your *Naani*—bless her soul—had all decided to find justice in a punch? All the men in this family would have broken noses."

"I had to stand up to Jay . . . and for once, I had to stand up for *myself*."

Auntie Sharmila sported a grim look. "Do you know when I got married, I was nineteen . . . *nineteen*. My mother pulled me out of college a few months before I was supposed to graduate, and I married your Papaji in a ceremony that my parents couldn't afford. They had to sell part of their land just so they could get me married and settled."

"I know," Mira muttered.

"I had dreams too, you know. And I would have *loved* to date a white American . . ." her auntie mused, with a distant look in her eyes. "But I didn't. I sacrificed my happiness, over and over, for the sake of my husband, for the sake of my in-laws, for the sake of my children . . . because I knew what my parents sacrificed for me. I couldn't let them down, so I fought to survive."

"But Mummyji," Mira interjected softly. "I don't want to survive. I want to *live*. I want to be happy, and I want to live my life."

Auntie Sharmila pursed her lips. "I see. And what about us? Your family, your parents?"

A NEW MANTRA

"I love my family. I don't want to have to choose..." Mira breathed out, holding back her tears. "But if I have to choose, then I choose *me*. And there's nothing wrong with that. Running's taught me that self-love isn't selfish."

"*Running?*" her auntie cried out. "All of a sudden you're talking about sports?"

"Do you know, Mummyji, I could barely run a mile when I first started running, but it wasn't because I didn't have it in me. It was because I didn't believe in myself. I didn't respect myself or my body. I didn't love myself enough. But the more that changed, the better I became as a runner." A soft laugh escaped Mira's lips as she considered her auntie's flummoxed look. "Anyway, I'm sorry if I've made you unhappy; you don't deserve it. But I have a new mantra—I am now my favorite person in the world. And I won't apologize for that." With that, Mira turned around and walked away, her heart happy, and her soul as light as a feather.

Chapter Twenty-Six

ALL THE RESEARCH pointed to the importance of a mock run, especially before a long-distance race. Mira tried not to think of Andy, but his advice to her from the past came to mind. He'd stressed the need to plan this "rehearsal race" in a way that she'd be able to physically recuperate from it in time to run the actual thing. Mira locked eyes with her calendar and decided that two weeks before race day was when she'd complete her rehearsal race. She chose a Saturday, so she'd have Sunday to rest before going into work. This was going to be painful. And she was nervous. And then she became doubly nervous when she realized this wasn't even the real race—just a preview of the actual one. If this was enough to freak her out, how would she complete the actual half-marathon? Quickly distracting herself with the homemade oatmeal-raisin bar she held in her hand, Mira tried to think positive thoughts. Maybe she'd go out and get some run clothes for race day—*feel* pretty during her first ever half-marathon.

The week of her rehearsal run, Mira followed the *Runner's World* guidelines to a T as if this were the week of her actual race day. She drank lots of coconut water for those natural electrolytes. She carb-loaded, without misusing the term, focusing on healthy carbs with lots of fiber and lots of vegetables, just the right amounts of protein, and fruit to quell her petulant sweet tooth. She continued running that week but tweaked her routine, whereby she ran a short three-miler on Monday, took a break doing low-impact yoga on Tuesday, then jogged an easy six-miler on Wednesday, and wrapped up with cross-training on Thursday. Friday, she went out for a long hike with Laila. Saturday was when she'd run her rehearsal race. Friday night, she made curried ramen noodle soup with vegetables and tofu. She carefully injected well-balanced flavors into her broth—ginger, lemongrass, basil, with a shadow of curry powder, coconut milk, and a tease of soy sauce.

ON SATURDAY MORNING, Mira ate half a whole-grain bagel with peanut butter, per the combined recommendations of all the running gurus of the world. She washed it down with eight ounces of coconut water and then drove out to her usual trail. She was nervous. She knew this was just a mock race, and yet she felt the pressure. The fact was this was Mira's first official attempt at running 13.1 miles. And today was the day she'd find out whether or not she could do it. There was nothing "mock" about the impending revelation, and that's what scared the bejeezus out of her. What if she failed? What if she couldn't do it? What if today would prove that her months of training had been a waste? What if her failure today impacted her real race? What if, what if, what if . . . ?

Down at the trailhead, Mira attempted to tame her racing heart. If a practice race had the potential to unleash this kind of anxiety, then she didn't know what to expect on the actual race day. Strapping her smartphone onto her armband, she pre-set her app to record her run miles, pace, and runtime. She did a few customary knee-up routines—if nothing else, she hoped it would shake off her unwanted nerves. And then she took off, steady and slow.

This being her usual trail, Mira knew that a single loop was six and a half miles long. She planned to run the trail loop twice, and then run once around the parking lot to capture that elusive 0.1 miles to complete her total 13.1-mile half-marathon test run.

It didn't take Mira long to realize she was doing really well. By the end of her first loop and at the start of her second, Mira's nerves were calm and her mind floated inside a peaceful, thoughtless vacuum. The sounds of the gravel, chirping birds, and the wind engulfed her, and she focused entirely on them, instead of the miles she was clocking, or her pace. Soon, Mira was halfway done with her second loop and was on the home stretch. Pain and fatigue from running ten miles were making themselves known. Her calves were on fire, her arms were sore to the bone, and her feet—well, she couldn't feel them anymore, so that was good. She devoured oxygen through her mouth and felt she could make the remaining three miles, despite the pain. Mira smiled to herself. *This whole half-marathon's going to work out.*

As she approached the final mile, Mira defied her odds and pushed forward, kicking up her pace. The adrenaline surged again, which fueled her desire to finish her first 13.1

miles. At least then, regardless of what happened on race day, Mira could feel reassured that she'd given her training her very best effort. With the parking lot in sight, Mira began sprinting toward the imaginary finish line. Yup, she was almost there, but then—

A rustling sound distracted her from behind. She swerved ever so slightly, just to check her rear view. She was all alone on the trail, which wound through dense thickets. It was still pretty early for a Saturday morning, and although Mira knew there likely were a few other hikers out, she'd yet to pass another human. Oddly enough, there had been a black bear sighting on that trail just the week before. Mira even remembered spotting a sign that morning on the information board at the trailhead, posted by the Washington State Department of Fish and Wildlife, requesting trail users to be aware, respectful, and immediately report any bear sightings. Mira knew she was consuming extra energy every time she turned to check her back. But the idea of running down a trail with a four-hundred-pound spring bear briskly jogging behind her was giving her the heebie-jeebies. She was still a few hundred feet away from the parking lot, and Mira could hear the rustling sound getting louder. What caused her worry to spike was that the rustling appeared to pause every few minutes—very unlike a hiker. The trail straightened out ahead, so Mira could now catch a clear view of who (or what) was behind her. Still running, and still determined to finish, she turned to check her rear one more time. And then she felt her heart stop.

Andrew Fitzgerald was jogging toward her, a good distance away, but close enough to sound like a stalking bear.

Mira's brain was frozen, with no idea what to do next. Andy was smiling at her. And before she knew it, she felt herself pivot, and she began running toward him like a sun-starved flower. A flicker of a smile began to ignite her face. She'd missed him with every fiber of her being. She didn't know yet if she loved him. Or maybe she did and was too scared to admit it. But as she watched him close the distance between them, a second, more unpredictable feeling took over Mira's senses. The smile never made it to her face. Instead, a frown crested her temple. Andrew Fitzgerald had left her without the slightest indication of where he was going. This man had broken her heart. Who cared if he'd returned looking like a nerdy Chris Hemsworth?

Andy was a few feet away now. But instead of charging forward into his arms, Mira starkly turned on her heels, and began sprinting away from him, toward the parking lot. She ran as fast as her fatigued, Punjabi-Indian muscles could carry her. She knew she'd never stack up to Andy's elite-runner speed, but she wasn't going to let him woo her back by just showing up.

"Mira," Andy cried out. Yup, she'd missed the sound of his voice when it called her name, but nope, she wasn't going to stop. No way.

"No!" Mira yelled back. Why she would waste her breath on a word like that, she'd no idea.

The sound of Andy's feet on the gravel got louder, more determined. "Mira, STOP!"

"N—" she couldn't force out the rest of the word because she was both breathless and giddy.

"Would you stop, please?" Andy quickly caught up to

her, now running right by her side. *The fast bastard.*

Mira shook her head vehemently. "I-I'm not s-stop it . . ." She was aware of, yet helpless against, the lack of oxygen to her brain which was now causing her to spew gibberish.

Andy kept up with her, even though she was swaying with fatigue. "You've got to let me talk, please," he begged.

As they entered the parking lot, Mira was determined not to let Andy ruin her practice run. So, per her original plan, she decided to run once around the parking lot for the last 0.1 miles. She was stumbling and practically unconscious. But, damn it, this was going to happen.

Andy ran the round with her. "What are you doing, exactly?" he asked calmly. "You can't be trying to get away from me, running a circle around the parking lot?"

"N-not everything's h-ha 'bout you. Andhoo..." She panted, gulping precious air through her mouth. "This is mah mock runh..."

Andy said nothing, but continued to run quietly beside her until she finished and doubled over beside her car to catch her breath. Ripping her armband off, Mira ignored Andy's presence as she pulled her phone out and turned off her mile-tracker app. Hah. She'd officially done it. She'd in fact *overdone* it, running 13.5 miles. This was probably because she'd run toward Andy when she first saw him, and then away from him, when she remembered the heartache he'd caused her by shutting her out of his life.

"YES." She smiled to herself.

"How did you do?" Andy tried to ask, leaning in toward her.

Mira backed away from him instantly. "You don't exist," she replied, her voice low and firm. Her body ached in a thousand places, yet she fought the urge to melt into Andy's stately arms, which she knew he'd gladly hold up for her.

"Mira, I'm sorry." Andy's words floated up to her ear. "I'm really, *really* sorry."

Hunched over from exhaustion, she began moving in the direction of her car. "Andy, I really don't want to talk right now, okay?" she said, hurling the words over her shoulder as she walked away from him.

"Mira, please, I just want one chance. I don't deserve one chance, I know . . . but I *need* it. Please?"

She sighed and stopped for a moment. "Andy, there's absolutely *nothing* you can say to fix the fact that you walked out on me."

"I know that, and it's not why I'm here. I'm not here to justify my decision to leave without telling you where I was going. I was wrong. Period."

"Great. We're on the same page. Can I go now?" Mira asked as she used her clicker to unlock her car.

"Listen—*wait*," he cried. "I want to explain my side of the story." Andy paused to gauge Mira's receptiveness. The best she could offer him was a calm, blank expression, so he breathed out and kept on going. "Look, that night when Jay showed up and you asked me to leave, it felt to me as if you had made the decision to get back with him. I was so mad I didn't . . . *think*—"

"I asked you to leave because I didn't want you to end up in a fistfight with Jay. I was sure you were getting ready to punch him and—"

"I *would* have punched the prick."

"There, you see?" Mira pointed out, doing a pancake-flip of her palm. "So, I asked you to leave. I didn't think you'd take me *literally*, though . . . I didn't mean, 'Andy, get out of my life forever,' you know?"

Andy nodded. "I realize that now . . ." He paused. "So, what happened? After I left?"

Mira let out a sigh. "I punched the prick in the nose and told him to get the hell out of my life."

A look of pride mixed with disbelief adorned Andy's face, and he let out a laugh. "You *what*?"

But Mira chose to retain the frown on her temple. "Do you really think I was going to let Jay back into my life? It's like you don't know me."

"I *do* know you," replied Andy, his gaze steady on hers. "Which is why I was worried you might put your happiness on the back burner and get back with Jay to keep the peace with your family."

"That was the *old* me, Andy. I've changed. Running has changed my life. It may sound crazy, but it's true."

Andy smiled. "It doesn't sound one bit crazy to me."

"It's helped me feel stronger, smarter, more beautiful . . ." Mira breathed in. "This race has helped me find myself."

"You *are* more beautiful, more incredible, than anyone I have ever known."

Her lips remained an unaltered straight line on her face. "Why are you back . . . from wherever you went?"

"Whidbey Island," said Andy. "I ended up renting a cottage on a lake. That's where I've been staying these past few weeks. I needed to get away . . . clear my head."

Mira remained unaffected. "It actually doesn't matter where you went. You left me, just like Jay did."

Andy moved closer, just short of reaching for her hand. "Jay left you because he didn't love you. I left because . . . I *love* you, Mira," he blurted out.

Mira felt her brain explode. *What was that? What did he just say? Am I dreaming? Confused? Or am I so elated I want to attempt a cartwheel? Oh God, I need to lie down.* And yet, on the outside, Mira remained cool as ice as she replied, "Huh. That came out of nowhere."

Andy slowly extended his hand to touch hers. She didn't retract it, mostly because she wasn't done freaking out inwardly. He held her hand sandwiched between his palms. "The truth is, I fell head over heels in love with you the first time I laid eyes on you—the day you forgot your purse over a giant cookie," he said with a warm laugh. "I'll never forget that day because that was the moment I fell in love for the first time ever. It took me some time to realize what was happening . . . I've never been in *love* before, so I guess I had no way of really understanding what I was feeling—"

"So, you sentenced yourself to solitary confinement on an island somewhere, and now you've returned as some kind of love-*swami?*" Mira frowned.

"Not a *swami* . . . just more self-aware." He shrugged. "I should've told you how I felt sooner; I admit that was an error on my part. But then I waited because I wanted to solidify my financial future before having a serious talk about our relationship with you—I guess I preferred not to confess to both love *and* bankruptcy all in the same conversation."

Mira raised a brow at him. "I don't know what to say, Andy. It surprises me even more that you took off on a woman you say you love. To me, that's worse, not better."

Biting his lower lip, Andy nodded back. "That's a fair point and, again, I'm not making excuses here, but it took me a little while to understand the rules of the game."

Mira squinted back at him. "And you expect me to sit around and wait for the rays of wisdom to shine on you? This is exactly what Jay did . . . he broke my heart, left me, and then returned, expecting me to just take him back. I'm sick of it. I'm tired of being treated like some kind of doll."

The grim look on Andy's face was unmistakable. "So, I blew it then?"

"I'm sorry, Andy. I'm not that person anymore . . . the one who crumbles like a cookie because a man walked out on her. I've been there and done that . . . once. And once is enough for me. You and I had a lovely time together, and I'm really grateful to you for helping me with my race training and . . ." Mira breathed out. "But I'm not going to melt into your arms at your command. I'm done getting my heart broken. You took me for granted and now it's too late." She looked at her watch. "I've got to go. I just ran 13.5 miles and I'm starving."

When he spoke, his voice sounded like that of a man who had just been gutted. "OK. I respect your decision, and I won't bother you again. But . . . could you wait here just one moment? I want to give you something."

Before Mira could mouth the words "I don't think so" Andy had dashed off to his car, which was parked a few feet away from hers. While she waited, Mira stroked the feeling of catharsis she felt inside herself. She'd believed (in theory) that running had changed her. It had helped her gain the self-confidence she'd never had. But now, she'd proved it to herself, by saying, "No, thank you" to Andrew Fitzgerald. *Bravo, Mira Sood.* She cleared her throat as the initial effects of her decision (a feeling of liberation) started to wear off, replaced by its side effects (self-doubt).

A moment later, Andy was standing before her again, holding a big brown bag. He smiled, the kind of smile that pressed those lingering side effects of rejecting him deeper into her forehead. Mira felt a headache coming on, so she massaged it with a frown. "What's this?" she asked, keeping her voice flat and steady.

"Open it," he insisted, in his buttery-deep voice—the same one he'd used to whisper her name in bed. Yup. She'd likely miss that very much. She reluctantly took the bag out of his hand and peeked inside. Her heart instantly skipped a beat as she pulled out a shoe box. Inside it rested a pair of neon-blue-and-pink Brooks Running shoes—the pair she and Andy had seen on their very first shoe-shopping "non-date." The pair she'd fallen in love with, but (still) couldn't afford to buy. The pair she knew "was the one" to wear for the race. A tiny bubble of guilt rose up in her chest and snagged itself in her throat. Mira tried to swallow it down, but it felt prickly. She shook her head at him and returned the bag. "I can't accept that."

The softness of Andy's face was replaced by hollow disappointment. "Mira, you deserve this," he protested. "Don't do it for me. Take it because *you* deserve this. You deserve to wear these shoes in your first half-marathon."

Mira considered Andy's argument. All her life, she'd played by the rules. Never lied, never broken the law, never borrowed money without paying it back in full, with interest; never talked during movies, never drove over the speed limit, never, never, never. And yet, she got cheated on by her husband. Frankly, she was tired of always doing what was expected, not what was good for her. She deserved the shoes. She deserved to wear them to the race. And it was time she threw her dusty old rule book out, or maybe place it on a high, high shelf for a bit. "Thanks," she said, and accepted the bag.

The most radiant (and dangerously handsome) smile burst across Andy's face. "Thank you, Mira," he replied softly, and extended his hand to her to shake. "I'll miss you," he conceded, tipping his head to one side.

"We had a good run, no pun intended," she replied quickly, trying not to look straight at him. Why? Because that would be like taking a walk down the snack aisle at the grocery store on an empty stomach.

"Yup, we sure did . . ." he replied softly.

"I'd better get going," said Mira and spun around to jump into her car. She drove straight out of the parking lot, overriding her instinct to glimpse at Andy one last time in the rearview mirror.

After a soulful shower, Mira threw some mirepoix, along with some cloves of garlic, olive oil, and a can of chunky tomatoes, into a giant pot, added in some vegetable stock, along with a handful of elbow macaroni, salt, and pepper. She threw the lid back on and let the whole thing simmer on low while she planted herself on the sofa. Her body ached sweetly from her mock half-marathon run. Her heart ached also, but Mira pretended not to notice that part. The decision had been made, and her heart needed to get with the program.

Pulling the shoes to her chest, Mira examined them up close. They looked incredibly well made—a fact that had been painfully reflected in the price tag the first time she'd seen them at Sporting Goods.

"What d'you have there?" asked Laila as she approached her cousin.

Mira smiled admiringly at her babies. "My new running shoes."

Laila frowned. "*Running* shoes?" she replied, sitting down next to her cousin. She uncovered the second shoe that lay swaddled under white paper and examined it. "I've never seen running shoes that looked like . . . well, *this* good."

Mira cleared her throat nervously. The situation was dangerously close to warranting an explanation, which she absolutely didn't want to give. Laila would chew her to cud if she ever found out that Andy had given her the shoes.

And that's when Laila fired the shot. "Where'd you get 'em?"

Mira knew she was a terrible liar. But that didn't mean she wasn't going to try. "I got them, er . . ."

Laila's gaze shifted from the shoe to Mira. "Yes?"

This was shameful. Mira sighed and conceded quickly. "Andy gave them to me, but—"

"*Andy?*" cried out Laila, slicing through Mira's attempted explanation.

"Look, we broke up, okay? I mean . . . we weren't even

officially going out, but we—I told him I don't want to see him again. And please don't make me talk about it anymore."

Laila folded her lips inward as she noticed how Mira sat cradling one of the shoes in her arms.

"OK, but before I drop this conversation, I want to ask you one question," said Laila.

Mira studied her cousin briefly. "Fine. What?"

"Are you sure about your decision?"

"Yes." The word ricocheted off Mira's tongue with apparently no effort at all. Which likely meant her brain and heart were finally aligned. *Phew.*

Chapter Twenty-Seven

SPRING – *March*

AT THE START of the final week before race day, Mira picked out her race outfit—a pair of navy-blue capri pants and a fuchsia-colored, long-sleeved tank top. They had been her favorite wear through her training days. Her new shoes had been broken in, and everything felt ready to go.

Friday, the day before race day, she drove out to BigFoot Athletics to pick up her race swag containing her bib and tracking chip. This gave her the opportunity to study the other racers who had also arrived to pick up their bibs and swag. *Yikes.* she mused to herself. They all appeared pretty self-confident, like they had done this before, only a few million times. They paused to chat each other up, slapping shoulders and fanning themselves with their race packets. It took a great amount of optimistic thinking on Mira's part to stop herself from feeling as if she'd just taken the training wheels off her bike and was now off to race at a goddamn velodrome.

Mira sheepishly stepped up to the counter where volunteers were handing out race packets and offered up her driver's license. "Hi, I'm here for my race packet?"

The volunteer studied the card briefly, filtered through

the neatly stacked race packets and pulled one out, handing it to Mira. "Here you go. Have a good race." She smiled.

"Thanks." Mira smiled back, feeling a little less like an outsider.

That night, Mira lay in bed thinking about the next morning—the day of the race. The day she both dreaded and anticipated. When she'd first begun training, she'd had next to no confidence. Midway through training, she'd been sure she'd signed up to make the biggest mistake of her life by attempting to run a half-marathon. And now? She felt ready. She felt strong. *BREATHE*, she said to her heart. She had everything she needed to nail this race.

SATURDAY MORNING, RACE day, Mira hugged Laila goodbye as she left the apartment. "Are you sure you don't want me there when you take off?" Laila had asked.

"No, I'll just see you at the finish." Mira had smiled back. She was too jumpy to have company. Alone was probably best, at least at the start.

Mira arrived at Lake Union Park at 6:30 am, an hour before time. The parking lot was mostly empty, but for a few cars scattered around. A few racers were running light-footedly around the parking lot. Mira stepped out of her car and re-pinned her bib to her tank top for the fiftieth time. She'd readjusted the damn thing so many times now, she had a dozen or so pinpricks all over her finger from the accidental stabbings. "Shoot." Mira winced, feeling another jab to the old pointer. She sighed with dissatisfaction as she gave the pinned-up bib one final glance. Leaning into her car, she pulled a pen out of the glove compartment and wrote the word "BREATHE" in big bold letters on both palms.

Perfect. Now that that was settled, she could move on to the next challenge—she needed to pee. Drinking a sixteen-ounce glass of smoothie a half hour before her departure from the house might not have been her brightest idea. "Damn it," Mira muttered under her breath as she approached the restrooms. While the parking lot was fairly empty, there was a curiously long line outside the restrooms, including the porta-potties that speckled the park entrance. *Damn it, damn it, damn it.*

It was seven o'clock by the time Mira stepped into a restroom stall. She still had thirty minutes before the race, but she was unnerved by how *not* smooth sailing everything had been so far. Then again, this was her first race (of her *life*), so maybe the choppy logistics were unavoidable.

Done with her bathroom break, Mira felt revived and decided to walk in the direction of the starting line. A crowd (a massive one) had already begun to gather. Thousands of people, from every walk of life, huddled close together as the cloudy March day breathed a chilly breeze, while eager family and friends gathered to support them from the sidelines. Music played on the jumbo speakers, and the race pacers took their spots in the crowd, each one holding up a placard that displayed their goal runtime: 1:30, 1:45, 2:00, 2:15, and 2:30. Mira wondered whether she should use a pacer—she had found from her research that a pacer helps a racer meet a certain goal time. But the trick was to select the correct pace group. Too fast, and she wouldn't be able to keep up. Too slow, and she would probably fall short of her expectations. Or should she forgo a pacer altogether—her race, her pace? The slowest pacer proposed to finish the race in two hours and thirty minutes. Would that be overshooting the mark for Mira? Was she fit enough to run a half-marathon in two hours and thirty minutes? She did the math in her head. Her finish time when she ran her mock half-marathon was two hours and fifty-nine minutes. Which meant she'd have to improve her pace significantly to keep up with the gal holding the placard that offered a two-hour, thirty-minute finish time. But not trying was just as bad an option. Maybe she could run faster when running an actual race? After all, the collective energy of the crowd, the pumped-up spirits of the racers, the music, the hooting and cheering of the bystanders and race volunteers was infectious. Mira made a quick decision. Walking over to the pacer who held up the two-hour, thirty-minute placard, she took her place in the group—at the very back of the class, but still close enough to notice the pacers' calf muscles twitch with anticipation. *Lord, help me.*

Mira checked her watch. Ten minutes to go. Final announcements were made, urging racers to take their places at the starting line, and requesting onlookers to clear the way. Mira's heart was thumping loud enough to cause her eardrums to vibrate. A countdown to the race began: Ten. Nine. Eight. Seven. Six . . .

The runners steadied themselves. Mira breathed out to calm her nerves and read the lettering on her palms: BREATHE. This was it. Three. Two. One. And they were off.

The elite runners who occupied the starting corrals were the first to take off, jetting forward at lightning speed. They soon disappeared out of sight, even before the last of the racers had crossed the starting line. Mira stayed close to her two-hour-and-thirty-minute pace group. Their pacer was a brusque brunette with a shoulder-length braid and calf muscles that flexed and danced with each stride. She casually chewed gum and chatted up another racer from the group, looking as Zen as if she were sitting at a bar.

The racecourse was a mostly flat loop that first wrapped around beautiful Lake Union, followed by an extended loop around some paved trail through the park itself. Total: 13.1 miles. Race volunteers stood at every 0.5 miles for the first two miles, cheering the racers on. Police cars blocked off streets to accommodate the easy flow of race traffic, and Mira felt . . . alright. The thumping in her heart had subsided, and her breathing felt less strained, more regular. They were at mile 0.6, but at least she hadn't prematurely passed out from all the excitement.

The racers flowed alongside Mira, as paces between them sometimes collided, and other times coexisted. The urge to outrun a fellow racer was a constant temptation. And Mira did on a few occasions. But she reminded herself that this meant nothing against the ultimate goal—to finish her first half-marathon. A respectable runtime was more of a perk at this point.

Mile three. The racers had already thinned out. There were some racers who were trailing; there were some that had outrun the others and were out of sight. The racers who had graced the starting corrals were close to the finish line. Mira swallowed hard, feeling the dry prick of her throat. She knew there were rest stops and rehydration stands at every two miles. Foolishly, she'd chosen not to use the one she'd passed at the second-mile post. So now, she had to wait until mile four to hydrate. To make matters worse, this new and improved pace was just not working for her. Actually, it was killing her. She'd run less than a fourth of the total race distance, and already, her feet ached like they had run ten miles. There was no way she could keep this up much longer.

And then, to her horror, her pacer kicked up the pace a minute later. Mira was now beginning to hyperventilate. This race was quickly turning into a disaster. She was blowing it. All her training, through all those months, all the effort, the runs after work, her (suspiciously) excellent mock half-marathon run, were all for nothing. Clenching her teeth, Mira pushed through the pain and fatigue. Her feet were making it very clear to her that they were not on the program—it was as if she were running with a five-pound bag of russet potatoes tied to each foot. Her calves were crying out for her to stop. And this whole experience was forcing her to admit the sordid bottom line—she had overshot the mark. She'd taken the outcome of this half-marathon for granted because things had been going so well. The fact was, she'd never run a half-marathon before. So she needed time to understand how to play the game—*WOAH.*

Mira felt a lightning strike of realization inside her head. Andy's words came flooding back—he had made a mistake because he'd never experienced love before. He'd needed time to learn to play the game. It was too late to wonder now. But maybe, just *maybe*, should she have given Andy that second cha—*mile four*. Mira's silent contemplations came to a screeching halt when her eyes caught sight of the milepost and the heartwarming sight of the hydration station next to it. She pulled to an unceremonious stop under a tree, a few feet away from the volunteers who were handing out hydration gels and small cups of ice water. "Water first, please," they said, trying to dissuade racers from seeking a revival shortcut by simply chugging down tubes of the electrolyte-rich gels and forgetting to wash it down with enough water.

Mira didn't need to be told twice. She grabbed the cup of water like a kid on a Popsicle stick. She instinctively downed the contents and immediately doubled over, coughing as half the ice cubes from the cup journeyed down the wrong pipe. *Super*. Not only was she not going to finish the race, she was also going to choke to death on ice at freaking mile *four*.

Slowly recovering from her embarrassing and slightly dizzying feat, Mira sucked air in through her funneled lips. This race, so far, had been a total and complete disaster. No, correction: a *stinking* catastrophe. Plus, she was beginning to feel emotionally hijacked by guilt over kicking Andy to the curb for taking off on her. Because all of a sudden, she found herself empathizing with him. Thanks to this day and this race—her sickening performance—she now understood what he'd been trying to say to her. His reason for leaving that day no longer appeared irrational or even unfair. Too late, but there it was.

Mira quietly watched a few racers stampede past her. And she knew, in that moment, what she needed to do. She needed a new game plan. Her pacer, leading the two-hour thirty-minute finish time group, was long gone and well out of sight. Excellent. Because it meant Mira was now free to run the way her Punjabi-Indian body was born to run—slow, yet gritty, like homemade phulka-roti.

Wiping sweat off her brow onto her sleeve, Mira took off at a much slower pace, pounding the gravel on the trail as she consciously monitored signs of rebellion from her body. Nothing. She smiled and kept on going. But just as she passed the five-mile marker, Mira began to, once again, feel the ache in her calves and the rawness of her feet as they wrenched inside her new shoes. Great. The threat to her finishing the race was once again imminent. But Mira was no quitter. If her body wasn't going to participate, she'd recruit her mind. Isn't that what Andy was always saying? The memory of him was gut-wrenching, but she forced herself to recollect the best of his advice in that moment: *Stay focused, breathe, and let your mind take over your body,* he would say, in that deep, calm, caramel-custard voice of his.

Go, Mira! She could literally hear him now. *You got this.* Hmm. It was as if he were standing at the top of a hill, shouting out to her. This could only mean one thing, Mira thought to herself, mortified—she was hallucinating. The pain, coupled with fatigue, was creating wishful sounds inside her head. It meant the fight to the finish would be harder. Mile six. *Keep up the pace, you've got this, Mira!* echoed Andy's voice, following a few quiet moments of running. Mira physically shook her head against the sounds. This was getting ridiculous. What next? Was she going to involuntarily start taking her clothes off?

"Chase the pace, chase the pace, Mira!" She turned intuitively in the direction of the voice. And her racing heart came to a full stop. "ANDY?" Yup. Andrew Fitzgerald was wearing a neon-green reflective rain jacket, standing up on a hill a few feet away from the racecourse, and holding up a giant poster with the words "GO, MIRA! YOU GOT THIS!" written on it in giant, black lettering.

She questioned his insanely supportive gesture by shrugging back at him, smiling and tearing up, dizzy and elated. And she knew in that moment, as she watched him hold up that enormous handmade poster above his head . . . she was in love with Andrew Fitzgerald. She'd loved him longer than she'd cared to admit. She laughed out loud and wiped her tears on her sleeve. She still had a race to finish. Quickly waving back at him, Mira dashed forward with a renewed fire inside her.

Mile eight. The runners were crashing and burning around her like jaded fireflies. The miles were beginning to reflect on the racers—on their faces and in their strides. Some ran, partly hunched over, as if they were running directly to the E.R. with a case of appendicitis. Mira's body begged for her to quit. *Nope. Suck it up, Sood*, she said to herself and forced a smile into place as she accepted a cup of ice water from a race volunteer. By mile ten, Mira's adrenaline was beginning to kick back in. This was the home stretch, with only three miles left to go. She then caught a glimpse of Andy's Jeep, pulled up at the shoulder that lay parallel to the racecourse trail. "Go, Mira. You're almost there," he cried out, clapping his hands. And the words fired up her inner guns. Race volunteers lined the course trail on either side, after every few yards. They clapped and cheered as Mira and her fellow racers hobble-charged toward the finish. Sandwich board signs were thoughtfully metered at every turn, with encouraging messages to the racers. "Some people won't even DRIVE 13.1 miles today" or "Short-lived pain for Eternal Bragging Rights" or "Free Ice Buckets at mile 13.1" or the real classic "RUN now, RUM later"

It was getting harder to push, but Mira allowed herself to be distracted by the volunteers cheering. She tottered down the trail, past a runner who was hunched over and hyperventilating, gripping his knees with his palms. Her glutes ached so badly she was sure her butt cheeks had both fallen off somewhere around mile nine. Her feet were so suspiciously numb they were no longer causing her pain, just apprehension. Every inch of her body was moments away from giving up the fight to keep running. The only string holding her grit together was the prize combo that awaited Mira at the finish line—her finisher's medal, plus Andy. Mile twelve.

Neon orange traffic cones lined the paved course that led straight back into the parking lot of Union Lake Park. This was it; she was almost there. Mira pushed forward, completely oblivious to the photographers who crouched down on the sidelines, snapping pictures of her and the other racers as they conquered the final mile of the race. Some runners appeared to still possess the presence of mind to smile back at the cameras. Mira could only manage a half-wave, followed by an involuntary groan. "Argh..." Man, was she hurting.

The course tapered as huge crowds of supportive family and friends lined the sides of the trail as Mira and the other runners approached the 12.5-mile mark. She forced her mind to take control again, and with the adrenaline pumping through her veins, she pushed for the final 0.6 miles toward the finish. She spotted tents, and she could hear loud music playing. As she turned the corner, she spotted Andy, standing in the crowd, yet distinctive, owing to his neon jacket. Right next to him were Laila and Seth. They were all three laughing and cheering her on. Shaking his head at her with that look she recognized, Andy cried out. "Go, get that medal, Sood!" he shouted.

Mira laughed as she turned to run toward the finish. And that's when she noticed the large digital race clock that was mounted right above it: 2:28. *No. WHAT?* Mira's already dead jaw dropped. This was impossible, and no way was she about to finish her first ever half-marathon (which had almost killed her), in two hours and twenty-eight minutes. The taste of glory was in her mouth. With every bit of energy she had left, and some borrowed from the crowd's collective spirit, Mira sprinted, running across the finish line and right into the arms of the volunteer handing out the race's finisher medals. "Congratulations." The volunteer smiled. Mira tried to mouth the words, "Thank you" but breathed air out instead. A second later, Laila and Seth appeared before her. "Hey, you just set a Sood record for most miles run in a lifetime." Laila laughed.

"Congratulations, Mira," Seth added with a smile.

She nodded back, trying to swallow air down her desert-dry throat. "Y-you guys an i-item, now?"

"It's official," Seth said, throwing an arm around Laila.

With a panting smile, Mira's eyes now began to search

the crowd for Andy. But she couldn't spot him anywhere. "Where's he?" she asked, turning to Laila.

Laila turned to the gathered crowd and then back to Mira. "I don't know, he was just with us a minute ago—"

Mira could barely get her feet to move an inch, but pulling their weight along, she began to frantically look for Andy. "Seth, do you know?" she asked him, looking over her shoulder. He shook his head. She couldn't understand it, but she continued to look for him in the crowd. Just as she began to give up hope, she spotted the neon-green jacket walking away in the direction of the parking lot.

"Andy," cried Mira. She couldn't even run after him because, well, that would kill her. So she limped toward him at her fastest post-race pace—three inches per minute. "ANDY..." she shouted, glad her lungs were still in one piece. "ANDY, STOP!"

He appeared to pause for a moment, and she heaved a sigh of relief when he turned. He waved from the distance, looking hesitant.

"Get over here, will you?" called Mira.

"I had to come," he explained as he approached her. "I know you said you didn't want to see me, but I wanted to be there when you ran the race. I'm sorry."

He stood a few inches away at first, so Mira moved closer to him. She considered his neon jacket, which oddly smelled of Clinique. "Is this Brooke's jacket?" she asked, her voice as hoarse as a freight truck driver.

Andy coughed up a laugh and scratched his chin. "It fits me great, actually. Plus, I figured you'd spot me in anything neon."

Mira nodded, allowing a few more seconds to pass between them in silence. "Shall we go grab a bench? I'd hate to pass out mid-sentence," she said with a smile. They walked over to the nearest hydration station to grab a couple of cups of ice water. Then Mira let her body collapse onto the nearest park bench, with Andy settling down next to her. She pulled out her medal, savoring the moment along with it—she had run and finished her first half-marathon, setting her own 2:29 PR finish time along with it. It felt surreal to her, as she lovingly traced her index finger across the embossed shape of a soaring bald eagle—the official Lake Union Park Half-Marathon mascot. This was epic. And almost too perfect to bear. Turning to Andy, Mira smiled. "Listen, I've had time to think, and I understand what you might have gone through when you took off like that—"

"But I was wrong to take off," he insisted.

"Well, you were just being . . . *human*," Mira said, with a tip of her head. "I didn't realize it until I ran the race today. You know, my mock-race performance gave me such confidence that I took the actual race for granted. When I started running today, I completely lost track of my pace and well, my overconfidence received a well-deserved smack. Like you, it took me time to understand how to play the game."

Andy frowned back, looking confused. "But your runtime was amazing."

Mira shrugged. "I wasn't expecting it to be, though. At mile four, I was sure I wouldn't even finish."

"Wow, no kidding . . ."

"And there's one more thing I realized today," said Mira, coyly knitting her fingers into Andy's. She then looked him in the eye and spoke the words that had been inside her all this while. "I love you."

For a moment, he said nothing. His mouth lay open and his eyes were wide with surprise, so Mira continued. "I'm not sure how you feel about me, whether you still feel the same way—"

Andy's mouth closed on hers, extinguishing any remaining words before they could slip out. An electric shudder dove down her spine as Mira melted into his arms, returning his kiss with unmistakable intent. They laughed like highschool sweethearts and hugged each other as if one of them was about to go off to war.

"I love you, you crazy, crazy Sood," Andy said, holding her firmly in his arms as if he never intended to let her go. "And I know I might be pushing the limit here, but there's something I want to ask you."

Mira's heart jumped to her throat as she gazed skittishly into those hazel-brown eyes of his. "Yes?" she asked meekly.

Andy suddenly let go of her and stood up tall, and before Mira could comprehend what was going on, he was down on one knee before her. A second later, like a magician performing the crowd-pleaser trick, he pulled out a small, red velvet box from the back pocket of his jeans. Mira's heart was ready to explode. "What the—?"

"Mira, will you marry me?" asked Andy, and opened the box to reveal the world's most beautiful vintage engagement ring with a large square-cut center diamond that glinted even under the clouds.

"Andy—" gasped Mira. "You didn't just pull that ring out of your back pocket?" she cried out.

"I bought it while I was on Whidbey Island . . . when I realized what I felt for you, and I've been carrying it around in my pocket ever since." Andy shrugged. "I was planning to pop the question the last time I saw you, but—"

"Oh God." Mira cringed, recollecting how their last meeting had ended.

This made Andy smile as he continued to stay put on his one knee. "What do you say, Mira?" he asked her.

An incandescent smile bloomed across her face. "Yes, Andy, of course I'll marry you! Oh my God!" She knelt down beside him as he slipped the ring on her finger. A perfect fit it was too. She kissed him unabashedly and to her heart's content.

Mira eventually found Laila in the crowd and broke the news to her and Seth.

"No way! Congratulations, you guys," cried Laila, as she hugged her cousin and then Andy, with Seth following suit. "You've almost turned me into a believer," added Laila, taking a closer look at the engagement ring.

"Thanks, Laila," Mira said, returning the hug. "Who knows, maybe you'll be next?"

"Oh God, no. I love you guys, but I know this is exactly the kind of thing that will never happen to me," Laila replied with a firm shake of her head. "And even if it did, I would never, never, *ever* marry anyone who Auntie Sharmila would approve. Else, what's the point, right?" She laughed before turning to lock arms with Seth. The two of them began walking toward the parking lot.

"Never say 'never,'" Mira yelled back, waving to Laila.

With her arms interlocked around his neck and her legs

belted around his waist, Andy ultimately ferried Mira on his back toward his Jeep. As her head serenely rested on the back of his shoulder, Mira thought about how her life had appeared to have defied the laws of science—turning from ashes to paradise. Of course, this was just the beginning of a whole new journey for her and Andy—one that rested on hope, not guarantees. But that thought no longer scared Mira. And even though she couldn't predict the future, her happy heart had everything she needed right there in that moment.

The End

Don't miss Laila Sood's story in book 2, *A Rebel's Mantra!* Coming in July 2022, pre-order now!

Join Tule Publishing's newsletter for more great reads and weekly deals!

If you enjoyed *A New Mantra,* you'll love the next book in…

The Sood Family series

Book 1: *A New Mantra*

Book 2: *A Rebel's Mantra*
Coming in July 2022!

About the Author

Sapna lives in Seattle, WA with her perfectionist husband and perfect daughter. Her name in Hindi means "dream" and true to its meaning, Sapna finds gratification in dreams and storytelling. She was born in southern India, raised in northern India, and spent the better part of her adult life in the United States. She, therefore, unabashedly clutches her Indian roots while embracing the American in herself. She loves to cook traditional Indian food and, yes, she uses cilantro in practically everything. When she isn't cooking, writing, or being intellectually stumped by her daughter, she may be found running down the nearest trail by her Pacific Northwest home. The inspiration for her debut novel, *A New Mantra*, has been her own journey as both a woman of color and a runner; the latter being a sport that was introduced to her by her husband.

Thank you for reading

A New Mantra

If you enjoyed this book, you can find more from all our great authors at TulePublishing.com, or from your favorite online retailer.

CPSIA information can be obtained
at www.ICGtesting.com
Printed in the USA
LVHW012128190622
721627LV00003B/350